**"What sacrifice can a teacher of infants provide?"**

Sorcha had no answer. The queen lifted an eyebrow.

"Do you love your land of faerie?" her mother asked.

"With every breath in my body."

The queen nodded. "Then you shall leave it."

Sorcha stopped breathing altogether.

"The least you can do for me is to reclaim the Dearann Stone," her mother said. "To do that you must travel through the great gate into a place so inhospitable your faerie soul shall shrivel."

There wasn't a whisper of breeze on the plain. Every fairy to the far horizon held still, stricken.

"And if I fail?" Sorcha had to ask.

"Then none of us will be left here to accuse you, will we, little Sorcha? For the earth will have died."

**Books by Kathleen Korbel**

Silhouette Nocturne

*Dangerous Temptation* #2*
*Dark Seduction* #34*

*Daughters of Myth

---

## *KATHLEEN KORBEL*

Kathleen Korbel lives in St. Louis with her husband and two children. She devotes her time to enjoying her family, writing, avoiding anyone who tries to explain the intricacies of the computer and searching for the fabled house-cleaning fairies. She's had her best luck with her writing—from which she's garnered a *Romantic Times BOOKreviews* award for Best New Category Author of 1987, and the 1990 Romance Writers of America RITA® Award for Best Romantic Suspense, and the 1990 and 1992 RITA® Award for Best Long Category Romance—and with her family, without whom she couldn't have managed any of the rest. She hasn't given up on those fairies, though.

# KATHLEEN
# KORBEL

∾⚬∾

## DARK SEDUCTION

𝒮𝒾𝓁𝒽𝑜𝓊𝑒𝓉𝓉𝑒® 𝐵𝑜𝑜𝓀𝓈

nocturne™

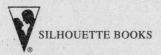

SILHOUETTE BOOKS

ISBN-13: 978-0-373-61781-4
ISBN-10:    0-373-61781-X

DARK SEDUCTION

www.silhouettenocturne.com

**Printed in U.S.A.**

Dear Reader,

When I tell people I'm writing a trilogy about fairies for Silhouette Nocturne, some inevitably say, "Really? What's so frightening about fairies?" They're obviously thinking of the wrong fairies—probably Puck or Peasblossom from *A Midsummer Night's Dream*. Funny, tiny fairies that sit atop bluebells.

Well, Irish fairies are different. Think something more like the elves in *The Lord of the Rings*. With attitude. Irish fairies can be of any size and disposition. There are funny ones, but there are also terrifying ones. Take the *leannan sidhe*, the fairy seductress. She seduces mortal men into sexual slavery. (And yeah, one of the sisters in the series is a *leannan sidhe*—and she's a good guy. Well, sort of.) Or take the fairies who infect dreams and bring madness. I've given those fairies a name: *Dubhlainn Sidhe*, Fairy of the Dark Sword. They're here, too.

As you'll be able to tell from the first word of *Dark Seduction*, fairies can be very dark indeed. Especially to the poor humans who get in their way, which is exactly what happens to poor Harry Wyatt. Whether he gets free—with the help of Sorcha, the second of the Queen Mab's daughters—is the question.

Yours,

Kathleen Korbel

Again
for Kieran

for the world's more full of weeping
then ye will understand

# *Prologue*

He could smell her. It was dark, with not even enough moonlight to illuminate her bedroom. But he didn't need light to know where she was. He could smell the soap on her: citrus and aloe. He could smell the shampoo in her hair and the detergent on her nightclothes. He could smell *her*. Her scent, that dark, private musk that had been calling to him the whole evening, until he could use the darkness to climb through her window.

He smiled, there in the darkness. He knew she was waiting for him, even though she was silent. She was breathing, soft currents that wafted across his over-heated skin. She wanted him, too. She'd watched him all evening over drinks. She'd smiled with her perfect white teeth and her sloe eyes. She'd sent out the scent of pheromones, and he'd responded.

She lurched awake and he stopped her. "No," he whispered, settling his body against hers.

He laid his hand over her mouth and thought how soft it was, how cool and smooth her teeth were against his palm. He thought how hard he was for her, hot and ready and shaking with the effort of control.

He would have her tonight. She knew it, and he knew it, and it made him impatient.

"You know who I am," he breathed in her ear.

He felt her tremble and nod.

"You knew I would come."

She nodded again, and he could smell the first taint of fear on her.

"Don't be afraid." He slid his free hand along her soft, sleek throat and traced the edge of her clothing. Something silky and light, something that just asked to be ripped away. "I'm going to make it so good for you."

He knew he was breathing faster. Her heart was pumping faster, and the first tang of perspiration hovered in the air. Sweat had broken out on his forehead. He couldn't wait. He knew she couldn't, either.

"Now," he told her, filling his lungs with the smell of her sex.

She lifted a hand. He thought she would reach up to touch his face. Instead she reached for his hand, trying to dislodge it. He wouldn't allow her to. He knew she didn't really want him to stop. He chuckled and said, "No. Not yet."

He hooked his hand around the neckline of her gown and almost came when he heard the fabric rip. He yanked hard and felt the garment disintegrate beneath his fingers. She was his for the taking. Her skin tightened with the chill. He could imagine that her areolae were pebbling, just waiting for his tongue. He leaned over and tasted her skin, salt and sweet air. He took possession of her breast and thought of what a feast it would be, there in the dark where they were strangers, even though they weren't. Where he was in control, because she wanted it that way.

He lifted his hand away from her lips so he could kiss her, slide his tongue into her mouth and lap up the last vestiges of sleep. But she yanked her head back.

"What are you doing?" she demanded, her voice suddenly shrill. "This isn't the way it's supposed to happen."

"It happens," he told her, "the way I say it does."

And he wrapped his hand around her slender, vulnerable throat.

She bucked against him. "You bastard," she rasped. "Stop it now."

Rage flared in him. Hunger. How dare she? How *dare*—

He tightened his hold on her throat. Her pulse beat frantically against his fingers as the rasp of the air in her throat thinned to a whine. He couldn't wait. He couldn't stop. *Yes, like this. With her struggling for air, for life. Like this.*

He reached down to yank open his pants, even as he felt her struggle against him. *Because* he felt her struggle against him. She was his, and she'd better know it now. She'd better understand that he was in control. He was the one with the power. He was smiling as he squeezed her throat, tighter and tighter, as he reached down…

Harry Wyatt lurched straight up out of his bed, his heart hammering. Sweat soaked his sheets, and his hands shook so badly he couldn't so much as rub the images away from his eyes.

He'd had the dream again. Again he'd woken just in time, before his subconscious betrayed him. He didn't know how much longer he could survive it. The horrific taste of violence lingered on his tongue. The terror that always followed swamped him, leaving him cold and nauseous.

Awake, he would never so much as consider something so vile. Asleep, he couldn't seem to stop. And he was still hard as a rock.

What was wrong with him? What in the name of God was he going to do to stop it?

He swore he could still smell her on his hands.

# Chapter 1

There was a storm coming. Sorcha, daughter of Mab, Queen of Fairies, stood out on the wide, sweeping Plain of Gates, what the mortals called Carrowmore, and considered the clouds that massed at its horizon. The wind worried at the assembled faerie gathering, tugging at dresses and hair, fanning gossamer wings and sending shadows skimming across the grass like dark birds.

The day was warm, but Sorcha shivered. She wasn't the kind of fairy who saw portents in everything. That was the job of young Kieran, the seer for the clan of the *Tuatha de Dannan*. But there was portent in this wind, and it was ill. For the first time in centuries, the fairy clans were at war and it was partly her fault.

"Well, now, my young Sorcha," the queen said, turning to her. "What say you?"

It all came down to this. If only her older sister Nuala were still here to save her from it. But Nuala had escaped, although the queen called it exile, forfeiting her throne and immortality for the mortal she loved, leaving Sorcha behind to pick up her mantle.

"I am honored, my queen," she said, doing her best to stand strong before the majesty of her mother, "but my answer remains the same."

The queen stood at the crest of the long slope, so that the great central stone tumulus framed her and, beyond it, the turbulent sky. Her hair, that fey, otherworldly yellow that inspired poetry, swirled in the fretful air like a battle pennant. Her white robes gleamed in the half-light and the gems on her hands glittered. Her head was bare this day and it shamed Sorcha. The crown of the *Tuatha de Dannan* was empty of its great bloodred Coilin Stone, for it had been stolen. Sorcha had been its guardian.

Mab needed no crown to display her power, though. The assembled ranks of faerie trembled before her. From the grave marching fairies, with their gray robes and shadow-woven hair, to the sprites, who hovered in anxious rainbow-hued clouds, and all in between, the earth fairies of the *Tuatha* waited in hushed silence for the pronouncement of their queen, and none more anxiously than Sorcha herself.

"But I've said it, little Sorcha," Mab said, her voice a hum on the wind that made even the distant trees tremble. "You are to be queen."

Sorcha, so much smaller than her mother and standing down the hill from her, as was right, bowed her head. "I am not worthy, my queen, and we both know it."

"You would have Orla be queen?" her mother asked,

and Sorcha didn't know whether her mother was furious or amused. "My same daughter who brought our own enemy to rob us of the great Coilin Stone?"

Well, Sorcha had to admit, the queen had her there. She took a quick peek over to where her younger sister stood ramrod straight beside her and wondered what was going through Orla's mind.

"I fought bravely, my queen," Orla protested, her voice yet proud, even for her crimes, her cat eyes hot and her head unbowed.

"And so you did, Orla," the queen acknowledged. "Even though you wouldn't have had to fight at all if you hadn't invited the *Dubhlainn Sidhe* to pillage your own house, now, would you?"

"I didn't—"

The queen lifted a languid hand, and her daughter froze. Sorcha, standing next to her, felt her sister's indignation like a blast of heat. Oh, would Orla never learn? They would both pay for this disaster, Sorcha for not protecting what was hers to protect, and Orla for handing it away in the hope of gaining power. They might as well face it like the daughters of royalty they were.

"And how is it you'd do penance for the loss of my Coilin Stone, Orla?" the queen asked, her voice slyly sweet.

For a moment Orla stood silent, her heavy raven hair lifting in the wind. "What would you have me do?" she finally asked.

The queen tilted her head and smiled, and all knew the smile was not kind. "Foolish girl. I will have you reclaim it."

Even Orla grew pale. "From the land of the *Dubhlainn Sidhe?*"

"Do the *Dubhlainn Sidhe* not now possess our great Stone?"

Sorcha saw her sister swallow. "Aye, lady."

The queen nodded. "Then it is there you must go. But not, I think, quite yet. Is my seer here?"

From two steps behind Sorcha, a young boy stepped forward. Kieran himself, with his wise eyes and impish smile and shock of bright red hair. "I am here, *a bhantiarna*," he said without fear, for only the seer could tell the truth to the queen and not suffer for it.

"Remind my daughters, seer," the queen said, "just what is at stake."

For a moment the boy considered his queen, as if counting the cost of their loss. Sorcha could count it already, in the faces she missed in the throng that filled the plain. Warriors lost in the effort to beat back the armies of the *Dubhlainn Sidhe.* Friends and mentors laid out for the funeral pyre and then internment atop Knocknarea, where the old queen's cairn challenged the sky: light, air and peace. There was keening in the wind for those brave ones, and Sorcha felt it in her soul. Already the lack of their precious Coilin Stone had cost them the sun. She couldn't bear to think what else would be forfeit.

"This you know, my queen," Kieran called out in the singsong cadence of the bard, his small body perfectly erect, his hands folded in front of him. "Three stones rule us, formed by the ancients and set in our crowns. Donelle the Ruler, he of magnificent blue who resides in the Land of the West, where the temptation of him cannot entice us to destruction. Coilin Ruadh the Virile, who resides in the crown of Mab, queen of the matriarchal *Tuatha de Dannan.* And crystal clear Dearann the Fruitful, to balance the patriarchal power of the *Dubhlainn Sidhe,* the faerie of the air."

Like the assembled races, Sorcha listened, rapt at the age-old telling, knowing the words by heart, but sustained by their acquaintance.

"It has been years on years since tragedy befell the *Dubhlainn Sidhe* and their Dearann Stone was lost to them."

"The *Dubhlainn Sidhe* were careless, seer," the queen reminded him tartly.

"No more careless than we, my queen," he responded, his voice calm. "For we allowed the loss of the Lady Dearann without comment or help in her recovery, and the male *Dubhlainn Sidhe* grew dark and resentful for loss of their power, for want of the balance of their feminine stone. We grew lax, not anticipating that the *Dubhlainn Sidhe* would seek recompense. Now they have the great Coilin Stone, which will gain them not just power, but masculine ferocity. There is no female power left to balance them, my queen."

"And if the balance is not restored?"

The child thought a moment, then sighed. "The *Dubhlainn Sidhe* grow stronger. They have already lost the gentling influence of the Dearann Stone. Now they gather the masculine power from the Coilin Stone, and it gives them no restraint."

"And what of the *Tuatha?*"

"Our power will wane, and with it all feminine power. And without that, how will there be rebirth?"

Even the queen became perfectly still at Kieran's words.

"If we cannot reclaim the stones and restore the world's balance," he finished, lifting his hands in helplessness, "there will be no spring."

Sorcha had known the truth of the seer's prediction long before he stated it. Even so, the gravity of his high, young voice struck her heart. No spring. No lambs or bluebells or sweet green grass. The birds gone. The earth herself, their dear mother, dying for want of a soft hand.

She couldn't bear it. She wanted to hide, to weep, to keen like the *bean sidhe* in grief. But she was a princess of the blood, so she stood still before her people and waited.

"And what would *you* do, my Sorcha?" the queen asked, turning her gimlet eyes on Sorcha, "to save our mother earth?"

"What would you have me do, *a bhantiarna?*" Sorcha asked, as her mother knew she would. Her heart clamored in her chest and her belly hurt.

"I would have you be queen."

Sorcha had no courage. It was why she should not be queen. She knew it. Her mother knew it. Her gifts were small and private, not terrible and great, such as a queen would need. An eye for the stone and weave a fairy should wear to display her power. A way with words to tell the stories to teach the young. A love of every plant and flower that grew. Not a taste for power, nor the stomach for ruthlessness.

She shook with the silence that stretched across the great plain, even the wind suddenly dying, as if waiting for her answer.

"You would desert your people at this time?" Sorcha asked her mother.

It was the bravest thing she'd done in her life. And the most foolhardy. The queen reared back as if struck. The throngs of faerie shuddered and stared. Arwen, the queen's consort, stepped forward to give physical support to his queen, but Mab held him off. She stood alone on the crest of the hill and faced down her daughter.

"Sure, I think I'd be careful about accusing the queen of cowardice, little girl," Mab whispered.

Sorcha felt it in her chest, where dread lived. "A great queen is needed at this time, lady. Not an insignificant teacher of infants."

There was a stirring in the ranks. The queen quelled them with a look. Then, for a long moment, she considered her daughters.

"I had three daughters," she said. "Shouldn't that have been enough to satisfy any queen she would have an heir? And yet here I stand disappointed, and my people without a future. Isn't this a time when there must be testing?"

There was no answer.

"Aye," Mab answered herself, and smiled. "If you can't be heirs, you can at least be sacrifices. For we know that when the earth is upended, the only thing that will suffice is a good sacrifice."

Sorcha wondered, did her mother know that her daughter was shaking? That she was so afraid, she couldn't even gain the muscle power to run? Did it please her mother to terrify her so?

"You've already taken my power as the *leannan*

*sidhe,*" Orla objected, her voice quavering just a bit. "What else do I have to give?"

The queen lifted an eyebrow. "Why, your freedom, my Orla. Your very life, if I so choose. You think that losing the power to seduce mortals is the worst that can befall you?"

"What would you have *me* do, my queen?" Sorcha interrupted, proud that her voice sounded calm. It was better to draw her mother's fire than let her incinerate Orla on the spot for her defiance.

"You, Sorcha? What sacrifice can a teacher of infants offer?"

Sorcha had no answer.

"Do you love your land of faerie?" her mother asked.

"With the very breath in my body."

The queen nodded. "Then you shall leave it."

Sorcha stopped breathing altogether.

"The least you can do for me is to reclaim the Dearann Stone," her mother said. "To do that you must travel through the great gate into a place so inhospitable your faerie soul shall shrivel."

There wasn't a whisper of breeze on the plane. Every fairy to the far horizon held still, stricken.

"You know where the Stone is?" Sorcha asked.

The queen shrugged. "I might have a suspicion."

"Send *me*," Orla insisted.

The queen turned to her youngest. "Ah, no, Orla. I have *much* better plans for you. Sorcha shall go. She will search for our stone where it lies lost amid the mortals and bring it back so it can be traded for the Coilin Stone. And when she comes back, she can again tell me how she will not be queen."

"And if I fail?" Sorcha had to ask.

"Then none of us will be left here to accuse you, will we, little Sorcha? For the earth will have died."

Sorcha was not even allowed to return to her home to pack anything to help her. The queen assured her that nothing she owned would help anyway. The *bean tighe,* healer for the fairies, sneaked a small pouch of herbs into Sorcha's pocket when her mother wasn't looking. The elven warrior Xender, who protected the queen herself, slipped Sorcha a delicate elven blade forged in mystical fires. And Orla, still deathly pale with waiting to know what her sacrifice would be, passed on some of the oil she rubbed on her own sleek body to attract the mortals she had once so enthusiastically seduced.

With her small cache and her trembling heart, Sorcha walked to the Plain of Gates, thirteen different portals into worlds not her own. Whether the queen saw the gifts or not, Sorcha didn't know. Mab said nothing as she walked to the head of the faerie horde and paused. The silence stretched out across the plain, across the suddenly still sky. Finally she stepped before the gate that would take Sorcha into the land of mortals.

At least, Sorcha thought with relief, a world she would recognize. A world on her earth, in her time. She stepped up next to her mother and waited for the command to go.

"Take this with you," her mother instructed, handing over a soft leather pouch. "Inside you will find a crystal. If necessary, leave it for the Dearann Stone. No mortal will be able to tell the difference. And no mortal will see it unless you so will it."

The queen laid her hand on Sorcha's forehead, in the age-old blessing of a mother to her child. "Look for the one who is us," she said.

Nothing more. She turned Sorcha toward the gate into the other world and stepped back.

Sorcha saw Kieran standing to the side. "Will I see you on the other side?"

The little boy shook his head, his eyes grave. "I cannot help you."

He didn't say why. Sorcha was afraid she knew, though. Kieran was a changeling, a human child with a fairy heart who divided his time between the two worlds. But his mortal place was in Ireland, at a place called Rathkeale, where his parents awaited him in the Castle Matrix. The queen had said the place Sorcha was to go would be inhospitable. There was no place in Ireland inhospitable to fairies. She would be going beyond safety. Beyond belief. And she would go alone.

*"Slan,"* she said. Farewell. And then, before she had the chance to reconsider, she stepped through the gate.

The change was cataclysmic. The gentle sun vanished. The warm verdant grass froze. The hills she'd left disintegrated into a wasteland.

Sorcha almost stumbled to her knees, her head spinning from the crossing, her ears ringing with the pressure change that always happened when moving from her world to another. But worse this time. Devastating.

It was cold. Sorcha didn't know what to do with cold. It was wet. She'd never been wet in all her days. The wind, a sharp knife of misery, carried rain on it and soaked her in her slight fairy attire. It howled and keened and moaned, a living thing bent on tormenting her, and she saw nowhere to escape it.

She was standing out on another hill, a long, sloping expanse that rose and fell like the sea, but a gray sea. A gray ocean without color or warmth or comfort. There were a few trees, but they were leafless, sere, scratchy sticks that stretched toward a hostile sky.

She took a wild look around her, terrified, upended, alone. Her heart thundered in her ears and her breath rasped in her throat. Her skin, which had never suffered more than the gentle cool of the gloaming, shrank against the elements. Her heart, her great fairy heart, shrank within her.

"To me!" she cried in a long, ululating wail. "All faerie folk and free, to me!"

The call of battle, the call of the clan. The desperate cry for a familiar voice.

Her answer was the wind. The cold north wind, with no faerie voice on it, no faerie warmth in it, no faerie taste to it.

This wasn't just another world. It was an alien world, without fairy comfort, without magic. With only the bitter wind and empty hills.

She didn't know what to do. She didn't know where to go. Surely she would be dead before she could find another life, much less the Dearann Stone. Surely her mother, that cruel queen, had simply meant to offer her up to an indifferent earth.

This earth that would remain cold and empty when the spring refused to come.

"Forgive me," she moaned, sinking to her knees, there on the bare earth. "Oh, forgive me, *mathair.*"

But the earth, that verdant comfort that had never failed her, refused to answer. From toe to knee there was silence beneath her. Even when she lay down, full onto the ground, her face to the earth, her fingers spread wide to encompass it, she felt nothing. No whisper of life, no hint of warmth. All about her was dead and she grieved for it.

She didn't even hear the stranger approach.

"Here! What are you doing? Get up!"

Startled, Sorcha looked up to see long legs in front of her. Thick boots, sturdy pants, long, sleek limbs. Tall limbs. She kept looking up and then up and still he went on.

A man.

A mortal, dark and fierce and glowering at her.

Sorcha stumbled to her feet, her instinct that of flight. This man was her enemy, surely, in this terrifying place.

"I—I… Forgive me…" she gasped, and stumbled. Her feet were too numb from the cold to hold her up, her senses still in too much upheaval.

She reached out for balance and ended up crashing into the mortal's chest. He grunted, struggling to stay upright. He reached for her, but it was too late. In a tangle of limbs, the two of them tumbled over and their momentum carried them rolling all the way down the long hill into the rocks at the bottom.

"Ooomph!" he grunted again, coming to a halt right on top of her.

Sorcha couldn't breathe. Her poor body felt as if it had been flayed, and her brain was still spinning. And that lump of a great mortal was lying on top of her, as if she were a feather mattress.

"Please…" She shoved at him, but it was like trying to move granite. "I…can't…breathe…."

"Oh. Sorry."

He lurched up, a hand on either side of her head, until he balanced himself over her, lifting his weight but not his control. "I…"

But then he stopped, staring. Sorcha couldn't help it. She stared back. A mortal he might be, but he was magnificent. Taller than even the *Tuatha,* stronger than the elven guards, fiercer than the *Dubhlainn Sidhe.* Dark and sharp-edged, with high cheeks and a taut jaw and a rapier of a nose. A face on which even a scowl was a thing of beauty. And Sorcha revered beauty.

But that wasn't what silenced her. It was his eyes. Dark-fringed, wide, crystal-bright. And green.

Fairy green.

Sorcha's heart leapt in her breast. She felt joy bubble up in her, the relief of a saved life, the delight of finding that she'd been wrong. There *was* another familiar face in this alien place.

A warmth flooded her such as she'd never known, in heart and in head and deep in her belly, where his met hers. A current of something hot and primal sparked, there on the inhospitable hill, darkening his eyes and crackling through her limbs.

She opened her mouth to say something. What, she didn't know. She never got it said. Instead, he kissed her. Warm lips and hard, scratchy jaw and sleek hands in her hair, pouring his life into her, waking her, warming her, welcoming her with the most primal force in all the world. She greeted his kiss with an open mouth, welcomed the invasion of his tongue, feasted on his heat and his strength and his hard, heavy ferocity. She stopped breathing or thinking or questioning. She simply wrapped herself around him and welcomed herself home.

When he pulled away, his face still perilously close, they simply stared at each other, both panting for air. He seemed stunned. Sorcha didn't know why.

"Ah, how lovely," she said, lifting her hand to his face. "You're the one I'm to be looking for, then."

"The one you're looking for?" he asked, his voice oddly hushed, his eyes still deep and dark.

She smiled. She laughed. "Of course. Didn't the queen herself tell me to look for the one who is us? And who would be quicker to recognize the mark of a fairy than I? Your sister thanks you for her welcome, *mo dearthair.*'"

"What?"

She gave him an even larger smile. "Ah, pardon. I forget it's the mortal tongue I need. I merely called you my brother. I thank you, my brother, for my welcome."

For a second the stranger stared at her. Then, shaking his head, he dragged her to her feet. "That's it," he said. "I'm calling the police."

# Chapter 2

"Police?" she asked.

Harry saw the confusion in the young woman's eyes and huffed in frustration. It wasn't enough that he had another of those damn movie freaks wandering his property. He had one who thought she was actually participating in the film, like a fairy version of a Renaissance Fair. *Reality? What is reality? No, no, I'd prefer to live in a fantasy world like the people in the movie.*

Well, *damn* the movie. He wasn't putting up with it a moment more. Not even when he still couldn't quite pull himself away from the heart-stopping kiss they'd just shared. All right, then. The kiss he'd just taken.

It hadn't meant a thing. Surprise. Sudden human contact out on the edge of the moors. A hit on the head. God knows he'd bounced enough down that bloody hill.

He'd been stunned. Nothing more. *Nothing.*

He grabbed her by the arm and began to haul her up the hill. Which was when he realized that she was shivering like a wet pup, and barefoot. *Barefoot,* for the love of God. Didn't these people have a ha'penny of sense among them?

"Just what did you think you were going to prove?" he demanded, shucking his anorak. "That fairies could survive a Yorkshire winter? Well, they can't. That's how I know they don't exist. They *never* existed, damn it."

"But of course they do," she assured him in the most musical voice he'd ever heard as she stood there letting him drape her in his oversize coat. And then, bloody hell if she didn't smile as if she'd just discovered gold. "Aren't you the living proof of it, now?"

"And there'll be no more of that, thank you. I don't care what that bloody movie said, there are no fairies here. No fairy houses or trees or mists or any other damn thing. Nothing but a horse farm in the middle of nowhere. Now, where do you live?"

They still hadn't moved, although he couldn't figure out why. Since that thrice-damned movie had come out about his family, he'd been picking lost children off his land like ticks, all of them looking for what the movie promised: the proof that there really was a fairy world out in the middle of nowhere, that magic had survived the age of technology. And every one of them had been a right pain in the arse.

But this one…he couldn't quite get a handle on her. Or himself. Her skin was so cold she should have been in a coma, but it felt like silk. Her curly blond hair straggled into her eyes but shone like spun gold. Rain dripped down her neck and onto that pitiful excuse for a dress...that betrayed a lush young body. A lush young body that had just been pressed knee to shoulder with his. Her breasts were heavy and full for a woman of her size, the nipples damn near popping right through the thin dress the color of a dawn sky. Silver—no, blue. No, lavender.

He shook his head, disgusted. He was freezing, he was wet, and he was standing there mesmerized by a pair of breasts in a gossamer dress. And a smile that lit the cold, hostile moors like a sunburst beyond the clouds.

"I asked you," he grated out, trying his best to intimidate her, "where the hell do you live?"

"I live in the land of the other, of course," she said, as if he should know better. "Beyond the gates and the shadows under the hill."

He couldn't seem to argue with her. He couldn't let her go, that curious heat still snaking up his arm from where he held her. He wanted her, and that was the most absurd thing that had happened since this whole mess had started. Right there, in the rain, in the open, he wanted to just take her to the ground, finish what he'd started, and pour himself into her as if she could somehow save him. How idiotic was that?

"Come on," he growled, turning her up the hill and trying hard to ignore the rock-hard cock in his slacks. "You're going to catch your death out here."

She stumbled after him as if it were the most natural thing. Every other one of the trespassers had argued, fought, implored. She was smiling. Damn her.

"Did you say it's, what? Winter?" she asked, skipping up the hill like a deer, even while encumbered with a coat that hung to her knees. Her bare knees. Her glorious, pale, sleek knees.

*Bloody hell.*

He sighed. "Yes. For another four months."

"And the mother earth always dies now?"

That stopped him. "Do you mind?" he demanded. "I'm not in the mood for games. Save the role-playing for your friends."

She stood there, wide-eyed and silent. Then she looked around. "This is what it looks like, so, without spring?"

She sounded absolutely lost. How could that hurt him? He was probably coming down with pneumonia and already delirious.

"November comes every year, lass," he said, walking again, his hand still around her arm. "Right on schedule."

"But spring won't come," she said back. "Not unless I recover the Stone."

That brought him to a dead stop. "Don't," he growled, finger in her face. "There is no stone. No fairy diamond. It was a *movie,* damn it? What part of that confuses you?"

Good God, her smile just got bigger. "Ah, thank the goddess. Herself my mother wasn't wrong. You know what I've come for."

He simply didn't have any words for her. Not any she would believe, evidently. Just like the others.

No, not like the others. He hadn't felt compelled to kiss any of the others, nor protect them from anything. He'd hauled them up to the manor and handed them over to the overworked police, then wiped his hands of them. Hell, his grandmother didn't even know half of what had descended on them since she'd made that pact with the devil and allowed the filmmakers access to her and the estate, so they could retell the fable of the cousins who had gone out to photograph fairies and brought one home.

There was something about this one, though. Something guileless in those wide spring-green eyes that made him want to protect her. Something in that musical voice and the lush lips that made him ache with wanting for things he'd never had.

And he made it a point never to do that.

So he led her all the way up the hill and down the next one, where he'd been walking off his last six months in the city, and he never took his eyes from the forest of chimneys that peeked through the distant trees.

It took a good twenty minutes for them to traverse the back lawns. Before him rose the back of the Abbey, a collection of mismatched wings that stretched back to the original abbey the Wyatts had claimed from Henry VIII. From true gothic to faux gothic to a bit of Elizabethan and Jacobean, the old girl boasted just about every architectural monstrosity in the book. At least Robert Adam had saved the inside. For a time, anyway. But Harry made it a point not to think about that, either.

He guided his charge toward the kitchen door, just as he had all the others. He'd just pulled it open against the harsh wind when the girl balked like a fractious horse. "Oh, no," she said in a bare whisper as she gazed up at three stories of gray stone. "I don't think I can go in there."

He turned to see that her oddly rosy cheeks had gone chalk white. Her eyes were round as saucers.

"Why not?"

"It's stone, isn't it? Fairies don't live well in stone. We can't see out, you see, to what is living. We have to see the earth, feel her power beneath our feet, hear the wind…."

"Believe me," he said. "You'll hear the wind just fine in here. It's draftier than a privy in a gale. And there are plenty of windows to look out of—see?"

Fifty-four rooms full of them, all added in times when the Earls of Hartley had been a force to reckon with. Now held together with chewing gum and baling wire and every penny he scratched out of London. He wished he could say why he still loved the old place so much.

She gulped and shook her head. "Is it any warmer in there?"

"Absolutely toasty."

She actually laid her hand against her chest, as if reassuring herself that her heart still beat. "All right, then, I'll come. For a bit, anyway. It is the sacrifice that is asked, after all."

Harry guided her through the door. "So it is."

Poor crazy girl. Poor crazy, lush, exciting, heart-stoppingly sensual girl he still wanted to get on her back.

Mrs. Thompson put a quick end to that fantasy.

"Eee, not another one," she stated, hands on predictably massive hips. Mrs. Thompson was a great cook, one who believed that the recipe must please the cook before the client. She was very well pleased. At least until another of their wandering fairy-searchers stumbled in. "Are ya daft, girl? You've nowt but your nightgown on. Get over here by the stove."

The girl seemed to be reassured by the great room and its high white walls. She even smiled at the vegetables Mrs. Thompson was chopping on the counter, as if delighted by the familiar.

"You need to get her some real clothes, milord," Mrs.

Thompson said, taking one of her kitchen towels to the girl's hair. "Lady Phyllida's things might work."

"Lady Phyllida might not want them to," Harry said sotto voce. "Besides which, they'd be miles too long for her. This is another one of our fairy brigade, Tommie."

"You think I can't see that? Go on, now, and have your grandmother pick something out. Lady Phyllida is off on a buying trip with the family. She'll never know."

Lady Phyllida, who had been Mrs. Trent-Larson for the last ten years.

Harry almost found himself grinning. "How do you think she'd look in jodhpurs? I think it's all Phyl owns."

Tommie snapped a towel at him. "Go on, then. You need this done before Miss Adderly arrives for dinner."

Gwyneth. Hell. Harry checked his watch and did his best not to moan. Oh, Gwyneth would simply love to share a house with the fairy princess here.

He left. His last sight of the girl was her smiling up at Tommie like a martyr caught in the Colosseum. Well, Tommie would fill her up with scones and tea and comfort so that by the time the police came to take her back home she would have forgotten why she'd come in the first place. Harry pushed his way through the green baize door into the dining room and headed for the stairs.

He hadn't been home long enough this time to adjust to the place. And it did take adjusting to. It was such a grand old barn, where once Adam had held sway. Stately, with clean lines and exquisite craftsmanship, from paneling to marble to plasterwork. A soothing symphony of comfort that had lasted over three hundred years intact. Until his grandparents and then his parents had gotten to it.

They'd ruined it. Defiled it. And still, he couldn't wait to come home to stand in these ruined rooms.

A faint sound from the kitchen got him moving again. He didn't have time to reminisce. He had a crazy woman to corral before his very twenty-first-century fiancée arrived. And to do it, he would have to make it safely past his grandmother.

By the second floor, he was tiptoeing. Predictably, it wasn't enough.

"Who is she?" came a querulous voice from his left.

Harry took two more steps.

"Harold George Cormac Augustus Be-ver-ly!" she hollered—it was the only word for it. "Get in here!"

Harry flinched. He could live with every other one of his names—even, when he was feeling generous, the Earl of Hartley. But Gran always had to tack on *Beverly*. And she kept repeating it in louder and louder tones, like a snooze alarm, until she cracked him. It was a ploy that had worked since he was twelve.

"Good afternoon, Gran," he greeted her with a bow as he stepped into her parlor.

It was stifling in the room due to an overworked radiator and a roaring fire. Furniture and bric-a-brac stuffed every free inch, representing every generation of Hartleys back to Queen Anne and beyond. A Neolithic spear held up the corner of the Adam fireplace; Jacobean footstools complemented the Victorian horsehair couch. Original tapestries hung alongside Poussin oils.

And then there was the throne. There was nothing else to call it. Carved black bog oak from Ireland, a good six feet high, with an impossibly straight back and unpadded seat, it was the only chair his grandmother would suffer herself to sit on. Harry considered it a testament to her refusal to age. The wheelchair she'd been reduced to was tucked back in the shadows.

He'd forgotten, though, that her fancy perch sat alongside a back window with a perfect view of the path he and the fairy child had taken.

"You stalking your girls like deer out across the moors, are you, Harry?" she demanded, squinting at him.

An anachronism, that was his grandmother. She belonged in a Jane Austen novel—if not Buckingham Palace. No more than four foot ten, she had the voice of a top sergeant, the family pride of a Plantagenet, and the horse sense of a jockey. She was deceptively sharp, decidedly opinionated, and dearly loved.

So he ignored her incendiary statement and bent to kiss her cheek. "I've been gone too long. I'd almost forgotten the dulcet tones of your voice."

She let out a bark of laughter that raised the head of her canine lap pillow, about five pounds of unidentifiable fur. "Queen Mab and I know a bald-faced liar when we hear one, dear boy."

Queen Mab let out a low growl. Gran stroked what Harry assumed was its head with gnarled fingers. "Now, who is Mrs. Thompson undoubtedly feeding in my kitchen?"

It was actually *his* kitchen, Harry thought absently. But one did not argue with the Baroness Waverly.

He grabbed a chocolate truffle from Gran's ever-present supply and popped it in his mouth. "Just one of those lost children who've been scaring the horses ever since you let that blasted film company make sport of us."

"No one has made sport of us, young man," she

snapped, slapping a small hand on the arm of her chair. "The story was mine to tell, and I told it."

Even as crazy as the subject made Harry, he struggled not to grin. "And made a tidy profit from it, too. That's the only good to come out of this fiasco, Gran. You can have all the coal you want up here."

"Don't be absurd. That money is for you, so you don't have to slave in that bank and can come home."

Once expenses were paid on the estate, it wasn't enough for him to take a vacation from the bank, much less quit it. Another thing she didn't need to know. "Work is good for me. After all, what would I do here? Phyl has the horses well in hand. I'd just waste my time wandering about shooting at things."

He got a distinct "harrumph" for that piece of nonsense. "Your cousin is an admirable woman."

"Because she listens to you?"

"She could do worse. I've raised some damn fine horses in my time, and you know it."

"Dear thing, nobody would ever challenge that."

Gran nodded, a brisk tuck of the head. "It isn't her legacy to keep, though. It belongs to the earls of Hartley."

"Of course it's her legacy, too. Her son is my presumptive heir."

"Not good enough. The title hasn't been away from the line since Henry the Eighth."

"Yes, I do know. And right now, this Earl of Hartley is doing his level best to make sure Phyl has everything she needs to run a successful breeding program."

And fix the roof. And keep his grandmother in coal. And finish tarting up the public rooms for when they opened the house next year.

Harry was thinking about how much work needed to be done when his attention was caught by a movement out the window.

His grandmother was saying something, but he missed it. He stalked over to get a better look out onto the back lawns. There. A shadow, moving beneath the trees. Harry ground his teeth. Bloody hell. It had better not be another fairy visitor. He'd already had enough for one day.

"Harry! Did you hear me?"

He bent closer to the window, but he couldn't see anything. Nobody walked out of the woods. Even so, for some reason the hair went up on the back of his neck, and he saw a flash of the visions that had been plaguing him. Felt that sick, surging fury.

He sucked in a breath and deliberately turned away from the window. "I'm sorry, love. I thought I saw something out there."

Gran waved his words off like insects. "Leave them be. They're not hurting anything."

Harry thought of the fey girl in his kitchen. "Except themselves."

"Bring her up here, Harry. I want to meet her."

That got Harry's attention. "Her?"

Another imperious wave of the hand. "The girl you bagged. I want to meet her."

"Oh, Gran, please don't. She's just a garden-variety eccentric, and she doesn't need to be encouraged."

For a moment his grandmother didn't answer. She considered Harry, as if debating something. He hoped to hell she couldn't see through his lie. An eccentric, maybe. Definitely not garden variety.

"I don't think so, Harry. There's something familiar about her. Something…"

Harry almost groaned out loud. "Gran," he said gently. "No. If Gramps and Mother and Dad couldn't find a fairy after all those years of looking, do you really think one is going to just wander up to the door and introduce herself?"

"Why not?" she demanded. "Do you think I would have worked so hard with the horses to keep us going if I didn't believe in your grandfather's dream?"

Dream? More like obsession. Nightmare. Ruin. No matter how hard Gran had worked to bring money in, it had gone out six times as fast. "Don't you think we've beaten this topic to death? Let me get that girl out the door, and then you can tell me all about this new mare Phyl's gone to purchase."

His grandmother collected herself, straightened, let the silence stretch into discomfort. It was rare these days that she played the baroness card. Harry saw her lay it out and sighed.

"Harold George Cormac Augus—"

"Yes, yes. I get it. As soon as I get her into something other than that soaked handkerchief she called a dress, I'll bring her up to pay obeisance."

Gran didn't so much as nod her head. "Mary will meet you outside with some of Phyllida's togs."

Mary, Gran's nurse, maid, friend and legs, met Harry at the door with a big smile on her homely black face and handed over a neatly folded pile of clothing topped by shoes. "I hope she has small feet," she said in her lovely singsong Caribbean lilt.

Harry reached down to relieve her of her burden. Mary

was only three inches taller than his grandmother. "I'll have to stuff newspaper in these to fit her."

He carried the clothing back down all three flights of stairs, his attention on the lithe young woman he'd left in Tommie's care.

Who was she? he wondered. It occurred to him that he hadn't even asked her name. Did he really want to, or was Gran right? Were some fairy tales too sweet to question? He was beginning to believe that he didn't want to find out that his captured fairy was actually a lonely secretary who'd seen *The Fairy Prince* one time too many. Although, if he thought about it, there was something less vulnerable about the sound of that. Maybe if she were a secretary he wouldn't feel as if he were defiling her by lusting after her.

Maybe he could lust after her successfully.

He stood there for a long moment, images washing fast through his head. Dark room, dark hours, dark thoughts. Her captive to his hands, to his needs. Willingly going where he would take her.

He wasn't sure how long the humming went on before he became aware of it. Sad, haunting, an ululation of mourning, it seemed, rising from the kitchen. His fairy girl. Her voice wrapped around him like smoke, sensual and stirring and somehow soulful.

He realized that he'd come to a halt in the formal dining room. How appropriate. It was one of his grandfather's greatest masterpieces. Where once Adam had decorated with plinths and cornices and classically inspired medallions, Nicholas Harold Wyatt, the seventh Earl of Hartley, had painted trees. Hundreds of them, rising from the green-carpeted floor like a forest in the long room, the branches stretching up and across the high ceiling until they twined into a living roof lit with the twinkling of a dozen or more recessed ceiling lights. It was a great hall to match the fairy world he'd painted in the rest of the downstairs rooms. Salons and music rooms and a ballroom had been transformed into an alien world with magical hills and dales populated by odd little houses and magical beings, their own Middle Earth.

It was the world described to him by his own grandfather, the old man had often said. A canvas so absurd that Harry felt shame anytime a stranger crossed the threshold. And yet, absurdly enough, one that made Harry feel so homesick he couldn't bear it. As if it weren't this house that was Harry's home but the woods painted on the walls.

He hated these rooms. Hated the waste of talent on these walls, the waste of money, the lost years of attention to a once-proud estate. And yet, wherever he went in the great old house, he found himself passing through the public rooms on the way, just to feel those trees over his head.

She was humming again. Harry snapped to attention and headed for the green baize door in the rear wall. One thing he knew for certain. When he took his guest to see Gran, he was taking her by way of the servants' staircase. The very last thing he needed today was his surprise guest asking about the landscape in his front hall.

"Here we are, then," he said, stepping down into the great kitchen. "Hope these will do."

For a minute he couldn't find her. Even Tommie seemed to have disappeared. All Harry saw was the pile of vegetables that sat out on the butcher-block table waiting to be thrown into the soup and the fire that crackled in the old hearth. Tommie, for all her size, felt the cold, so she always kept that thing roaring. Considering how little he could afford to pay her and how good her cooking was, Harry had no problem indulging her.

But right now he was standing in the middle of the floor with clothing in his hands and a sudden anxiety building in his chest. Where was the girl?

"Tommie?" he called, turning.

He hadn't made it far when he realized there was a bundled blanket on the floor, right in front of the fire. And that, at the sound of his voice, it had begun to turn.

"Ah, you're back, then," she said, with a delighted smile.

The fairy girl was crouched before his fire in an old horse blanket, as if waiting by a campfire. She was pale and shivering, but her hair was dry.

"Take that thing off," Harry demanded, stepping forward. "It probably itches like mad. Try—"

*Oh, good God.* She didn't just take the blanket off. She stood up and let it drop to the floor. And beneath it she was stark, staring naked.

# Chapter 3

She didn't even make it all the way to her feet before she lost her balance. Harry dropped the clothing and reached for her, sure she was about to pitch right into the fireplace. It was a mistake. The minute his hands touched that silky skin, he was flooded with the shock of pure lust, the kind that only haunted the darkest of nights. He shook with the effort to control himself. He inhaled the almost exotic scent of open air and spring and…was that cinnamon? Although how she could smell like Christmas cookies, he couldn't figure.

She was perfect, crafted for sensuality, with lush curves and tiny ankles, and the most delicious breasts he'd ever seen, full and high and crowned with soft pink nipples. And she was, God help him, a natural blonde. He couldn't seem to take his eyes off that nest of curling hair that made him itch to take her. Throw her to the floor, right there on the cold tile and the scratchy horse blanket, and bury himself so deep in her that he would never find his way back out.

He was panting, sweating with the effort to keep hold of his perilous control. He swore he could smell the arousal rise in her, a faint musk that incited images of conquest. *Now,* he thought, looking into eyes so wide and dark he thought he could fall right into them. *Here.*

He saw it in his head: tangled limbs and encroaching shadows, and the shock of satisfaction in those great, dark eyes. He heard it: harsh breathing and escalating moans as he pleasured her with urgent hands and a rock-hard cock. Deeper. Deeper. Harder, until she *screamed,* she screamed, there in his arms, on the floor, on the cold stone floor before the flicker of an unnecessary fire.

He had no recollection of pulling her to him, didn't remember taking hold of her hair to pull her head back to give him access to her. He didn't even know how her mouth opened beneath his, but it did. He kissed her, hard, deep, ravaging her mouth as thoroughly as he would her body. He felt the flush of her aroused skin against him, those full, firm breasts swelling against his chest, her belly welcoming against his rampant cock. He rubbed against her; he imprisoned her in iron arms; he sated himself on the taste of honey and cinnamon in her mouth. He cupped her bottom in his big hands, dragged her closer against him, and he thought of holding her down, of tying her down, of forcing her down, so he could take his fill of her. So he could control her, keep her, quiet any protest from her.

Except she didn't protest. She wrapped herself as tightly around him as he did her. She whimpered, but the sound was one of need, not fear. She opened and accepted him, met his tongue with her own to tangle in a dance of pure erotic pleasure. And it wouldn't have stopped until they were both naked and sated if Harry hadn't, at the last moment, heard the gasp of distress from the doorway.

He didn't know how he did it, but he yanked himself away. Gasping as if he'd been running, he pushed her toward his cook, who was standing there with a look on her face he hadn't seen since he'd been caught in the barn with one of the local girls when he was fifteen.

"I brought some clothes," he rasped, turning away. "Get her into them."

And then he stalked out the door into the teeth of the storm.

Sorcha's legs couldn't hold her up. With a whimper of distress, she simply folded back down onto the floor.

What had happened? How had she come to feel this disordered? She'd been sitting there on the floor, curled up in that torture of a blanket, trying to collect warmth from the fire, when she'd heard him behind her. It hadn't occurred to her that he would react so. After all, naked wasn't a state a fairy was unfamiliar with. It was natural so, a way to better enjoy the delights of Mother Earth, every inch open to the breeze and the sun and the mist of the morning. Mortals didn't seem to see it the same way.

Mortified, Sorcha curled back into herself.

"I'm reet sorry I left, child," the cook said behind her. "But who'd know the master would think to…to…"

Sorcha didn't lift her head from where it rested on her bent knees. "That isn't the way mortals usually greet each other, then?"

The cook seemed to have nothing in her but a sputter.

It wasn't the feel of him against her that troubled Sorcha. She was a creature crafted for pleasure. It was one of the dearest joys of her world to join in physical delight. It was a sacred ritual, wedded to the praise of the seasons and the joy of rebirth. And she had discovered joy in his arms, indescribable and unmatchable, something she'd never known, not even on the highest holy day when the fires burned on the hills and the fairy folk danced for the new year. But she'd seen something in his head that wasn't right.

Not joy. Not comfort. Fury. Aggression. Self-loathing. She couldn't tell exactly; evidently that gift was muted in this other world. Back in her land, she would have seen every image, heard every thought. Here she just got impressions. And those impressions frightened her. They'd frightened *him*.

"Coom now, child, get dressed," the large woman urged, pulling Sorcha to her feet. "You'll catch your death of cold if you don't."

Sorcha managed a smile, even as she considered what she'd seen and heard in the man's heart. "Ah, don't be after worryin' yourself. Fairies never fall ill. At least not in the way of mortals. We only pine if caught too long away from our home."

As she would surely pine if she couldn't find the Dearann Stone and get it back to her mother.

"Well, you'll not be pining away in my kitchen. Get thee dressed now."

Sorcha considered the pile of material the woman had picked up from the floor and shook her head. "I do thank you, Mrs. Thompson. But I'd like my own clothing back, please. That's my attire. Picked on my naming day."

"And not made for a Yorkshire November. Besides, it's still wet. Now, here. Wear this at least till yours dries."

Again the woman proffered the pile of clothing, and Sorcha couldn't think how to refuse. It seemed so important to her.

"Ah, it's the denim, then, is it?" she asked, reaching out to take the folded pants. "I recognize it, so. Didn't my sister's consort wear it when he visited? He's mortal, too, a great handsome one altogether, and was fierce attached to the things."

The cook helped her step into pants and then raised her arms to settle a soft concoction of lamb's wool over Sorcha's chest. "Now, then, get those shoes on," she said, rolling pants and sleeves up at least three times each to fit Sorcha's smaller frame.

Sorcha took a moment to acclimate to the clothing mortals wore, so heavy she couldn't feel the air around her. But warm. Warmer than the fire. Almost as warm as the man's embrace.

No. No, she couldn't say that in all truth. Nothing could match the scorching heat of his mouth on hers.

"I thank you," she said to the woman as she stared at the shoes. They seemed hard and unyielding, and that wasn't a feeling fairies could tolerate. "But no. I can't separate myself more from the mother."

The woman just stood there with the shoes in her hands, making that funny little "Eeee" sound in her throat. "What about socks?" she finally asked, and held up little foot snoods of brightly colored cloth: red and blue and green.

Sorcha smiled. "Aye, I think those might be nice."

She'd no sooner gotten them onto her feet and noticed how much warmer the stone floors were through them than the man returned. His hair was wet, as if he'd dunked it in a trough, and his posture was rigid. She heard the loathing in his mind again, the hot frustration, and she wondered at it.

"My grandmother would like to meet you," he said without preamble.

"Eeeee," the woman said again, sounding doleful.

Sorcha looked at them both and realized that they still didn't believe her. She probably shouldn't be surprised. After all, it wouldn't be a test if it weren't to be difficult. "Sure, I'd be that happy to see her. Can you be after tellin' me her name?"

He looked chagrined at that. "It seems introductions haven't been made, have they?"

"Now, that's not true at all," Sorcha said. "I'm known to Mrs. Thompson here, aren't I?"

Mrs. Thompson looked even more dour than he did at the information.

"I am Harold Wyatt, Earl of Hartley," he said with a stiff little bow. "My grandmother is Beatrice, Lady Waverly. And you?"

"Ah, so it's the titles we're sharing, is it?" She tilted her head, well acquainted with court etiquette. "I am the Princess Sorcha, Daughter of Mab, Queen of the *Tuatha de Dannan*."

"Well, this just gets better and better, doesn't it?" Mrs. Thompson said with a sly grin.

"I'll handle it," Harold Wyatt snapped. "Now, if you don't mind, it's getting late and Gran isn't the most patient woman on earth." He held out a hand toward the doorway. "Shall we?"

Sorcha slid the fairy purse into her pocket, but they didn't see her. Then she turned to follow.

"Should I trust you?" Mrs. Thompson demanded, evidently of Harold Wyatt, hands back on her hips.

He gave her a glare that should have melted the woman's hair. "Thank you for your concern, Tommie. We'll be fine."

"It might not have impressed itself on you at the time," she answered, "but the girl has a fairly lethal-looking knife strapped to her leg."

Harold Wyatt shot Sorcha a sharp look.

"It's for use against the *Dubhlainn Sidhe*," she said. She was about to reassure him that that kept him safe, as well, but found herself hesitating. Didn't the *Dubhlainn Sidhe* specialize in fury, terror and aggression? Could that be the fairy blood that flowed in Harold Wyatt? And what if it was? What should she do?

For now, all she could do was follow as he led the way up a set of narrow stairs. Not that she'd ever climbed any before. They were such a mortal invention. Fairies simply flew, if they needed height. But there would be no flying in this place. She could feel the weight of disbelief weigh her down. Not to mention the closed-in space. Sure, it took her breath. Or was that the power of the man who climbed ahead of her?

"I'd appreciate it if you don't encourage my grandmother," he was saying, his voice echoing oddly up the way.

"Encourage her how?" Sorcha asked, reaching out to run her hand along the wood rail, the only familiar surface she'd met in this cold stone place.

"She wants to think that this is all real. She's spent her life listening to it, after all. Her husband spent all *his* life trying to prove it, and then his son and daughter-in-law after him. I can't force her to face reality—it would be too cruel. But for God's sake, don't go telling her about fairy places and fairy spells and crap like that. She's a proud old woman, and I won't have you making fun of her."

Sorcha stopped between one step and the next. "I don't understand. What would I be makin' fun of?"

Harold Wyatt whipped around on her, and there was such a heat in his eyes. "The idea that her grandfather was a fairy prince. She believes it, so it's what she told the movie people, and they've created a whole damned industry from it. Well, he wasn't. He was probably a gypsy or an Irish horse trader who bamboozled a vulnerable heiress. But that just isn't as good a story, is it?"

A fairy prince. Sorcha could barely keep silent. Could she be right? A *Dubhlainn Sidhe* prince could easily have made off with the Dearann Stone. And there had been no strange disappearances from the *Tuatha* in the last few centuries. Was that where this Harold Wyatt had inherited his darkness?

"And where is this grandsire of yours, who thought himself royalty?" she asked.

He looked a bit taken aback. "Good Lord, he's been gone for at least sixty, seventy years."

Sorcha slumped a bit. Ah, it would have been too easy, any other way. It would have been nice, though, to simply confront the man who claimed to be a fairy and ask if he knew where the Stone might be. She wanted to be home, so. She wanted spring to come again. She didn't want to spend the rest of eternity in this bleak gray-brown world being tormented by this tormented man.

"And you think this is what I should say to her?" Sorcha asked. "That her grandfather was a liar?"

He shoved an agitated hand through his hair. "No. God, no. Just don't tell her you're the Princess Sorcha."

"Then *I* should be the one to lie?"

His glare was uncomfortable when he turned it on a person. But such pain there was in it, he probably didn't even know. Sorcha so wanted to lift a hand to that rough cheek in comfort. "Yes," he said, his voice taut and furious. "If you think you're lying, I don't care. Say hello, tell her how nice it is to meet her and then leave. I won't allow anything more. Do you understand?"

Sorcha tilted her head, as if that could help her comprehend him better. "What have they done to so hurt you so, *maneen?*"

He stiffened as if shot. "*Hurt* me? Nobody's hurt me."

"Ah, but I think they have. Your heart is in turmoil, and I think it gives you no rest. Is it such a fearsome thing to think fairies live?"

"It's *foolish.*"

Except his voice said more. It said *dangerous. Frightening. Heartbreaking.*

Sorcha shook her head. "Then it's sorry I am, Harold Wyatt, Earl of Hartley, for you'll never know the peace I think your grandmother does with just that bit of belief."

For a long moment he couldn't seem to answer. He

just stood there on the step above her, his hands out as if to brace himself with the walls, a tower of anger. Sorcha knew, though, that he would not hurt her. He only wanted to hurt himself.

"Don't. Encourage. Her," he grated out, and turned back up the stairs.

And Sorcha could do nothing but follow.

Sure, she didn't know what she'd expected of this grandmother of his, but it wasn't the woman who greeted her when Harold threw open the door onto an ornate, overstuffed, over-hot room. She was a wee bright thing, an apple doll in silk and tweed, with a face like a *bean tighe* and a spirit like fire, and she sat like a queen in the center of her realm. Sorcha was smiling before they were ever introduced. She wanted nothing more than to curl up at this grandmother's tiny feet and rest.

The dog on the old woman's lap would have none of it. It started to bark the minute Sorcha crossed the threshold.

"Mab!" the old woman snapped.

Sorcha whirled around. "Where?"

"What?" the lady demanded.

The door was empty of queens of any kind. Sorcha let her heart rate settle.

"Gran's dog," Harold Wyatt said with a curious curl to his lip. "Her name is Queen Mab."

Sorcha was startled into a laugh. She turned back to peer with delight at the little ball of excitable fur. "Ah, I wouldn't be tellin' herself that, if you don't mind. I'm not sure she'd think it was quite an honor."

"Herself?" the woman asked, her voice too big for her little body.

Sorcha couldn't help but smile. "The queen."

"Well, girl," the old woman said, tapping a gnarled hand on the arm of her chair. "What do you have to say for yourself?" Unaccountably, that was when Sorcha really took note of the chair the old woman sat in. Intricately carved, it rose a good six feet behind that little gray head, a great throne for this little ruler.

"Ah, Goddess, can it be?" was all Sorcha could think to say, breathless with wonder at the deep, dark gleam of wood. "Could I touch it, do you think?"

"Touch it?" the woman asked. "Good heavens, whatever for?"

Sorcha couldn't wait for permission. She stepped forward to run her hand up the side of the chair that had been carved in the most ancient celtic designs: mythological beasts wrapping endlessly onto themselves and surrounded by knotwork.

"And who wouldn't want to honor the spirit of black bog oak?" she breathed, tracing the living lines of ancient races. "A magic, rare wood it is that carries the record of generations in it. The very memory of my people." She closed her eyes for a moment, as the recollection of all those centuries washed through her fingers along with the spirit of him who had raised it and decorated it. She opened her eyes, tears crowding her throat. "Oh, a great heart must have crafted this."

Harold Wyatt almost came at her. But Sorcha didn't attend to him. She'd put tears in the old woman's eyes and it wasn't what she'd meant to do.

"Oh, please, Gran," she begged, hand out. "I'm sorry."

"Her name isn't gran," Harold Wyatt barked.

His grandmother waved him off. "Oh, Harry, don't be such a stick. I like her calling me gran. And you must call Harry by his name, too. Understand?"

Sorcha smiled. "Harry? Ah, a much more friendly name altogether, isn't it?"

The little woman laughed like a clap of thunder. "And Harry needs all the friendliness he can get, girl. That's the truth."

Sorcha nodded, not exactly sure what the problem was to begin with. "You'll accept my apology, then, Gran?"

"Apology?" the little woman barked, straightening to an impossible rigidity. "For what? For telling me my Nicholas had the hands of a genius? That the gift he gave me for my wedding day is beautiful? Well, it is. And there's nothing wrong with your saying it. Now, sit down, child, and tell me your name."

"It's Sorcha," Harry said, easing a bit closer.

"I didn't ask you, Harry," Gran snapped, then pointed Sorcha to one of the spindly-legged chairs that had been placed across from her. "Sit down, Sorcha. You look demmed silly in those socks."

Sorcha obeyed and perched herself on the chair before lifting her feet for consideration of the bright, happy colors that encased her toes. "Sure, we have nothing like this where I live," she said, wiggling her toes.

"And where is that?" Gran asked.

Sorcha's head snapped up. She caught Harry Wyatt's glare out of the corner of her eye and ignored it. Instead, she let her focus return to her feet.

"Not…nearby," she said with a smile she hoped disarmed as she rubbed at the odd blue material of her pants. "It's terribly sorry I am that I've intruded on your privacy."

"You're Irish," the woman said, as if it were an accusation.

Sorcha actually smiled. "After a fashion, so I am."

"Well, good. That accent's a breath of fresh air around here."

Sorcha wanted so badly to ask, *Where? Where is here?*

It was as if the old woman had heard her. "This is Yorkshire," she said. "England."

Sorcha's spirit deflated a little. *Ah. England, where the faerie had suffered so from disbelief that they'd all but vanished. No wonder her mother had warned her.*

"Do you like it here?" the old woman asked. "In this house?"

Sorcha opened her mouth and tried to lie. *Oh, yes. It's grand. All stone and…stone.* The truth of it was, the place was beginning to suffocate her again. She felt hot, restless with the loss of the earth beneath her feet. Even the glorious aura of the chair didn't soothe her. "I'm not used to something so big, sure. It's fierce large, isn't it?"

"The stone walls bother you?"

Goddess, was that a knowing light in those old blue eyes? Sorcha felt worse by increments. "Ah, well, they…" But she couldn't think of a good lie.

The old woman laughed, an oddly young sound. "Oh, I know my grandson told you to humor me. Don't worry. All I wanted to do was see the color of your eyes."

Sorcha couldn't look away from her.

Harry's grandmother nodded her head, her face seeming to glow. "They're green, aren't they? Like spring grass in sunlight. I had a feeling they would be."

Sorcha looked over at Harry, but he was watching his grandmother as if she'd suddenly hissed and spat.

"Your eyes are blue," Sorcha softly said to the old woman.

She got another bright, winsome smile. "I know. I inherited none of the blood, it seems. Except for my way with horses. Like Harry and his cousin. But Harry has the eyes, doesn't he?"

He did. Fairy eyes.

The old woman believed her. The old woman who might just be as pixilated as a mooncalf. Sorcha's heart sped up. She was still feeling disoriented, suddenly cold in this furnace of a room, even as something dripped down her back, but she tried her best to pay attention to what Harry's grandmother was saying.

"My Nicholas and I were first cousins, you know." Gnarled hands stroked the fanciful wolf's head that bared its teeth from the end of her chair arm. "The families intermarried like the Romanovs. Harry's parents were second cousins or some such. But grandfather sired the lot of us, so the bloodlines are strong."

"Gran," Harry Wyatt protested, coming to his feet.

"It's *my* story," the old woman informed him without looking away from Sorcha. "I assume you've not seen the movie?"

"Ah, no. I'm afraid not."

The old woman nodded, as if expecting that. "No matter. His name was Cathal. That's all we know. He took my grandmother's name, since she was a hereditary baroness. Nothing unusual there, if you're marrying up."

"Except he wasn't," Sorcha said. "Cathal is a royal name."

The old woman had a smile like a sprite. "A prince of the blood, she told me. After he died, of course. Couldn't admit it while he was alive. He would have been a circus freak. But if you knew him, you just… knew. He was…" Her voice drifted off, her attention away, back to earlier days, magical days, Sorcha thought. The old woman's face grew younger and it was something poetic.

"Gran," Harry Wyatt said, his voice softer than Sorcha had ever heard it. "Mary's here. It's time to rest."

Another old woman entered the overcrowded, over-hot room, another descendent of magic, Sorcha thought, although she didn't know what kind. Almost as small as Gran, but with wrinkled skin the color of the bog oak and wisdom in her mien.

"Look at her eyes," Gran said without looking away from Sorcha.

The other woman bent to pick up the dog named Mab and straightened to smile at Sorcha. "You're right," she said to the old woman. "But I knew you would be."

Ah, there was music in her voice, like wind through trees. Sorcha smiled. She wished she felt better. She would love to quiz the two women before Harry dumped her back outside. She wished…

"It's settled, then," Harry's grandmother announced as Harry pulled a wheeled chair out from behind a screen.

"What's that, Gran?" he asked, lifting her as easily as a child and turning to settle her into the chair.

It was then that Sorcha saw how wasted and small her legs were, how limp. It made her sad for this vital little woman who must once have walked her realm like a force of nature.

Gran was smiling like a hawk. "She's staying."

Harry Wyatt almost dropped her on the floor. "No, Gran. She's not."

Sorcha should have protested. Should have apologized. But suddenly she couldn't seem to form words. She was hot again, so hot she thought the mortal clothing would suffocate her. Her head hurt, as if somebody had turned a vise on it.

"Harold George Cormac Augustus Beverly," Gran snapped. "You would dishonor the legendary hospitality of the Wyatts?"

"*And* the Waverlys. She doesn't belong here."

"And she belongs out in that storm?"

Sorcha was sure she could hear it, roaring around the house and drowning out the voices. Her head itched again. A pressure was building and she couldn't breathe.

"I'll drive her to Hartley. She can stay at the Green Man."

"No, Harry. She won't."

"I'll be fine altogether," Sorcha protested, thinking how tinny she sounded, how she should fight to stay here, where a fairy prince might have lived. Suddenly she didn't have the energy. "I'd be grateful for my own clothing, though. It was given to me on my naming day...."

Both of them turned on her, obviously ready to shout at her.

She forestalled them when the pressure became too much. Too much. Ahhhh...

"Chooo!"

Her head exploded. Then the world simply disappeared, and she felt the floor hit her face.

* * *

Gwyneth Adderly was a very modern British girl. She didn't mind when people called her self-made, because she was. She'd made it through school on scholarships, since her parents lived on nothing more then the memories of past glories and prestige. Her great-grandfather had been a viscount and a good friend of the Duke of Windsor. It had been enough for her parents to live on. Not her. She'd parlayed her schooling and drive into an associate partnership at a futures trading firm.

It was what had brought her together with Harry. Both of them had chosen to live in the real world, not the fantasy one inhabited by their elders.

Just like his grandmother, another relic who preferred to live in a highly imaginative past. Gwyneth's family had gauged themselves by royalty. Harry's had relied on fairies. It was enough to give a modern girl the hives.

Gwyneth always paid her obeisance to the old girl, though. After all, Harry seemed to dote on her. Today, though, Gwyneth wasn't feeling quite up to fairy stories and noblesse oblige. She was still shaking from the near miss she'd just had on her way up the drive. She'd been pushing her way through an ugly autumn storm all the way up from London, only to have it get unaccountably worse the minute she'd passed through the gates to Waverly Close. And then, as she'd swept around the long curve by the oak copse, a person had run right out in front of her car. She was sure of it.

She'd seen him quite clearly. Dark eyes, pale, pale hair, lithe and otherworldly, he'd appeared out of nowhere, all but running right under her bumper. Except he hadn't. He'd leapt out of the way. Straight up. Over her car.

She'd obviously been mistaken about that last part. After all, she'd stopped the car and stepped out, just to make sure, only to see nothing but the empty lawns that swept up to the gray stone of the Close. She checked the car's bonnet, but it was unmarred. She could almost believe she'd imagined it, except for what she'd seen in his eyes, just for that flashing moment when he'd turned to her. Something compelling. Something frightening. Something that upended her firm pragmatism in ways she couldn't explain.

The minute she got to the front door, she reported the incident to Sims, the Wyatt butler.

"A…man in the park dressed like…Robin Hood?" he asked, his round, red face a bit slack with the obvious effort of maintaining his poise.

Gwendolyn focused on shaking the water from her umbrella before handing it to him. "Yes. Robin Hood. What part of that confuses you?"

"Why, nothing, miss," Sims said with a quaint little bow. "I will alert the archers immediately."

Gwyneth glared at him. "Make fun all you want. But what if the idiot ends up dead in the park and the Earl is blamed?"

"He will, in turn, I'm sure, blame me for allowing such a miscreant to invade his property."

Gwyneth glared at him. "And so he probably should, you old goat."

She didn't wait for more. Instead she turned for the great stairway, trying not to shudder at the dreadful murals that wrapped around the walls and all the way up the stairwell. Fanciful trees, prancing gray horses and flowers in a thousand shades. Oh, she wished she could get her hands on this mess. But it was just another indignity to be suffered in the name of survival. There would be hordes of guests tramping through the state rooms soon, all paying for the privilege of seeing the home of the Fairy Prince. Which meant the murals had to stay.

Not one of them would survive above the ground floor, though. That she vowed. She would *not* spend the rest of her life surrounded by fairies, even if they were painted. This was a historic site, one that deserved elegance and dignity, and she was damned well going to see that it got both.

"It's an Adam masterpiece," she growled out loud as she climbed the steps. "Not Bilbo Baggins's house."

"Indeed, madam," she heard sotto voce from Sims below her. "I fear Mr. Baggins would have been quite lost here."

"I heard that!"

"Of course you did, ma'am. Haven't we all commented on the superhuman quality of your hearing?"

She leaned over the railing to fire a challenge back at him, to find him conveniently gone.

Snotty bastard. Just because he'd been born here and was the latest in generations of Waverly dependents, he thought he could say just what he thought. Especially since Harry had put him in charge of the new staff they'd hired to prepare for the masses.

Ah, well, she thought, sliding her hand up the sleek mahogany banister. This was what happened when modern English girls met the price of fantasy.

But that was a matter for later. For now, she needed

to get past those bizarre walls on the ground floor and reassure herself with Harry's blessed pragmatism. She sprinted up the steps, already knowing exactly where she would find him at this time of day. She even prepared the delighted greeting she'd give the old baroness. There was no reason to hurt the old woman with any home truths, like the fact that her family had ruined a once-proud country estate, not to mention an even prouder family name.

But she and Harry were about to change all that. That thought inspired a true smile just as she reached the half-open door to the baroness's rooms.

"Good God, Harry," she heard his grandmother bark. "What did you do to the gel?"

Gwyneth pushed open the door to find Harry on the floor in a rather inappropriate embrace with a small blonde woman.

"Yes, Harry," Gwyneth echoed. "What did you do to the girl?"

## Chapter 4

The first thing Sorcha thought when she woke was that she had exploded. She was sprawled on the floor. She must have hit her head; it was suddenly stuffy and thick, as if the blood were congealing inside it. Worst of all, she was cold. Dear Goddess, how could she be so cold in this close little room? Then the pressure began to build up in her head again, and she realized she'd been wrong. Being cold wasn't the worst thing.

"Oh, how do you stop it?" she asked, trying to rub it away.

"Stop what?" Harry Wyatt asked.

She couldn't manage an answer. The pressure wouldn't go. Just rose and rose, taking her breath, stopping her nose up, burning until she couldn't help it, she—

"A—chooo!!"

—exploded. Again.

She grabbed the sides of her head, sure they would be in pieces. She whimpered, terrified of this thing that was happening.

"Is it the *Dubhlainn Sidhe* laying this curse on me?" she demanded, and thought her voice sounded pinched and tetchy. "Will they torture me until I fail?"

"Torture you? What are you talking about?"

She barely heard him. "Didn't I tell her I wasn't worthy? I am a fairy of small talents, quiet moments...." Finally she opened her eyes to find the Earl's face just above hers. He seemed to have gathered her in his arms. Shouldn't that make her warm? "My head," she whispered, and then sniffed, for some reason. "How many pieces is it in now from the explosion?"

The burning was back, searing her nose, her eyes, her throat. Building again, building...

"Explosion?" he asked.

"Please," she begged. "Tell me what you see. What dread magic has been visited on me. A—choooo!"

"Good lord, Harry," a new voice intruded. "Not another one."

"Hello, Gwyneth," Harry's grandmother said.

Sorcha was too busy hanging on to Harry to look away. "But my head..." she protested. "My...my throat. There is poison inside. I know it."

"Not really, child," Gran said, sounding sympathetic. "It's a virus, that's all. You have a cold."

Sorcha tried so very hard to understand. She certainly was cold. What did it mean that she *had* a cold? "And the explosions?"

"It's called a sneeze," Harry said briskly and hauled

her to her feet. "Which you know damned well. Now, if you don't mind, the play's over. It's time to rejoin the real world."

Sorcha rubbed at her head. "Is this a mortal ill?" she asked, swaying where she was.

"Oh, Harry, how awful," the new woman protested. "Can't the police do something about these people?"

"*This* person," his grandmother said, "is my guest. Is that a problem, Gwyneth?"

Sorcha finally got her eyes open to see a very tall, very slim, very tight-lipped woman standing in the doorway, staring at her as if afraid she'd stolen something.

"No, of course not," the woman said, but she didn't mean it. Sorcha could see it in the set of her shoulders. She was furious and frustrated.

"Not a believer, then, is she?" Sorcha asked Harry's gran.

The old woman grinned. "Sorcha, my dear, I'd like you to meet Gwyneth Adderly, Harry's fiancée. Gwyneth, this is Sorcha. She'll be staying for a few days."

"Gran…" Harry warned.

"At least until she's feeling better. She's ill, Harry."

Sorcha obliged her by sneezing again. It took her balance from her, and she had to hold on to a chair to stay upright. "I'm sorry…I just…"

"There she goes again," the woman Gwyneth said, just before Harry grabbed her under the arms.

He dragged her to a chair, sat her down and shoved her head down between her knees. "You are *not* about to faint on me, young lady. I don't have time for it."

"Ah, I'm that sorry…" she managed, wondering if

her head was going to fall off and roll away. "I don't feel well at all."

"She looks terrible," his grandmother said. "Feel her forehead, Harry."

"I will *not*—"

"Harold Marcus—"

"I'll do it," the dark lady said in that soft, whispery voice that made Sorcha feel calmer.

She didn't move for fear that her head would break. She could see Harry's feet in front of her. In great, thick shoes, they were, tied and strapped, barricading his feet from the air. It was no wonder he couldn't feel Mother Earth, Sorcha thought distractedly. No wonder he had no real whimsy in his eyes like his grandmother. If Sorcha were his grandmother, she'd make him take off his shoes altogether.

"I refuse to be party to this," the Gwyneth woman snapped. "First the man in the park, and now this. It's just too much, Harry. You have to stop it."

"You tell me how, Gwyneth," he snapped right back.

Sorcha felt sad for him. She felt sorry she was causing such stress. And something about the way his fiancée had talked about a man sent a frisson of warning down her back.

She would have said something, but she couldn't gather the energy. It seemed she was simply going to disintegrate right here in this little pile on a stiff chair in a stone prison.

"Child, you all right?" the dark woman asked.

"Oh, aye," Sorcha answered, hearing the unfamiliar rasp in her voice. "I just feel…"

The gentlest of hands lit on her forehead, offering cooling and calm. Sorcha sighed with it.

"You might want to call a doctor," the woman said, her voice still unspeakably peaceful. "This girl's burnin' up."

"Give her some aspirin," Gwyneth said, sounding almost frantic. "A decongestant."

"Ah, no," Sorcha protested, getting her head up. The room spun, and she held on to the hand of the kind woman, bracing herself with that calloused gentleness. "Mortal remedies aren't for me. Who knows what they'd do, now?"

"Oh, I don't know," Gwyneth said, sounding frustrated. "Take away your fever and stop your sneezing?"

Sorcha struggled to get in a breath. She felt her energy ebb. Goddess, could this mortal cold overcome her fairy life so quickly? Desperately, she fumbled in the pants where she'd stashed her bag, but her fingers were clumsy and her breath short.

"Somethin's real wrong here," the kind woman said.

"My herbs," Sorcha begged. "They're in a bit of a bag. If I can get to them…"

She felt fingers fumble alongside hers. She heard voices echoing and felt the frustration in Harry Wyatt's heart.

"Oh, for heaven's sake," he said, and slapped her pouch into her palm. "Here. Do you mix them with anything?"

"No." She desperately tried to focus. "One is for fairy ills on mortals, the other mortal ills on faerie. Oh, which is it?"

She squinted, separating the two packets and trying to read the *bean tighe's* horrible handwriting. It was harder to breathe, harder to see, and she felt another of those fierce awful sneezes coming on. She couldn't allow it, not with the most delicate herbs in both worlds in her hands.

"Ah…here." Her hand was shaking hard, but she separated out a pinch. No more. She slid it under her tongue and closed her eyes against the pain of it. *Nothing is worth the cure that doesn't hurt,* the *bean tighe* was wont to say. Well, this herb sent shock waves through her whole system.

She was struggling to get her herbs put away. "I can't…" There were tears on her face, tears in her lungs and heart. She wasn't sure she'd been in time.

Big hands took the pouch from her, calloused hands that knew work, but were gentle and delicate as they closed away her precious medicine.

"I thank you, Harry Wyatt," she whispered, and managed to look up into his face, his dear, troubled face that she would have liked to know better. "And I'm sorry. I think, after all, I've failed, and there will be no more spring. Forgive me."

They were the last words she managed. Her strength vanished, and her eyes slid closed. This time she felt Harry Wyatt collect her into his arms before she could hit the floor.

"Yon fairy bower is prepared, my lord," Sims intoned.

"Knock it off, Sam," Harry said. "Did you call the doctor?"

"Indeed I did, sir. He said he'd be over after his surgery. In the meantime, he suggests aspirin and decongestants."

Harry followed Sims down the hall to one of the habitable guest rooms. His shoulders were aching. Fairies were heavier than they looked. This one might not be big, but she was dead weight.

She was also pale as death. He could hear a slight

wheezing when she breathed, too. He had no business being worried for this latest entrant in the fairyland sweepstakes. But, God, he was. He'd never seen anybody get so sick so fast. And it was a dead certainty she wasn't faking it. Her skin was still hot enough to vaporize water.

So what if she was a bit delusional? So what if she was going to make his next few days a living hell, what with his grandmother insisting the girl was a fairy and Gwyneth insisting the girl go?

All he wanted was a little time away from the pressures of the city. He wanted to walk his land and rest in the battered old leather chair in his library. He wanted to pretend that Waverly Close wasn't just one disaster after another. Instead he got to pretend that a fairy princess had come to visit.

Brilliant.

"I will *not* be part of this," Gwyneth said behind him, sounding frightened. He didn't blame her.

"What would you suggest I do, Gwyneth?" he asked, his voice sounding as weary as he suddenly felt. "Throw her out?"

"Call the police," she said. "Just like I told Sims to do with the other one."

He knew he should ask. She wanted him to. Sorcha must have had a co-conspirator they'd left back out on the moor. Well, let somebody else take care of him.

*She smelled like rain and cinnamon.*

Well, where in the hell had *that* come from? He almost closed his eyes and just breathed in. It wasn't a sensual smell, not exotic or dark. But somehow it snaked in under his defenses and made him want to touch her.

Her breasts were pressed against his chest. Her skin was so soft he wanted to drop his face against it and rub, and her hair, that unbelievable silk, tickled his arm.

From one step to the next, one breath to the next, he was suddenly ravenous for her. And here he was traversing the main hallway of the second floor like a bloody parade, with his butler leading the way and his fiancée and his grandmother and her companion bringing up the rear, Gwyneth and Gran still arguing over the best disposition of the girl in his arms.

"You can't expect Harry to give consequence to one of these creatures," Gwyneth was protesting.

"I can and I will," Gran answered. "It's still as much my home as his, Gwyneth, and I'll have my say."

"But she could be *anyone*...."

"She *stays*," he growled, whirling on them. "Do. You. *Understand?*"

Gwyneth flinched as if he'd slapped her. Suddenly he didn't care. He wanted them all gone. He wanted this woman all to himself, no matter that she was unconscious with fever and as vulnerable as a human could be. He wanted to be on top of her. He wanted to be inside of her. He wanted to make those huge green eyes widen and darken and close, close with languor, not with illness. He wanted to hear her shriek his name....

His grandmother slammed her cane against the wall. *"Harry!"*

He stopped, his breath shuddering in his chest. His grandmother was looking aghast, and he wasn't surprised. He was hard again, just with the scent of this fairy girl in his nostrils. He was trembling with the effort it took to keep from shoving every other living soul down the stairs and shutting himself away with her. He was going mad; he knew it. And it was evident that now everybody else did, too.

"Mary," he said, his voice still low and harsh, "if you would stay with her once we get her settled…? Gran, I'll take you back to your room."

"I think that would be wise," his grandmother said.

Gwyneth didn't seem to have any words at all. She looked shaken. There were tears in her eyes, and she seemed unable to hold her hands still.

"I have some business to attend to in York," she said in a thin voice. "It might be best if I take care of it now."

Harry snapped off a nod. "Yes. I'll see you after, then?"

"Yes."

Sims held the door open to the Chinese room, and Harry stepped through. He wasn't overly fond of this room. Too overdone by one of his distant aunts. Silk birds on silk walls, and a bed the size of a battleship swathed in more silk, all of it crimson. Birds under glass and parasols stuffed in ginger jars. His poor fairy child would have a seizure when she woke to all of this.

He laid her on the bed and stopped himself from climbing in after her. He took a deliberate step back and let Mary by. The woman named Sorcha looked lost on that monster of a bed. Harry knew he had no business being attracted to her. But she had breasts that made a man's hands itch and hips that just called to his cock. And her scent. A common thing, sea air and cinnamon, but suddenly mesmerizing. So uniquely her that he wanted to bend over and sip it.

He could actually see the scene in his head. He could hear her gasps of pleasure, feel her long, delicate fingers trailing down his naked skin. Smell the sweat on her skin as he drove into her.

"Good God, Harry," his grandmother snapped, smacking her cane against the back of his knees. "Snap out of it."

The sting of the cane was quite adequate to deal with an errant daydream. Harry came back to attention and backed farther away.

"Go apologize to Gwyneth before she leaves," Gran suggested.

Harry looked over to see not condemnation, which he'd suspected, but sympathy. Did she understand? Could she explain it to him? He dragged a hand through his hair and closed his eyes. He struggled hard for his legendary control.

"What's happening?" he demanded. But only to himself.

His grandmother heard anyway. "You're facing the unexplainable," she said, her voice more gentle than he thought he'd ever heard. "Don't be alone with her. Not for a moment. Not until we know exactly what brought her here."

He pointed a shaking finger at her. "I love you, Gran. But do not mistake that for complicity. She's not one of your fairies. She's a confused girl, and she's going home as soon as she's well enough. Do you understand?"

"More than you think," she said with a smile, and turned her wheelchair around.

Harry stood in the door of the bedroom watching her go and couldn't think how to answer. Finally he realized he had no choice but to intercept Gwyneth before she left. He had to explain what had just happened.

He had to *try* to explain, anyway. That was if somebody could explain it to him first.

It was time to ease the storm. Darragh, who held clouds in his hands and set loose the lightning, was tired of being cold. Storms were a different thing altogether in this land of mortals. Not something of majesty and power, but a burning, stinging misery that did nothing to help the earth. And no matter how angry and frustrated a fairy was, he was not allowed to injure the earth. It had nothing to do with the fact that he was cold and wet and shivering.

So he calmed the clouds and the wind. Then, for good measure, he opened the bright metal door of the automobile he'd seen the beautiful woman wield and slipped inside the back. He'd seen automobiles, of course. He'd always been fascinated by them, sleek beasts that had all the benefits of a horse without the attitude. But he'd never actually been inside one. The seats were soft as doeskin and the air warm. It would be so easy to sleep here. So much more comfortable than waiting outside that great pile of stones for Sorcha to reappear.

She was his way to the Dearann Stone. She was the key. And after he'd gone to all that trouble to follow her across the gates into this living hell, he wasn't going to lose her.

He might have slept a little; he wasn't sure. Before he realized it, one of the doors opened, and he saw gleaming blond hair over the back of the seat.

"Great, hateful cow," she snarled as she climbed in. "'Don't hurt the fairies. Don't confuse the trespassers.' As if it weren't patently obvious that girl is nothing but an escaped lunatic. Who could ever see *her* perched on a bloody flower?"

She threw some kind of satchel over the seat and hit Darragh square on the head. He almost yelled at her. But then he caught a whiff of her scent, a brisk, sharp tang that was new to him. She was still muttering as she fiddled with something up there. Darragh thought it might just be worth his while to see what she would do. She certainly didn't seem to like Sorcha. She might just like to meet somebody who felt the same way.

He would wait a bit and see. And in the process get a ride in this marvelous creation.

"Gwyneth's a bit angry," Harry admitted. The faint handprint that could still be seen on his cheek said as much.

His grandmother smiled, but she didn't look happy. "And you're surprised, are you, Harry? After that display in the bedroom, I'm surprised she didn't heave a chair at you."

They were sitting down to dinner in the small dining room, *small* being a relative term. This room was decorated in just as many trees as the other, just not as tall, and with a few structures painted in the corners that looked for all the world like something from a Disney movie. He hated it here. He couldn't stay away.

"I'm afraid I've been under a bit of stress lately," he said, rubbing at the bridge of his nose. "Work and all."

"Not to mention a beautiful woman who sets off your libido like Guy Fawkes rockets dropping into your lap."

He was already shaking his head. "I'm sorry. I can't explain it. I already told Gwyneth that."

His grandmother snorted. "I'm sure she understood."

He couldn't help a wry grin. "Would you?"

"Absolutely not. If your grandfather had tried something like that, he would have had to wear a hat to hide the lumps. I'm sure it was just insult to injury that she had to admit she thought a man flew over her car."

"Jumped. He jumped."

"That's a Jaguar coupe, Harry. One does not jump over a Jaguar coupe. She sounded as fascinated with him as you are with little Sorcha."

"I am *not*—"

"That's what Gwyneth said. But she was awfully flushed when she said it. When Sorcha wakes, we'll have to ask her if she brought along any friends when she came over."

"Came over from where?" he demanded. "Liverpool?"

His grandmother just smiled and dipped into her soup. "I don't suppose you've heard anything from that worthless physician."

"Just that he has other priorities before coming out to the big house for a cold."

Grandmother shook her head. "It's not a cold, Harry. At least not one the likes of which *I've* ever seen. Mary is worried for her."

"Then we should get her to the hospital."

"No." She shook her head again, focused on her spoon. "They'd kill her for sure."

Harry wasn't sure how much more he could take of this. "Please," he begged. "Don't put that girl's life at risk because you want to play fairies."

If she could have, his grandmother would have surged to her feet. Her color was high, and her eyes glittered. "I know it's been a disappointment to you that the estate has suffered. I know you would do anything before admitting that your parents, or indeed your grandfather, could have been right. It would negate every iota of logic you've held on to for your whole life like words from the Bible. And I know it's far more comforting to think of your grandmother as a charmingly eccentric recluse with a penchant for fanciful stories. But I'm afraid you're about to be surprised, Harry. And if you can't keep an open mind, you could very well be shattered against the walls of your logic."

"She is *not*—"

"Pretending. She is *not* pretending. You've certainly seen enough of those to tell the difference. And my instincts say that the young blond gentleman dressed like Robin Hood who went sailing over Gwyneth's car was not pretending, either."

"Oh, no," Harry heard from the doorway. "Blond, you said?"

Harry leapt to his feet. Sorcha was standing in the doorway, Mary right behind her.

"What are you doing out of bed?" he demanded, stepping up.

He pulled himself to a halt when she walked into the room. She looked perfectly fine. A little wan, slow to move, but awake. Alert. Smiling. "I am well, thank you," she said with a look behind her. "Thanks to Mary's help and the *bean tighe's* herbs, I…oh…oh, my…"

Harry instinctively looked behind him, but her focus was on the walls. Up to the ceiling, where the recessed lighting twinkled like stars. She stood stock still a foot inside the door, and there were tears in her eyes.

"Oh, Goddess, it looks just like home."

"You think so?" Gran asked.

Sorcha turned her attention to the old woman and smiled, a couple of tears slipping down her cheeks. "Ah, I do, so," she said. "It's the small hall, then, isn't it? The wee fairies reside here where they can't be all over trampled. See them? Up there in the ceiling, where they can flit and flirt with each other? The trees are a bit different is all, and the mountains. Ours are softer, gentler. Sure, aren't these broad-shouldered and sharp?"

It was all Harry could do not to throttle her. "Stop it," he commanded.

She didn't seem to hear him. "Oh, mother, I miss it so. But how did you do it? How did you know?"

"My grandfather described it," Gran said, her own head back to take in the view. "My husband painted it."

The two women were beaming at each other. Harry wanted to break something with his fists.

"Are you sure you're well, child?" Gran asked her. "Mary?"

Mary smiled and took her regular seat. "Wish I had me some of them herbs. She was six inches from dead, I'd swear it on my mother. Then, poof! Up she sits and apologizes for the fuss."

"I don't want to be a bother," the girl said.

Harry saw new shadows under her eyes and wondered if that was from whatever she'd been through for the last four hours. He was *not* going to worry about her. He was just not.

"You said something about the blond man?" he asked.

She took her time in answering. She couldn't seem to take her eyes off the tops of those trees. Harry wished like hell he knew why. Then maybe he'd know why he couldn't, either.

"Oh, aye." Finally she faced him. "I heard you mention him."

"You know him?" Grandmother asked.

"What color was his raiment?" Sorcha asked. "Can you tell me?"

"Gray," Harry said, even knowing he shouldn't. "Silver-gray, Gwyneth said."

Sorcha seemed to deflate. "Then he's followed me over. Ah, this is fierce bad."

"He? He who?"

"Oh, I'm that sorry. You don't know. Darragh, son of Bran. He is the storm keeper, and he is beautiful. He has dark, dark eyes, and isn't his hair the exact shade of moonlight?"

"That sounds just about how Gwyneth described him," he said. "Why is it bad?"

She shook her head. "Because he'll be looking for the Stone, too, so. And he won't want good things for it. He'll want to steal it away with him. He was shamed, you see, for helping my sister Orla in trying to take the throne. The queen exiled him. He must think this will get him back. Or find him a place with the *Dubhlainn Sidhe*."

"You love him," Gran suddenly spoke up.

Sorcha smiled at her and shook her head. "Loved," she said. "A sad state of affairs altogether, for wasn't he my sister Nuala's intended consort? When he was replaced by the mortal she wed, he sought his own way to power. And in doing so, caused my own exile here." She sighed, looking so sad. "And now it's his enemy I must be. For I must find the Stone first."

"Stone?" Gran asked. "What stone?"

"The Dearann Stone. A rare, bright stone of perfect clarity that holds the female power of faerie in its depths."

"The Fairy Diamond?"

"Gran…"

"You know it, too?"

"Of course I do, girl. It's right upstairs."


Gwyneth parked the car in a lot alongside the York Minster Hotel, where she was to meet a partner in a futures trading firm who was interested in her. She wasn't in the mood for the meeting anymore. She was still trying her best to overcome the day she'd already had. With trembling fingers, she reached up to move the rearview mirror, so she could get a look at her hair. Instead, she saw a face.

Not her own. A man's, peeking over the seat behind her. She shrieked.

"Ah, now, don't do that," a soft voice whispered in her ear. A lovely voice. A voice that made her want to smile and dance.

And how bloody absurd was that?

"How did you get in the car?" she demanded, slipping the keys out, and preparing to open the door and run like hell. She must have some kind of weapon at hand. Maybe the keys, right to the eyes. She'd seen it once on the telly.

"I've been here all along, lass," he said with a sparkling smile. "I just didn't let you see me till now."

Gwyneth twisted around so suddenly that she was sure she dislocated at least one vertebra. "You're the one!" she accused. "You jumped over my car!"

She should be screaming at him to get out, screaming to any passerby for help. One look in his other-worldly face stopped her. His eyes were deep, gray like storm clouds over the Atlantic. His face was as fine as a sculpture, pale and honed and aristocratic. His smile was…oh, bloody hell. His smile was enough to make a sensible girl slide right off her soft leather Jaguar seat.

"Sure, there was no jumping involved," he said. "I was fascinated by your machine and what did you do but almost run me over with the beast? Well, a fairy has no choice but to take flight at such a time." Reaching out an elegant hand, he brushed her English blond hair back from where it swung in her eyes and smiled that same heart-stopping smile at her. "But now I'm thinkin' I'd much rather investigate its owner. What else on your mortal realm smells as fine as you do?"

As lithely as a dancer, he lifted himself from the backseat and took her face in his smooth, impossibly gentle hands. Gwyneth stared at him, frozen in place. Odd places on her body began to hum, and she was smiling at him even as she thought she should be running down the street in pursuit of the last dredges of her sanity.

She was engaged.

She was paralyzed. She was about to let a complete stranger kiss her in the middle of a parking lot, and she couldn't remember how to care. Oh, bloody hell.

# Chapter 5

Sorcha thought she was still ill. Surely she couldn't have heard those words.

"The fairy diamond is here?" she asked, just to make sure. "Here in this house."

"Of course it is," Harry Wyatt snapped. "Isn't that why you're here?"

Surely her journey couldn't be over so soon.

The thought surprised her. She should have felt relief. What she felt instead was disappointment. She wanted another kiss from Harry Wyatt. She wanted to talk to him, to make him understand what he refused to. She wanted to see him smile. She wanted to see him smile at *her*. But now she wouldn't have time.

"I was sent here to find it," she said, her voice hushed. "But I didn't know…may I see it?"

One of the great ruling stones here, in this prison of disbelief. The mother light of the faerie, hidden so long that the *Dubhlainn Sidhe* had despaired of it. Although wasn't it just like men altogether to never have found the thing? They probably hadn't even tried. One day on this side of the gate, and she was actually to see it.

She wiped her hands on the legs of her pants, trying to maintain a bit of calm. Harry and his grandmother seemed to be carrying out a completely nonverbal argument with no sure winner. Sure, Sorcha wasn't entirely certain which one had the redder face.

"It's just to pay my respects, don't you see," she wheedled, the weight of the false stone heavy on her hip. "After all, if it is the…fairy diamond, then it would be Dearann the Fruitful, she who brings us spring and children. She it is who ripens the harvest and brings mares to foal. Without her, the earth would not turn to summer."

"Don't let the local vicar hear you say that," Harry Wyatt suggested. "He has this odd idea that God might be in charge of things like that."

"Well, of course she is," Sorcha said. "But even she uses a bit of help now and again. And her most lovely Dearann Stone is a bit of help. You see?"

Harry scowled. "*She* is a chunk of quartz," he snapped. "And that isn't anything to see."

"Don't be absurd, boy," his grandmother snapped right back. "It's a legacy from your great-great-grandfather."

"Shares in a railroad would have been better."

The old woman thumped her cane against the floor. "I understand your frustration, Harry. But since you never met him, I will not have you disparage my grandfather. Now, you can stay here and pout all you want. Mary and I are going to take the girl to see the stone."

"We've just sat down to dinner."

"It'll wait."

Harry slapped his napkin onto the table and got to his feet. "I'll go along," he said. "After all, I should probably keep an eye on the silver."

He grabbed hold of his grandmother's chair and turned it for the door, Mary jumping to her feet to follow. Sorcha backed out of his way just in time. Then she accompanied them down the hall.

Oh, and weren't there more surprises along the way? How could she not have seen them on her way to this room? Sure, she had been so focused on seeing Harry Wyatt again, on once again flirting with that incredible attraction, that she might have overlooked the smallest bit of heaven in this prison.

But to have missed this, a world of murals, painted as if from her own memory, with tiny stars in the ceiling that looked so like sprites that she fought tears, and herds of moon-pale horses with the fairy light in their eyes pacing the corners.

She might be going home soon. She might be able to walk among her own trees and settle down on the grass with the children, dance in the great hall of a banqueting night. She might be able to reacquaint herself with every beloved fairy in the realm. But she would be doing it alone.

Being alone hadn't bothered her so much before. She'd always trusted that she would find someone for herself, even when she'd pined for Darragh in her lonely little house in the glen. She'd believed that there would be someone to take the edge off her loneliness.

Never, though, could she have anticipated what it would really mean.

She'd never realized that men could be so...overwhelming. Even Darragh, with his storm-dark eyes and beautiful faerie body, had never struck her so. She'd seen him as a companion, a muse, mayhap, someone untouchable and worth worship. Never had she thought of him in the sense she suddenly did Harry Wyatt. And Goddess knew she'd never been afflicted with such stunning mind images with him or any male.

Sure, she should have learned better from her sister and her mother, but who knew a man could so set a woman's blood to churning just with his scent, or that a fairy might want to offer up almost anything for one more kiss? Who could ever know how neatly a woman's body could fit against a man's?

She knew now. And so it hurt to follow the rigid back of the man she suspected she would carry in her heart when she returned to her land.

"Slow down, Harry," his grandmother demanded. "The girl isn't up for footraces yet. She's still pale."

"Ah, no," Sorcha said with a big smile. "Aren't I in the pink of health?"

No, she wasn't. Not yet. She was still feeling a bit muddled from the mortal illness, her head echoing oddly and her chest tight. She felt trembly and uncertain, a foal on new legs, but she wasn't sure whether that was left over from the illness, the cure or the surprise. She just knew she couldn't allow Harry an excuse to cancel the trip upstairs.

"The walls..." she said.

"Beautiful, aren't they?" Gran asked. "And see the

horses? Nicholas said they were fairy horses he'd painted, but they're our horses to the nose."

Sorcha saw the intense longing on the woman's face. "You don't ride anymore."

Harry brought his gran's chair to a screeching halt. The old woman held him silent with a hand. "Not since I came a cropper at a five-bar gate about twenty years ago. Why?"

Sorcha looked again at the moon-pale horses on the walls. "Would you like to? If I can find the right horse, of course."

"What the hell are you talking about?" Harry demanded.

"Ride?" Gran asked. "Do you see my legs?"

Sorcha nodded. "Ah, sure. But I'm thinking you have horses here who would do. Well, if they agreed, of course. Sure they're fierce proud—"

"How dare you?" Harry demanded.

"No, truly…"

Gran stilled Harry with her hand. "We'll talk about this later, child." She sounded firm, but Sorcha saw the new light in her old eyes. She just smiled and followed as they walked on. And then, while she was still caught in the logistics of what she planned, Harry surely punished her for her words.

He came to a halt and stepped through a door, pushing his grandmother ahead of him, Mary on their heels. Sorcha had already followed before she realized that he'd just led her into a small box. Then the door slid closed.

"Oh, I…" She couldn't breathe. Goddess, she was caught in a cage of metal. It seemed that Harry took up what little air there was, and there was a grinding noise that hurt her ears. Then, suddenly, the box moved.

"It's an elevator, child," the old woman said, as if that would help.

Sorcha kept nodding. She put her hands out before her, as if she could test the weight of the air. It pressed on her. It bound her, and she was terrified she couldn't get—

The door opened onto another hallway. "Oh."

Sorcha set tentative feet onto the carpet and pulled in the breath of her life. She almost went down on her knees in thanks. Such a prison, that little box was. So tight and airless. Not to mention that moving about. Straight up, and all on its own. That wasn't a carriage a fairy could find comfort in. She stepped a bit closer to Harry, wishing she could fortify herself with his solid strength. Almost certain he would have none of it.

"You all right, girl?" Gran asked, peering closely at her.

"Aye." She pulled in an unsteady breath, trying to calm her racing heart. "It was just a surprise. Sure, there's nothing like it at home. So then, Cathal didn't build such a thing."

Gran laughed. "Good heavens, no. Harry was sweet enough to install it for me. Grandfather built…no. I'll let you see it later, shall I?"

"Did he really live in this place of stone?" Sorcha asked. "I can't imagine one of the fey people surviving here for long."

"You're laying it on a little thick," Harry said.

His grandmother frowned.

"I'm sorry," Sorcha said. "Laying what on, please?"

Harry never looked over at her. "I believe it's called blarney."

Sorcha grinned. "Ah, no. That's where the cousins live, not us. We're Sligo bound. Do you know it?"

"Never been there."

"Harry doesn't find Ireland as compelling as others do," his grandmother said, with a peculiar look on her face.

"Ah, isn't that a shame, then?" Sorcha said. "For there's no sweeter air or kinder rain."

Gran nodded. "That's what I keep telling him."

"She says I'll run across family there," Harry said with some disdain. "The kind that sits on flowers and plays the harp."

"And so you might," Gran said.

Suddenly the entire procession stopped. "If that were possible, don't you think somebody might have succeeded sometime in the past sixty years?" Harry demanded, his face taut and impatient.

"Maybe they weren't looking in the right places," Sorcha suggested.

And wasn't that a mistake, then? Harry shot her a look of pure venom. There was such resentment in him. Such fury and frustration. And yet, deep in the fire of that look was attraction. Hunger.

Suddenly Sorcha was swamped again by the mind-images. Harry bent over her, his eyes black with arousal, his chest bare and glistening with sweat, his hair tangled from her hands. She could smell the arousal on him, could hear the rasp of his breathing. She could feel the touch of his eyes on her own bare skin, and wasn't it the most wonderful thing she'd ever known? She froze there in the middle of that great hallway, only feet from her goal, because she couldn't look away from the hand Harry lifted in her own mind to touch her.

"We'll never get there at this pace," his gran snapped.

The images vanished like bubbles, leaving Sorcha

even weaker than before, her heart beating hard in her chest, her hands itching for the touch of what she'd just imagined. What Harry had imagined, as well. She could see it on him, in the dilated pupils and flare of his nostrils. He was as aroused as she was.

"Stop that," Harry said.

"Stop what?" Gran asked.

"Faith," Sorcha breathed, a hand to her chest. "Now I know why my mother and sister are so addicted to the thing."

"What thing?"

Harry turned and continued down the hall. "Nothing."

Even as upended as she was, Sorcha almost laughed. You could call it many things. Never, in all the millennia of faerie existence, could you call it "nothing." Indeed, didn't her mother and sister Orla cherish the chance to invade a man's mind and share such fantasies? Sorcha had never before felt the desire. Since meeting Harry Wyatt, she couldn't seem to stop.

He was having none of it, though. He pushed his grandmother's chair down the carpet as if mounting an attack. For a second Sorcha could do no more than watch him. For a second she completely forgot what they were doing here.

The Dearann Stone.

"Thunder and hailstones," she cursed and walked on.

That was all it took to dispel the last of the fantasy. It was the house that did it, and it wasn't something Sorcha liked at all. It was a great long hall they walked, hung in paintings and populated with statues, cold, dead things that looked like ensorcelled children. Sorcha shivered under the stares of them and wished herself away. She ached to have her feet on the grass again, even if the grass was cold and wet. This house simply bore in on her, even the rooms painted like her own world. And this hall was higher up, farther away from the earth and her comfort. It was no wonder someone had felt so compelled to paint it all over. How could a person feel the magic of the Dearann Stone past these walls?

Ah, the Stone. What would it feel like? she wondered. Her palms sweated in anticipation. Would it sing, or simply shine inside her? She only knew the power of the Coilin Stone, and that was masculine, a red, hard thrum that settled in a faerie's chest like fire. Dearann had to be quieter altogether, didn't she? Gentle, as a woman should be. As the earth was in the early days of spring, when the grass was so bright it hurt your eyes and the lambs gamboled on the green.

How could it have survived here, in this cage of rock? Sorcha called to it in her heart and heard nothing back.

"Sure, shouldn't I be feeling it now?" she said to herself, her hand once again to her chest.

Harry seemed to falter a bit and turned his head, but Sorcha couldn't read his expression.

"Feel it?" Gran asked.

"Aye," Sorcha said. "Aren't I the stone keeper? Isn't it to me they speak, so I know who belongs to them? I'm the one sees them safe and settled on the right hand."

Gran laughed, an abrupt bark of noise. "Girl, the Fairy Diamond would never fit on anybody's hand."

"Ah, no," Sorcha admitted. "Dearann is meant for no less than the crown of the *Dubhlainn Sidhe*."

Almost she said that they sore missed it. That the

world sore missed it. But the time wasn't right yet. It might never be the right time to let these mortals know the business of faeries. It was her own counsel she should keep, at least until she knew how she would deal with the Dearann Stone.

"The *Dubhlainn Sidhe?*" Gran asked.

"Fairies of the Dark Sword," she said. "The masculine to the Tua feminine. The air fairies of the South."

"*Dubhlainn,*" Gran murmured, as if testing it against her teeth. "*Dubhlainn.*"

Sorcha searched the well-worn features. "Is it familiar to you?"

Gran just shook her head. "I don't know. Could my grandfather have been one of them?"

"He could."

"He could also have fallen off a wagon of tinkers," Harry muttered.

Sorcha smiled. "Sure, it must be exhausting to carry such a furious anger around with you all the time."

Harry swung his gaze on her but said nothing. He didn't need to. Sorcha saw the pain beneath that anger. The fear and loss that shouldn't have been allowed within such sturdy halls.

He turned away when his grandmother reached up to pat his hand where it lay on her chair. "Pay no attention to Harry. He has reason enough to be surly. As much as I loved my husband and son, they squandered their birthright as much as any gambler on the horses and put our very home in jeopardy. But that's what this obsession is all about, isn't it?"

And it would kill Harry if he lost this place, Sorcha saw suddenly. This place he disparaged was as much a part of him as the hollows and dales of her home were to her. Ah, how could she hurt so for a mortal? It was as if it shimmered off him, this bone-deep fear. Fear of so much: the past, the future, the minute-by-minute present. How she wished she could ease that burden for him.

"Would you accept my apology, then, Harry Wyatt?" she asked. "My words were rash, and that they usually aren't."

He turned again, only a bit, as if afraid to betray too much. She saw it, though, the raw vulnerability that lived deep in the forests of his eyes. "I haven't been much kinder to you," he said. "We'll forget it then, shall we?"

She had no choice but to nod. It didn't relieve the pressure in her chest, though.

"Now then, girl," Harry's gran said, her voice brisk, "tell me about this stone-keeping business. What does it mean?"

Sorcha smiled. "Each fairy has a special place in our pantheon, gifts to give and enjoy," she said. "Each fairy's place is reflected in his or her raiment and silver-set stones." She held out her hands. "Mine, as you see, are opal and spinel, the color of my raiment that of the early dawn sky. My sister Nuala, who would have been queen, carried peridot and amethyst, and wore peacock. The queen by right is given emerald, moonstone and iolite to guide her people."

Gran leaned her head back to see Sorcha better. "What would my stones be?" she asked.

Sorcha couldn't help but smile. "Ah, well, I'd have to carry you to the stones to see them sing for you, now, wouldn't I? But if I could guess, wouldn't I grace you with the strength of a ruby and the grace of a pearl."

Harry's grandmother nodded, seemingly pleased. "I like that. Indeed I do. And Harry. What would you see on his hands?"

"She wouldn't see anything," Harry said. "I don't wear rings."

"Oh, don't be a spoilsport, Harry. Let the girl tell me."

"Jade," Sorcha said. "Onyx. And oh, I think the brightest chrysoprase. The color of spring, the cycle of the earth. For I think Harry well-rooted in the earth."

"How do you know?" Gran asked.

Harry was suspiciously silent.

Sorcha shrugged. "Ah, well, it isn't something I can define, I'm afraid, is it? I just feel it. It's my gift, small as it is."

"And Mary?" Gran asked.

Sorcha was pleased to smile again. "Ah, now, there are stones we don't see much in this far north land. Aquamarine for the water, I'm thinking. Coral for beauty, moonstone for the sight. For you have it, Mary, don't you?"

Mary said nothing. The shock in her eyes gave her away.

"Amazing," Gran said. "I can see exactly what you mean. I can't wait to see what stones you'd give my granddaughter Phyllida. Not to mention her children. Imps, every one."

"How you come by this gift?" Mary asked.

Sorcha shook her head. "Where does any soul-gift come from? I simply know that it is a necessary task, and it is my honor to perform it." She grinned. "Besides, it gives me the chance to stay with the children. And that is a great gift to me, altogether."

"You teach?"

"Oh, aye. Our history. Our lore and lessons. The craft of faerie and the specifics of each child's gift, so he may respect and cherish all."

"An important job," Gran said.

Sorcha shook her head. "Small gifts in a pantheon of majesty. But that's just fine with me, for what would I do with a grander gift?"

"You mean you don't want fame and fortune?" Harry asked. "A place on the evening news and a meeting with Oprah?"

Sorcha shuddered with the idea of it. "Fame?" she asked. "Ah, no. That's for others. Mine is meant to be a quiet life."

"Which is why you've dropped in on us like this?"

Harry's grandmother stiffened. "Harold—"

"Why *did* you come here?" Harry demanded, stopping just shy of the last door on the hall. Beyond, great windows opened to the undulating land beyond. "If you really are a fairy, as you want us to believe, what brought you here now, after my family's been on the hunt for you people for the last hundred years?"

For only a heartbeat, no more, Sorcha considered what she should say. What to give away to this man who could be so dangerous. Who had already taken the ground from under her feet. *Why, I've come to steal your treasure. I've come to betray your hospitality, one of the greatest sins a fairy can commit.*

"I've come to protect the Stone," she said. "Just as I told you."

"From what?"

"From Darragh. From destruction. From loss."

"Then you'll be glad to see it," his gran said, slapping at Harry's hand. "Right in this room, if Harry will just remember the concept of forward momentum."

But Harry wasn't finished glaring at Sorcha yet. "You know it isn't a diamond," he said to her. "We've had it tested, innumerable times, as it happens. It's a hunk of quartz. It's not worth stealing."

Ah, if he only knew.

"I would be the last person to harm the Dearann Stone," she said. "Now please. Could I see it?"

Harry looked as if he wanted to offer more arguments. Instead, he shook his head. "Fine. In here."

"It's the anteroom to my husband's suite," Gran said, her voice soft. "We're leaving it here until the state rooms are restored and ready for its display. But till now it's been where my father kept it, and his father before him, in a glass case that catches the afternoon light. It's—"

Gone.

The three of them stumbled to a halt just inside the door of a high, fairy-green room that had a few chairs, two lamps, and a round mahogany table set right in front of the window, where the sun could seek out the Stone in its glass case and shatter its light across the room. A glass case that was now on its side. Empty.

The Dearann Stone was nowhere to be seen.

## Chapter 6

For a moment there was nothing but stricken silence.

"Oh, crap," Harry muttered.

His grandmother laid a trembling hand against her chest. "Where is it, Harry? Where is Grandpapa's diamond?"

Without thinking, Sorcha stepped past Harry into the room. The room was warm, with carpets of deep greens and gold, and well-worn armchairs draped in throws. The sun slashed in a honeyed diagonal across the floor and gleamed off the toppled case, an unpretentious square of glass that seemed to simply sit on a wood base made of the same bog oak as the baroness's chair.

From where the box usually sat, there was a clear view over the hills and dales of this place, which surely must glow green in the spring, so that from her place here, the Dearann Stone could witness the fruits of her grace. A loving place to put her, but a prison nonetheless, keeping her from her own creations.

Sorcha closed her eyes for a moment and simply listened. Breathed. Felt. Struggled for calm past a clamoring heart.

Gone. It was gone. She was too late.

Still, there was hope. There *had* to be.

"It wasn't Darragh," she said, and turned to the old woman. "A fairy has not stolen the Stone."

"How do you know?"

"A fairy can always sense another's presence. There have been none here."

"I'm sure the police will be delighted to hear that," Harry said, and did his own search. "That means we only have to worry about the humans. And the humans who *think* they're fairies."

Harry searched under chairs and behind the high gold drapes that framed the windows. He even took a look out the window, as if expecting to see somebody standing out there, when they were a good three stories up a bare stone wall. Sorcha stood where she was, searching with every fairy instinct for the sense of the Stone. She could trace it, if only she could feel it.

But she couldn't.

She began to explore the room, eyes half-closed so the mortal world wouldn't confuse her, so she could better catch the embers of a fairy stone's power.

"Oh, Harry," she heard his grandmother moan.

Sorcha stopped then, to see the little woman staring at the empty case, as if looking on a dying loved one. Impossibly, she looked smaller, shrunken with the sudden loss. And Harry, who only moments before had been drawn up with outrage, went to his knees before her.

"Gran, don't," he said, his expression absolutely serious and sincere as he took those gnarled hands in his great ones. "The diamond is here somewhere. If we haven't managed to misplace the damned thing in the last hundred years, I sincerely doubt it's going to happen today. No stranger could have made it this far without us knowing."

And that was when Sorcha first began to fall in love with Harry Wyatt. He didn't believe in any of this. He hated it, was afraid of it. And yet, when his grandmother thought the gift of her grandfather had been lost, he didn't hesitate to protect her.

Gran reached out one of her hands and brushed a stray lock of hair back from Harry's forehead. "Thank you, dear boy. Call Sims. Ask him if he's seen anything unusual."

Harry gave her a wry smile. "More unusual than Miss Sorcha here and a blond man flying over Gwyneth's car?"

There were tears in the little woman's eyes, but she smiled back at him. "Please."

He never took his gaze from his grandmother's. "Miss…Sorcha?" he said. "Can you explain this?"

Sorcha wished she could have felt outraged at his implied insult. She couldn't. She understood full well the devastation that came with the loss of something precious. After all, wasn't that why she was here in the first place?

"Haven't I been with you?" she asked. "Sure, I didn't even know you kept it here till you told me. I didn't even know where here was."

Harry turned an accusing glare on her. "You didn't *admit* you knew it was here. What about your friend?

Seems pretty convenient that you get so sick we had to take care of you just about the time our Fairy Diamond goes missing."

"I've told you," she said. "Darragh hasn't…ah, I see. You still don't believe me, then, do you? You think I'm a mortal looking for fame and fortune after all."

"I think I can't ignore any possibilities."

His grandmother lifted a trembling hand to his cheek. "She's not lying, Harry. Trust me."

He kissed that tiny palm and smiled. "You I trust, Gran. Her, I don't. Miss…" He turned his hard gaze on her. "Just what *is* your last name?" he demanded.

"I have none," she said, trying to focus on more than one thing at a time: Harry and his grandmother; any evidence of the thief; the sense of complete emptiness in this room. "I don't understand," she said without thinking.

"What, child?" Gran asked.

Sorcha shook her head, her focus on that empty, over-turned case. "I'm not after feeling a fairy here. Well, not other than myself, of course. But sure, I don't feel the Stone, either."

Gran's attention sharpened. Harry swung full around, there on his knees.

"What are you talking about?" he demanded

Sorcha struggled with how to explain to mortals. "Every stone gives its sign. A sense, a…song, if you will, like humming under the skin. At least to me. I can recognize a fairy stone without opening my eyes." She shook her head. "I feel nothing in this room."

"Because it's been stolen," Harry said, and she heard something new in his voice.

For a second she only stared at him. What was it

about him, then, that suddenly looked so wrong? He still frowned. He still accused, just as he had all along. But her words had worried him.

"Do *you* know, Harry Wyatt?" Sorcha asked. "Why I don't feel the Stone?"

"Because there's nothing to feel," he said.

*Yet you'll look for it anyway,* she thought, and wished there were someone like Harry for her, who would so protect the people he loved without thought to his own needs.

"Even gone, it would leave a ghost of its essence behind," she insisted. "And yet I don't feel it."

"Ridiculous. When was the last time you saw it, Gran?" he asked.

The little woman rubbed one of her wrists, as if conjuring. "The day before yesterday, maybe? Little Lilly wanted to see it. You know how she is."

"Then it could have been taken anytime since then."

If possible, Gran shrank even more. Sorcha couldn't help it. She knelt down alongside Harry.

"How can I help, then?" she asked.

Gran's eyes were bright with unshed tears, and her hand trembled a bit as she patted Sorcha. "Dear girl. Would you go with Harry and look for it?"

Harry lurched to his feet. "She will not."

"Two heads are better than one," Gran insisted. "Please. I can't do it. This old barn is far too large. But the two of you could manage it quickly and efficiently. You could split up the rooms."

Harry snorted. "I'm not about to let her out of my sight."

Gran nodded. "Fine. Then do it together. You might want to check the grounds first. It looks like rain again."

"Gran…"

"She says she can feel it," Gran said. "Can *you?*"

Harry seemed startled. "What?"

Gran huffed with impatience. "Can you feel the thing? Does it hum for you?"

"Certainly not!"

"Then take the girl with you. It hums for her."

"Don't be—"

Evidently the old woman wasn't too crushed to level quite a look at her grandson. Sorcha thought it could easily curl a person's toes.

"What about the staff?" Harry asked. "We have a lot of new employees."

He got another huff and a wave of a hand. "Have Sims deal with them. They're all terrified of him. He'll sort them out. I'd put my money on one of those movie fans who've been trampling my rosebushes for the past six months."

"You're undoubtedly right."

"Now is not the time for recriminations. Just, please…find the diamond."

And that quickly, she was old again. It was Sorcha who patted her hand this time. Sorcha who smiled for her, and put every ounce of fairy magic she had into it. "Don't be after frettin'," she said. "I can't imagine your man here missing something the size of the Dearann Stone."

She prayed it was so. Especially since, for the first time in her life, she seemed to have lost her ability to feel one of the most powerful stones in existence. Ah, was there any other reason to escape this rock cage, if not this cold, bare mortal world?

"And once you sense it…" Gran said.

"Sure, I can follow it like one of your hunting dogs. I think that mortal illness must have interfered with my fairy senses, is all. Once it clears out completely, I'm sure I'll pick things up in a twinkling."

"Good," Gran said. "We can get started."

"We cannot," Harry argued. "None of us have had our dinner, and I, for one, am not traipsing around the gardens without an idea of what I'm doing. For all we know, Phyl felt an overwhelming urge to carry the thing to York with her."

"We both know better, Harry. At least call the police."

Harry opened his mouth, and then just shut it. Sorcha could almost hear the words in his head. *And do what? Tell them we've misplaced a sizeable chunk of quartz of no monetary value?*

Poor man. She so wished she could convince him that he was wrong about this, at least. She wished the Dearann Stone had sung for him.

"Tell you what, Gran," he said, climbing to his feet, the old woman's hand still in his. "If you'll go with Mary and finish your dinner, I'll start the search."

"But hurry," she said. "Won't you?"

"We will, darling. Now, go with Mary."

Gran nodded and took one last look at the empty case. Then she let Mary wheel her from the room.

Harry barely waited for the wheelchair to clear the door before turning on Sorcha. "Well?"

She wasn't sure what he was wanting. "Well?" she echoed.

He glared at her. "Listen, it would go a lot easier if you just gave the thing up now. I really am not in the mood to tramp through every one of these rooms and the twelve acres of garden that surround them looking for that hunk of rock, only to find that your blond friend has just put it up on eBay. Tell me now, and we can all go down and enjoy a bit of roasted partridge."

"I'm afraid you're wasting your time, Harry Wyatt," Sorcha said, beginning to feel frustrated herself. "I've told you. Darragh is no friend of mine, and I had nothin' at all to do with the Stone's loss. But I'm more than happy to help you look."

"While your friend gets farther and farther away?"

Sorcha refused to answer him, just set her hands on her hips.

Finally he relented. "You're sure it isn't here?"

Sorcha frowned. "You're sure you have the actual Stone?"

"I don't have anything right now," Harry snapped, then gave her an inelegant push for the door. "Come on. We have to ask the staff's help to search for the damned thing. Then you and I are going to spend some quality time in the gardens."


"Ole woman, you just lookin' for trouble," Mary accused, as she settled the baroness at her place at the long mahogany table in the small dining room.

Beatrice didn't even bother to smile as she picked up her spoon and resumed eating her soup. "She can help him find the Stone."

Mary sat down but didn't move to eat. "Dat's not what you want and you know it. Dat boy be engaged, Bea. Or didn't you see dat nice girl who's been here the last year or so?"

"Gwyneth *is* a nice girl," Beatrice answered without heat. "But she's not the nice girl for Harry. He thinks he wants normal. He doesn't want normal, though, Mary. He's not made for normal. It would kill him."

"Dat's not your decision to make."

"You'd rather just watch while he and that nice girl make each other miserable? She may be stiff and proper, but she doesn't deserve to be unhappy any more than Harry does."

"They'd end up paintin' over your murals, is what they'd do."

"And whitewashing Harry's soul in the process. He's not one of them, Mary. He's not a city dweller, or a drone in an office. He has such passion in his soul that just aches to be set free. I think this girl could do it, and I'm going to give her the opportunity."

"And den what? He wander 'round here giving tours to movie fans till he get his house sold out from under him when he can't pay the mortgage?"

Beatrice set her spoon down. "I don't know. I really don't. But I can't just watch him wither away for fear of the unknown. And that's what will happen if we let him marry his Gwyneth."

For a long moment Mary watched the baroness eat. "You didn't go and lose dat stone on purpose, did you?"

Beatrice lifted her head and pinned Mary in place with a glare of outrage. "That, my friend, is not an accusation I would take from anyone else. You know my feelings about the Fairy Diamond."

Her shoulders easing, Mary finally picked up her spoon. "Then you do believe she a fairy child?"

Beatrice let loose a bark of laughter. "Good heavens,

no. Not any more than Harry is, anyway. But she has a fairy soul, doesn't she?"

"Or a committable psychiatric disorder."

"You don't believe that, either, Mary."

But Mary kept her counsel to herself.

Mrs. Thompson tried to lend Sorcha her coat, but it was a dismal failure. The cook almost landed on the floor with the giggles. Not only was the coat too long, it was miles too big. Sorcha felt a little girl playing dress up with her father's clothes. Huffing in impatience, Harry swung his own jacket off his shoulders and helped her into it.

Immediately Sorcha was engulfed in his scent, a brisk, spicy aroma that conjured the outdoors, a sharp breeze over the moors. Oh, it hurt her, this thing, for he smelled like home, like the fairy wind that laid such a gentle benediction on a fairy's shoulder.

And yet, there was nothing gentle about Harry Wyatt—except, mayhap, his treatment of his lovely grandmother. Other than that, he was all sharp, hard angles, all energy and focus and fierce strength. And still she ached for him, for the feel of his skin against hers, for the benediction of his kiss.

How could that be? Wouldn't she simply batter herself against him like a moth against a wall? Wouldn't she be lost? Darragh, for all that she loved him no more, had a gentle heart—well, she'd thought he had. It was what had drawn her to him. Harry had the heart of a lion, and it frightened her.

And yet she wanted that, too.

"Fine, then, Phyl. Thanks," Harry was saying into one

of those little talking boxes people seemed to carry in their pockets like baby chicks. "I'll see you tomorrow."

Sorcha didn't bother to turn from where she was warming her hands in the kitchen fireplace. Well, the fingertips that peeked out from the cuffs of Harry's coat. "She doesn't have the Dearann Stone."

"No. She hasn't been near the Diamond Room in over a month."

"She lives with you all here?"

"In the estate manager's house. You'll see it from the back of the garden. Phyl is my first cousin. She and her husband, Edward, run the estate while I'm in town."

"Making enough money to keep it up," Sorcha said with a nod.

Harry glared at her for a second. Then he shrugged into another overcoat and turned for the door. "Come on. We're wasting time."

But they were forestalled by Sims, who came skidding through the kitchen door. "My lord," he said, his voice sincerely anguished. "We have completed a search of the servants' quarters. The Fairy Diamond has not been found. We are beginning on the state apartments now. The police have been notified and will be here in half an hour."

"You really called the police?" Harry asked.

The butler looked bemused. "It's the Fairy Diamond, my lord. Of course I called them."

"And they're coming."

Again the butler seemed confused. "It is the Fairy Diamond."

And he looked absolutely sincere, which made Sorcha feel even worse. The Dearann Stone was so important to these people: a part of their history and culture and tradition. And she would be taking it from them.

But maybe her mother was right after all. Maybe the replica stone she carried at her waist would be replacement enough. After all, no one seemed to sense the music in the real stone. Mayhap no one would notice its absence.

"What about the temporary staff?" Harry asked. "And the construction crews?"

"We're getting that information now, my lord," Sims said. "But we *know* everyone. They're all from Hartley. We made sure of it, after all the brouhaha over the movie."

Harry nodded. "Thank you, Sims. I know I don't need to remind you to keep this all very quiet."

"Indeed not, sir. I feel I am safe in saying that the last thing anyone wants in the neighborhood is more television cameras."

"Fine." Harry took Sorcha's elbow. "I'm sure you already alerted the grooms to search the stable block. We'll start in the gardens. Thank you, Sims."

Without another word, he pulled Sorcha for the door. She took a step after him and flinched. They'd strapped and tied her into their mortal shoes after all. Goddess, but her mother had figured it well what this exile would cost Sorcha. It wasn't enough that she had to search out a lost stone in a hostile place. She had to suffer one onslaught after another to her fairy senses to do it. And now her feet didn't just hurt, they were imprisoned and separated from the energy of the earth itself.

Harry opened the door then, and Sorcha was slapped with a blast of cold air. Worse and worse. She hunched into the coat, shoved her hands into the pockets and stepped past the door he held open into the back garden.

She hadn't noticed it when she'd first arrived. She'd been too cold and miserable. Now she took a moment to look around and saw that they were crossing a little patio area that thrust its way through what she thought might be the kitchen garden. The plants were dormant, but the earth was built up in tidy rows, all enclosed by a sturdy brick wall.

In the spring, she thought, there would be laburnum and wisteria cascading off those bricks. Beyond stood majestic plane trees, and beyond those she thought there might be a dormant rose garden, and acres of flower-lined paths that stretched across great lawns that slipped down to the wooded glen where a river meandered by. She remembered seeing it all from Gran's window. Even though the gardens were dormant, even though she couldn't feel a thing through these shoes and these mortal clothes, she longed to walk there.

"Let me know if you *feel* anything," Harry said, as he stepped briskly onto the path that led around the kitchen garden.

"It's a beautiful place," Sorcha said, looking around her. "Your family have cared well for it."

"No, they haven't. I've spent the last twelve years restoring it. They spent all their efforts trying to get to Fairyland. Which you undoubtedly know, since I'm sure you've seen the movie."

"Tell me the story," she asked, stepping off the gravel path so she might touch raw earth. "Pretend I didn't see it."

"You mean about the cousins who found the colony of fairies on their estate? And how they captured one on film and caught him, so he couldn't get back? And then, of course, how he conveniently fell in love with the cousin, who just happened to be rich and a baroness in her own right."

"And brought the Fairy Diamond with him."

"Oh, yes. We mustn't forget that part. The magical, dream-inspiring Fairy Diamond that generations of Wyatts and Waverlys thought spoke directly to them."

"But not you."

He drew up like an outraged virgin. "Of course not."

"You seem very certain."

He glared. "I am," he said, and strode off.

Sorcha followed, not bothering to keep pace with him. He marched across the lawns like a trooping fairy, which wouldn't do him any good for sensing fairy sounds. Sorcha meandered more slowly than the river. She ran her hand over the rough face of the brick wall and tilted her head back so she could see the clouds scudding above the trees. She suffered the cold for the chance to take her first good deep breath since arriving in this place.

And each step she took carried her farther away from the dichotomy of that great stone house. Claustrophobic and wonderful at the same time, for it had all that rock between it and the mother, yet its walls were alive with the memory of the land of the fair folk.

She didn't think she could survive here long. The pain of the contrast would be too strong, the sense of dislocation and loss. She thought maybe she would end up as surly and unhappy as Harry.

She'd just made it onto the lawns where the great hedges of flowers grew when she first felt it. Her heart sank. There was no question, then. Darragh had been here.

"There's been a fairy nearby!" she called to Harry.

He didn't look up from where he was poking into a long, high rhododendron hedge. "You can tell that, can you?"

"Yes," she said. "But I didn't feel it until we were well away from the house. So I don't think he's been inside at all."

Unless, of course, the rock interfered with that, too.

"Can you follow his scent?"

"I can. But I think we should be looking for the Stone instead. I don't think he has it."

Harry shrugged and walked on. Sorcha followed, peeking under the bushes Harry missed, perfectly certain they were on a fool's mission. She felt nothing, and she would certainly feel the Dearann Stone, especially out here in the open. It would resonate off each tree and blade of grass. It would call to her.

"It's not out here, Harry," she said. "I promise."

And not because she really wanted to get in out of this cold. Although Goddess knew she did.

"We'll try one more area," he said, straightening. "It's a favorite among the fairy-hunters."

He veered to the west, to where the lawns swept another quarter mile or so to another garden area, another wall of brick protected by more plane trees. Sorcha followed, limping now from the soreness of the shoes. Even in this cold, she wished she could take the things off.

She was so focused on her feet, and on the fact that her sense of the other fairy was somehow changing, that she failed at first to appreciate what lay on the other side of that brick barricade.

"This feeling of Darragh is darker than I remember,"

she mused, half closing her eyes as she stepped through the gate in the wall. "There's so much...rage...."

"Oh, excellent," Harry answered ahead of her. "That's exactly what I was hoping for. A fairy in the middle of a temper tantrum."

"Harry," she protested, wanting him to know that this wasn't a game at all, if what she felt was true. But she never finished the thought. She'd opened her eyes, and the scene before her literally took her breath. Harry had just led her through the brick wall into the far garden.

She laid her hand against her heart, tears swelling her throat. "He did this," she said, frozen in place. "Didn't he?"

Harry didn't bother to answer. He was bent over, searching the grass for the Stone. Sorcha lost sight of him, for she'd just stepped into a sacred grove. A carefully constructed garden that had been laid out around a beautiful wooden hall.

The landscape here was gentler than those wide empty moors beyond. It folded into a tree-protected glen, through which the river wandered. And here at its edge, where it was protected from the fierce north winds and the waters of the river could provide glittering music, Harry's ancestor had planted trees.

"He found every one of the nine sacred woods," she said, stepping reverently onto sacred soil.

She knew Harry was watching her now. She didn't care. Standing tall in reverence for the place, she spread her arms wide, palms up to cup the weight of awe in her hands. "Willow of the streams, hazel of the rocks, alder of the marshes, hawthorne of the field, birch of the waterfalls, rowan of the shade, yew of the resilience, elm of the brae, oak of the sun. All here to please the goddess, to reflect the gentle gifts of the Dearann Stone."

He'd planted them in a spiral, that long-ago prince, the pattern of life, and positioned the small hall in the center, like his own shrine made of living wood, of fairy wood.

"This is where the Dearann Stone first lived, isn't it?" she asked, dropping her hands.

Harry shoved his own hands in his pockets, his posture impossibly taut. "Which you would have known if you'd seen the movie."

She didn't answer. She was too busy bending over to pull off those horrible mortal shoes.

"Here, don't do that," Harry protested. "It's bloody cold out here."

"Not on this ground," she said, and for the first time since crossing through the gate from her world, she laughed with her whole heart.

With her first step, she felt the great life that drowsed beneath her feet. She felt the mother earth and the long-dormant traces of spring. She opened her arms as she ran into the circle, where only the yew held on to its green in this grim winter, and she began to spin.

"Stop that!" Harry yelled. "What do you think you're doing?"

But Sorcha wasn't listening. She was dancing to the earth and the power of the goddess and the memory of the beloved Dearann Stone, who had once resided here. She spun and leapt, laughter bubbling up, the relief of this place spilling tears down her cheeks and freeing her heart.

"Oh, sweet yew," she sang in her own tongue, even though she knew that only the goddess could love her voice, "who watches the ancients and graces us in the bleakest hours of winter, oh, sacred, sweet yew of the elders, sing for me, too...."

She finally spun to a halt at the door of the small hall. With trembling fingers she lifted the latch on the door to the building crafted from living trees, from each of the nine, woven into walls and a living roof, where birds nested and the sunlight shone. She stepped inside to find herself on a floor crafted from the finest Kerry crystal, with walls painted even now in bright symbols of life. There were chairs and a simple table in one corner, a comfortable bed in another, and a fireplace made of fieldstone that fitted neatly in among the tree trunks.

"He really was here," she breathed, overwhelmed by the sense of homecoming. "He brought his home with him."

"What are you talking about?" Harry demanded from behind her.

She swung around, her arms wide again, the tears streaking her face. "Oh, Harry, can't you feel it? He brought the sacred here, to this harsh place, and found a way to survive here. He must have loved your ancestress very much."

She stood there, her feet so warmed by the diamond-sleek floor, her heart saved from the winter of that stone house, her soul revived, and she saw in a flash of insight that Harry understood.

He *knew*.

"You've felt it, haven't you?" she demanded, stepping closer.

"Don't be ridiculous."

"What frightens you so, Harry? This is a blessed place, and you realized that."

"This is a folly. Nothing more."

Sorcha smiled the most ancient of female smiles and dipped her head. "He loved her very much," she repeated. "And she loved him enough in return to come out here to bear his children where the Dearann Stone could bless them."

Harry stiffened as if she'd slapped him. "Don't be—"

Sorcha couldn't help it. She lifted a hand to his strained face. "Is it such a terrible thing to believe?" she asked. "That a man and woman could love each other so much?"

He looked stricken, his beautiful green eyes as dark as a storm-tossed sea. His face was taut, his posture so brittle Sorcha wondered he didn't simply shatter.

*I could love you that much,* she thought, but didn't say it. Instead, she lifted up on her toes and laid her lips against his.

In an instant he had her in his arms, his kiss bruising, his heart hammering against her breasts. In another instant she was wrapped around him, her hands in his hair, her tongue tangled with his, her own heart bidding fair to outpace his. He shoved his hands up beneath her jacket, beneath the sweater they'd given her, and swept her skin. He lifted his leg between hers, and she rested there, rubbing against him like a cat.

She was consumed by him, by her need for him. She was hot. She was ravenous, setting out on her own exploration beneath coat and sweater and shirt to discover a sleek back, a taut belly, a hard, sculpted chest dusted in the most delightful springy hair. Oh, these mortal textures, so different from faerie. So rough and hot and urgent, until the images in her head matched those incited by her hands. She could hear their panting breaths, the slither and rub of material, and the whisper of skin against skin. She could smell the rising perfume of arousal, sharp and musky and salty, and it infected her with impatience. She could feel the rising tide of heat in her own anxious body, and the sudden, surprising shift of position as he laid her back on the thick comfort of the bed.

*Yes,* she thought, laughing into his mouth, his delicious, demanding mouth. *Yes, Harry, now. Take me here in this sacred place where we might make magic.*

It was as if he'd heard her. Suddenly Harry reared back and stumbled away from the bed. Left behind, Sorcha stared up at him, openmouthed. Her clothes were half-off and his looked as if he'd taken a tumble. Her mouth felt bruised and swollen, her breasts suddenly chafing against the sweater that only half-covered them.

"Harry?" she asked, afraid that her voice sounded small and pathetic.

He glared at her as if she were a lawbreaker. "I'm engaged," he snapped, still panting, his slacks still taut with the evidence of his arousal.

Sorcha closed her eyes. "Oh, Harry…"

Five minutes later, tucked in and tidy, the two of them walked back out of the grove, forcing Sorcha to put her mortal shoes back on her suddenly cold, miserable feet.

"I'm engaged," she protested into the sleek skin of his chest.

Darragh let his hands wander over her sweat-slick skin and smiled. "You might be wantin' to rethink that."

Gwyneth raised her head, and Darragh was delighted

to see the excitement rise again in her eyes. "I've never done this before. *Never.*"

He tested the plumpness of her lips with his finger. "Faith, you think I have? I've never met anyone like you before. Come to think on it, I've never been to a place like this before."

"You've never been to a hotel?" she asked, winnowing her fingers through his hair.

"Ah, now, where would a fairy find a hotel, then, girl? We have any tree branch or hayrack to rest in."

A building made of bedrooms, so she said this hotel business was. Sure, no fairy bower had ever felt so soft. Even with the windows closed to keep out the mother earth, Darragh thought he could drown in the comfort of this place and never need more. Except his Gwyneth. And on the name of the goddess, who could ever guess he would find a need for a mortal of any kind?

"You don't have to play this game," Gwyneth chuckled, an oddly husky sound in such a fine throat.

"Game?" he asked, distracted by the slope of her breast.

"Of course. You know perfectly well there's no such thing as fairies. It's all a myth the Wyatts made up to feel important."

Darragh pulled back, stunned. He couldn't help it. He laughed. "Ah, sure, aren't you going to be surprised when you have to admit the truth."

"What truth?" she scowled.

"That you know perfectly well there are fairies. For haven't you just been making intimate acquaintance with one?" He brought her face up again to kiss her most thoroughly. "And I'm thinking you might want to again."

She sighed and shook her head. "Really," she said,

her gaze sweeping over him with the kind of hunger fairies simply didn't possess. "I'm not like this."

He couldn't help grinning down at her. "Then you should be."

He kissed her again, until strange images appeared in both their heads of him taking her against the wall of a wooden hall. Of her arched against him, her head back, her hair tangled with leaves and twigs, her skin abraded and raw, her mouth open in screams of ecstasy. Dark, hot images that swamped her and opened her for Darragh's taking.

"I'm engaged," she said, but it didn't seem to matter anymore.

## Chapter 7

Harry woke to the sound of children outside his window. It had been a late, fruitless night, with everybody they could gather scouring the grounds in an effort to locate the bloody diamond. They'd had no better luck than Harry had had out in the gardens. In fact, the only thing Harry had collected had been a massive headache and an even bigger erection.

He'd had the dream again, over and over, until he'd tried to sit up the rest of the night to avoid it. And it wasn't the violence of the dream that frightened him this time—although it did frighten him and the more often he had the damn thing, the worse it got. But this time, the woman he'd stalked, the woman he'd tied down and taken over and over until he'd fallen exhausted over her damp, limp torso, had been Sorcha.

He couldn't get the image out of his head. Her full, ripe breasts laid bare with the ripping of her fairy costume, her golden hair sweat-soaked and tangled. Her lips red and moist and parted, her eyes wide and dark, her arousal turning inexorably to fear as the dream wore on to its inevitable conclusion.

And his own satisfaction at the results.

He wondered if his grandmother had any sleeping pills. If she did, he was damn well going to ensure a quiet night tonight. He simply couldn't bear much more of this.

And now he had to get up and start the search again for that bloody diamond or have to face his grandmother with his failure. Harry was well acquainted with failure. It didn't mean it got any more pleasant.

At least Phyl was back. He could use her good sense right now. He could use a buffer between him and that fairy child he'd stumbled over.

More images assaulted him: her twirling in her mad dance in the fairy grove; her wrapped around him as if trying to climb right inside him, as he'd fallen with her onto the bed he'd sneaked out there. Him pawing at her as if he needed nothing more than the feel of her skin to survive.

He didn't need to tell her that he was the one who kept up that little hall in the fairy glade, that some days it was the only place where he could sleep—especially lately. She would only read something more into it than the fact that in that little hall he was away from all the pressures of the great house. *She* would think it *meant* something.

After grabbing a quick shower, he dressed and headed down for breakfast and a report from Sims on their progress. Blessedly, Phyl was there before him.

"Why do I miss all the fun?" she demanded when she saw him.

Clad in her ubiquitous riding pants, boots and worn-out sweater, Phyl was everything his grandmother wasn't. Tall, lithe, athletic and just a bit horse-faced, hers was the body that went with his grandmother's commanding voice. Phyl had been cursed with a funny, whispery soprano that he sometimes swore only horses and her children could hear.

He bent to buss her cheek and give her a swat on the arse. "Can I help it if all the fairy children like me best?"

Phyl's long face lit with delight. "She's a pip, isn't she?"

"So you've met her already?"

Phyl laughed, and Harry thought of leaves rustling in the wind, which just made him shake his head. Poetry now. Damn that girl...

"I walked in to find her twirling around the main salon singing something in Gaelic," Phyl said. "When I asked her what she was doing, she said she was cele-brating her people. She seems to find our murals familiar. Something about her world but not her home, whatever that means. Bea and Theo are introducing her to the horses."

Harry groaned. "Great. I was hoping I could avoid that."

Phyl raised a wry eyebrow. "You think she's a horse thief?"

"I think she'll convince your children that she's a fairy, and they'll want to keep her. Like a pet."

"She *is* a pet, Harry. I can't wait for Lilly to meet her. She'll adopt her."

"Lilly adopts everyone."

As if called, a piping voice echoed down the stair-wells. "Ha-a-a-a-r-r-r-y!"

Harry spun around to see Phyl's nurse descending the steps with a pudgy, blond four-year-old in her arms. His heart melted into a gooey puddle, just as it did every time he saw his niece.

"Hello, my piglet!" he called out to her as he walked to meet them. "Where've you been?"

"Harry, Harry, Harry!" she crooned, proud of her ability to pronounce *R*'s. Her flat little hands were out to him, her round face radiant with delight.

Harry caught her up in his arms and buried his face in her baby-soft neck. "Lilly, Lilly, Lilly," he sang back, just to hear her chortle.

She yanked on his hair so he would look at her. Then she gave him a smacking kiss on his cheek. "'Lo, Harry."

"'Lo, Lilly."

"What about the diamond, Harry?" Phyl asked, as they walked toward the kitchen. "Any luck?"

"The only luck we've had so far is that the press hasn't found out about it. Be a tough go opening the house to visitors without the main attraction, now, wouldn't it?"

"And if you don't find it?"

He shrugged. "I'll find some way to duplicate it. Not one person's going to know the difference."

"Until some real fairy shows up and shouts fraud."

Harry snorted. "I'd love to see the charges. 'My lord, this hunk of quartz doesn't *hum.*'"

They'd just made it into the big kitchen when the

outside door slammed open and two more towheads careened in, followed at a slower pace by Sorcha.

"You're in your bare feet again," Harry accused.

She beamed at him. "Ah, well, I can't tolerate those hard things on my feet, Harry."

Clad in more of Phyl's rolled-up castoffs, she looked worse than she had yesterday. Her hair hung limp and dull, and there were definite circles under her eyes. And her skin…

But that wasn't something he needed to notice or comment on, especially since she was trying so hard to appear unchanged.

"You should see her ride bareback!" Theo cried, grabbing an apple from the counter and chomping into it. "She just jumped on Moonsilver and pranced around like a circus performer."

Harry moaned. Excellent. She had his nine-year-old nephew in her pocket already. And undoubtedly his five-year-old niece, as well. Bea was nodding and bouncing on her feet.

"She was *brilliant,* Uncle Harry!"

"That's wonderful, Bea. You pirates didn't tie Tommie to the mast, did you?"

"She went into town to shop," Theo said, tossing the apple core into the trash.

"'Lo!" Lilly called, leaning toward Sorcha. "'Lo! 'Lo!"

Harry stiffened. Sorcha caught sight of the little girl in his arms and her eyes went soft.

"Well, and what a great honor this is," she said, stepping closer. "Would you greet this unworthy soul?"

Fury hit Harry like a blast. "Don't you dare," he snapped. "Lilly isn't up to your nonsense."

"Ah, you think I'm after insulting your kin again, don you, Harry Wyatt?" she asked, reaching out her arms for Lilly.

Lilly, of course, went right into them.

"Lilly has—"

"You call it Down syndrome," Sorcha said softly, wrapping her arms around Lilly. "I know. And you think I would hurt a child who is so precious to the fair folk?"

"Precious?" Phyl asked, her voice small.

Sorcha's smile was pure sunlight. "Sure, what do we of the fair folk revere more than pure joy? And where could you find another mortal who could never lose their joy? These cherished ones are the only children who will never grow too old to see us. And they are welcome as revered friends in the land of faerie."

Harry opened his mouth, certain he had something scathing to say. He couldn't get it past the sudden inexplicable lump in his throat. Alongside him, Phyl actually had tears in her eyes. As for Lilly, she'd caught Sorcha's face between her pudgy little hands and kissed her on her nose.

"'Lo, fairy!" she cried.

Harry's heart damn near stopped beating entirely.

"Hello, my cherished friend," Sorcha said, returning the kiss for another bright laugh from Lilly. "And what is your name?"

"Lilly!" she crowed, although no one but the family could interpret it, because of all the *L*'s she still had trouble with.

No one except Sorcha, evidently. "Lilly," she repeated, nodding. "Ah, that's brilliant, isn't it? A lovely flower in a beautiful garden. Are you a flower, my Lilly?"

Lilly preened like a debutante. "Flow-*er!* Mama, I'm a flower!"

"But of course you are, my love," Phyl said. "Haven't I told you all along?"

Lilly thought about that. "Harry says I…a *pig*-let."

It was Harry's turn to clear his throat. "A very beautiful piglet, Lilly. And fine smelling, as well."

Lilly's laughter was pure and sweet as daybreak. And she kept patting Sorcha's face, as if she'd just made a great discovery. Harry couldn't bear it.

Never turning away from where her daughter was suddenly singing silly songs with Harry's fairy child, Phyl patted his arm. "You caught a real gem this time, Harry."

"I didn't catch anything," he groused. "She tumbled down the hill right into me."

All legs and fine breasts and glistening green eyes, laughter like birdsong and a spirit that couldn't seem to be quenched.

He deliberately turned away. "Well, Phyl," he said, stalking over to pull the skillet onto the stove. "Any ideas?"

"Not a one," she said, stopping by the fridge to pull out eggs. "I don't suppose you've had a chance to look over any of the other estate business since you've been here, have you?"

Turning on the burner, he snorted. "Hardly. I was taking my first walk when Peasblossom here fell into my lap."

"And Gran said you think there's another one of them wandering around?"

He shrugged, trying to focus on his eggs, rather than two very sweet, mostly off-key voices singing behind him. "Gwyneth spotted him as she came up the drive."

"Gwyneth," Phyl mused, looking around. "Isn't she here?"

Well, evidently Gran hadn't told her everything. He cleared his throat, trying like hell not to sound uncomfortable. "She was. She had an appointment with a futures trading firm in York. They're looking to offer her a job."

Phyl nodded as she handed over the makings for Harry's first breakfast and her second. Phyl ate like a trencherman. "That would be perfect after you're married. What about you? You going to try and get away from London?"

"There's nothing locally in investment banking that's big enough."

"And you couldn't work online?"

"Absolutely not. Half of what I do is handshaking. I make matches, just like Gran keeps trying to do."

Phyl grinned. "Worked for me."

"You've been in love with Ned since you were ten. Speaking of which, didn't he come back with you?"

Phyl waved off the question. "Oh, he's at a seminar till Thursday on how to promote the new project. I'm happy to let him do it. Leaves me more time for my horses."

"Horse!" Lilly cried out. "Ride! Harry, ride!"

"Later, Lil. I'm not dressed for it."

"'Lone, Harry. Ride 'lone."

Harry looked over to see the bright tears swell in his niece's eyes. "Now, piglet, you know I'd cry if I couldn't ride with you."

One fat tear slid down her round cheek. "'Lone." Could any word sound more mournful? It hurt every time he saw Lilly standing outside the paddock fence watching her siblings race around on their mounts, hurt even more than it did to see his gran watch them all out her window, alone in that blasted chair. He knew Lilly would never understand how dangerous it was for her to ride. But he knew....

"Harry, I can—"

Harry snapped to attention. "Don't," he said to the fairy girl, pointing a spatula like a weapon. "Just... *don't*."

She looked confused and a little hurt, but she kept her silence.

"This afternoon, Lilly," he said. "With me."

Lilly laid her head down on Sorcha's shoulder and stayed silent. Sorcha walked her to the window, where she pointed out birds.

Harry cracked a couple of eggs into the skillet. "Horses and fairies," he said to Phyl. "It fair reeks of a Disney movie. We need to find the diamond and figure out what to do with the fairy queen here."

"Not to mention all her friends who followed her over. Has anybody seen this man since Gwyneth?"

"No. Although Sorcha said she *felt* him. Whatever the hell that means."

"We saw him," Theo piped up.

Phyl and Harry turned to him. "When?" Phyl asked.

"Where?" Harry echoed.

Theo shrugged. "By the deer park. He was sneaking through the woods. Wasn't he, Bea?"

Looking up from where she was buttering a slice of bread, Bea nodded enthusiastically. "He looked like a fairy."

"And how does a fairy look?" Harry asked, striving for patience.

She actually seemed to consider it. "He was dressed like the fairies in my book. And he was pretty."

"So Darragh is still about," Sorcha said softly, still rocking Lilly in her arms. "Ah, I wish he'd go home."

"And when did you see him?" Harry asked his nephew.

"'Bout an hour ago," Theo said. "Bea and I were out hunting the foxes."

"Leave the foxes alone, young man," Phyl warned.

"Leave the fairy alone," Harry amended. "We don't know who he really is."

He did know that for some reason the new sighting unsettled him, which made no sense. After all, he'd had hundreds of sightings since that damn movie had upended his life, every one of them convinced they were fairies, too. This one, though...

He looked over at Sorcha. "Well?"

She shook her head. "Darragh might be confused," she said, "but he would never hurt the children. It's against every code of the *Tuatha.*"

"Yeah, well, you said he tried to steal power once before."

"Certain things are inviolate, Harry Wyatt," she said. "Even in my world."

Lilly gave her a big kiss, as if in punctuation.

"Even so, I'm putting out an alert." He shook his own head. "I can't wait to see how the police will respond to 'Be on the lookout for a white, blond male with dark brown eyes, dressed like a gray Robin Hood, who leaps Jaguars like Superman.'"

"Gray?" Theo echoed, then looked at Bea, who shook her head. "He wasn't wearing gray. And he wasn't blond."

Now everybody went still.

"Explain," Harry demanded.

"He was tall and thin, and had really dark hair. And he was dressed in black."

Sorcha sucked in a breath. "Black?"

Harry felt the dread grow in his chest. She'd just gone measurably paler. "Obviously that means something."

"Black," she repeated, crouching down before Theo, Lilly still in her arms. "You're sure, now?"

"Yes, ma'am. He kinda blended into the shadows, like a ninja."

She actually closed her eyes. "Ah, Goddess," she muttered, standing. "I should have known. Oh, I should have known."

"What should you have known?" Harry demanded.

Sorcha looked to each face before answering, and Harry suddenly saw a darkness in her, a slump to her shoulders, as if she'd accepted a new and terrible weight. "It means that it isn't Darragh the children saw," she said, sounding stricken.

Harry scowled. "You mean I have somebody else trespassing on my land?"

"Darragh would never appear in black. No *Tuatha* would. Isn't it the color of chaos, after all?"

"Then who the hell is it?"

Again she shook her head. Then she turned to the children. "If you see him again," she said, absolutely serious, "stay away. Call for us. Get help. But don't go near him. Do you promise?"

"Is he dangerous?" Theo asked.

"Oh, aye," she said. "I think he is. I think you must stay with your sisters and protect each other, while your Uncle Harry and I see to him."

"How?" Theo asked.

She looked almost grief-stricken. "I don't know. But we'll do our very best, now, Theo. You must believe that."

"Well, who the hell is he?" Harry demanded.

"I think," she said, drawing a steadying breath, "he might be one of the *Dubhlainn Sidhe*."

Phyl looked over at Harry, who waved her off. "You know him, too?" he demanded of Sorcha.

She lifted desolate eyes to him. "No," she said. "I only know *of* him. Of them." She shook her head. "I should have known. The *Dubhlainn Sidhe* are bringers of chaos and darkness, sowers of madness, the moan on the wind."

"Stop it," Phyl demanded. "You're scaring the children."

Sorcha lifted her hands. "I'm sorry. I can say it no other way."

"We need the Fairy Diamond," little Theo said, his face grave.

"No, Theo," Bea protested.

He turned on her, hands on hips. "We all need to be protected, Bea."

Harry completely forgot the eggs that were sizzling in his skillet. "Theo? Do you know something?"

Both children flinched. Both looked away. In Sorcha's arms, Lilly lifted her little arms. "Di-mond!" she shrieked. "*My* di-mond!"

Harry looked at the little girl, so happy, then at Theo and Bea, who were both looking absolutely guilty. "Theo?"

The little boy drew a long breath. Then he squared

himself, as if preparing to take a battering. "I had to," he said.

"Had to what?"

"Give it to Lilly. I had to protect her."

"Protect her?" Phyl asked, dropping to her haunches in front of her solemn son. "From what, Theo?"

But Theo didn't look at his mother. He looked at Sorcha. "I've been having bad dreams. I had to protect Lilly."

Harry could have sworn his heart stopped beating. His nephew looked at him now, begging him to understand. His nephew who had his eyes. His green eyes. Why hadn't he really noticed before?

*No!* That was absurd. There was nothing more to this than delusional fans infecting the minds of small children.

Even so, he went down on his knees right next to Phyl. "And in your dreams, Lilly is hurt?"

Theo's eyes filled with tears. "*I* hurt her."

Before Phyl could even react, Harry pulled Theo into his arms, holding him so tightly there could be no question of his meaning. "I understand," he said to the little boy. "It's a terrible dream. But it's not true, Theo. It's not true at all."

Theo pulled back just a bit to look hard at his uncle. "You're sure?"

"I'm positive. You could never hurt Lilly. You know that perfectly well when you're awake, no matter how terrible the dreams are."

"You've had dreams, too," Theo said, his voice very small.

Harry smelled the eggs burning. It was an excuse. "Phyl, pull the eggs off, please."

She stood, so that Harry had a bit of room to face Theo with what Phyl didn't need to hear. "I've had them, too. They can't hurt us, though, now that we both know. Okay?"

"How long have you been having the dreams?" Sorcha asked Theo.

Harry actually flinched. Somehow he'd forgotten that of course she would be listening.

Theo didn't seem hesitant at all in confiding in this perfect stranger. "The last week, maybe."

"And they got worse last night," she said, her voice quiet.

Harry looked over to see the same horror he felt reflected in her eyes. She'd handed off Lilly sometime in the last moments. Phyl was rocking her back by the stove, where Lilly couldn't be touched by what they said. Bea stood with one hand clutching the hem of her mother's sweater, her bread forgotten in the other.

"How do you know?" he asked Sorcha.

"The *Dubhlainn Sidhe* are the infectors of dreams," she said. "It is how they sow their madness. They've recently gained a great power, a darkness that would touch any who share their blood, which I think you two do. And now, if that is indeed one of the *Dubhlainn Sidhe* stalking your grounds, they have brought it here, through the gates. I'm so sorry, Harry. I'm so sorry."

Harry shut his eyes. He just couldn't bear to look at her right now. Not when the echoes of his own dreams still resonated in his head. Not when he could still hear her panic-stricken screams.

It was all so absurd. Coincidence and conspiracy theory all woven into a chapter of *The Lord of the Rings*.

Well, he wasn't going to succumb to this kind of madness. He was *not*.

"Apology accepted," he said, opening his eyes.

Let them think what they wanted. As soon as Theo put the Stone back, he would stop having the dreams. If he didn't, they would get him counseling or change his diet or something. Something that didn't involve this maddening woman who knelt next to him smelling like summer and spouting the most ludicrous nonsense he'd ever heard in his life.

"Where's the Fairy Diamond, Theo?" he asked, struggling to sound pragmatic and reasonable. "Surely you know by now that it needs to go back where it belongs. If nothing else, you've seriously distressed Gran."

"It's in Lilly's travel kit," the boy said, his voice very quiet.

"It's all right," Harry reassured him with one final hard hug. "You were trying to protect your sister. That is what the very best big brothers do. But now we need to put it back and see what happens. All right?"

Theo still looked frightened. Harry didn't blame him, especially if the little boy's dreams had been half as terrifying as *his* had.

"All right."

Harry and Sorcha got to their feet, and Harry held out his hand for Theo. It was time to put this whole business to rest. "All right, then, Theo. Let's be at it."

"It's up in the nursery," Theo said. "I wanted it to be close to her."

"Then let's go to the nursery and get it."

They trooped through the halls of his great house like a scene from the Pied Piper, Lilly singing again, and Bea

dancing around her mother. Harry and Theo and Sorcha
brought up the rear, all three solemn and nervous. Harry
even saw Sorcha wipe her hands against her jeans. Past
the halls where fairy horses pranced and up the stairwell
ringed in a fairy wood, they walked. Past the memories
of a mad old man who'd thought he'd been crowned
prince of the fairies, so they could reclaim the hunk of
quartz the old man had convinced the rest of the world
wasn't worthless and common, in an effort to protect
Harry's nephew's fragile heart.

Harry's own heart was beating hard, and he hated it.
He didn't want to do this, didn't want to reinforce the
delusions that had ruled this household for the last
hundred years. But delusions had power, so he would
use that power as he needed and then walk away.

The old nursery had lain dormant for years before
Theo's birth. During her nesting period beforehand,
Phyl had corralled Harry and Ned and Gran into helping
her turn it into a wonderland for her children, since she
spent so much time at the great house. And like a true
Wyatt, she decorated the whole thing in murals, these
from *The Wind in the Willows*. Lilly's travel kit was
tucked away in Mr. Toad's Hole, just past the physical
therapy equipment that helped Lilly overcome her
physical deficits.

"No nap," Lilly challenged from her mother's arms.
"No nap now, Mama."

"No, my piglet," Phyl assured her. "You're not visiting Mr. Toad just yet. You have far too much playing to
do before then. And a monstrous lunch to eat later, isn't
that right?"

Lilly nodded enthusiastically. "Monstrus," she sang.

Then she caught sight of what Theo was doing and frowned. "Mine, Theo. Mine, mine, *mine!*"

"I know, imp," he said, pulling out the bright pink backpack that was Lilly's travel kit. "But we have to give the diamond back."

"No!" Lilly shrilled struggling to get down. "*My* dimond! *Mine!*"

Theo pulled the cricket-ball-sized hunk of quartz from Lilly's backpack and held it up, and nothing happened. No crack of doom or flash of lightning. It caught the morning light coming in from the big windows, but other than that, it looked pretty unimpressive.

"Mine," Lilly whimpered, collapsing against Phyl's chest.

Sorcha stepped forward and bowed her head. Harry damn near snorted. No question now. She was a fake. She was acting as if she were in the presence of a deity, and it was nothing but a hunk of quartz. She reached out with both hands to accept the Stone from Theo and stood in reverent silence.

"Well?" Harry demanded. "Now what?"

She turned to him, and everything changed all over again. "I don't know," she admitted, looking back at the Stone in her hands with anxiety.

"You don't?" he retorted, about out of patience. "Why not?"

She faced him, and the ground seemed to shift.

"Because this isn't the Fairy Diamond."

# Chapter 8

Sorcha truly wasn't sure she could survive much more. She'd been through so much in the last days: war, loss, banishment, illness, nightmares. And yet she'd felt so hopeful. She would find the Stone. She would sneak it away from these kind people and return it to safety, so the world would realign itself. She would earn the right to go home where she belonged.

But now…

She wasn't strong enough for this. She didn't have the fortitude or the courage. She was just a teacher. Just a seamstress who lived in a tiny house by the river. She wasn't a warrior to face off against the *Dubhlainn Sidhe*. Not alone. Not without an army behind her, her mother at its head and her sisters alongside her.

She was alone. She was so very afraid. And she was about to fail all over again.

"What do you mean it isn't the Fairy Diamond?" Phyl demanded. "Isn't that the Diamond, Harry? Isn't that what we've had on display for the last hundred years or so?"

"Of course it is."

"Theo," Sorcha said, looking down at the solemn little boy who had his uncle's grass-green eyes, "have you ever noticed the Stone do anything…odd? Like, make you feel as if it's, oh, I don't know, singing? Humming? Especially when you held it. Have you known where it was before you saw it?"

Harry took an impatient step forward, but Theo wasn't attending. "No," he said. "Should I?"

She thought of asking Harry, as well, but it seemed pointless. Theo was nine. He'd certainly felt the arrival of the *Dubhlainn Sidhe* quickly enough. It was inconceivable to her that he wouldn't have felt the true Stone's presence.

She took a moment to consider the crystal that sat nestled in her left palm, for all the world like a glittering stone egg. Even with the interference of the house, even with the damage that might have been done by the mortal illness she'd had, there was simply no way she could *not* feel one of the three Filial Stones as it rested in her heart hand.

This stone was silent.

"If it isn't here," she said, "then where could it be?"

"If it isn't here, it doesn't exist," Harry said.

She pulled in a halfhearted breath. "Then all is lost. If the Stone isn't here, I know not where to look for it. And the *Dubhlainn Sidhe* have already breached the veil in my wake."

She felt tears welling in her eyes. She felt the expectations of her people all but crush her. She couldn't think what to do. She couldn't…

"Fairy!" Lilly called and leaned out from her mother's arms. "Fairy! 'Lo!"

Sorcha turned to see the little girl's frowning face. "Yes, my Lilly?"

"C'mere!"

Sorcha walked over to take the little girl from her mother's arms. Immediately Lilly cupped her face in her sweet little hands. "Smile," she said, sounding very serious. Then she gave her a big, gleaming smile, as if all Sorcha had needed was an example. Well, what could a fairy do but smile back?

Satisfied, Lilly patted Sorcha again, and then reached down to where Sorcha still held the Stone in one hand. "*My* di-mond."

"No, sweetheart," Phyl said. "It's Gran's diamond. She'll cry if you keep it from her. You don't want Gran to cry, do you?"

Lilly had to think about that for a minute. "No," she said with a shake of her head. "Go Gran. Now."

Sorcha fortified herself with a long hug from the little girl. It was a rare privilege to be able to bask in the joy of one of the cherished ones. That alone might save her from despair.

But then, what was she bringing to this beautiful little flower? Endless winter. Cold and darkness and loss.

And the heavy hand of the *Dubhlainn Sidhe,* who would have no restraint now that they had the Coilin Stone in their hands and no Dearann Stone to temper their power.

"All right, then," Harry said, reaching for Lilly, who happily changed hands again. "Here's the plan. We smile and give Gran her kisses, and hand over the Fairy Diamond. No talk of dreams or bad fairies or the possibility that this might not be her Fairy Diamond. Am I clear?"

The children nodded. Sorcha couldn't scrape up the energy to do even that. Harry scowled at her.

"If you can't figure out a way to keep from looking like you've just lost your last friend," he suggested, "might I suggest you stay behind?"

"No," she said, shaking herself. "I'll be grand. You'll see."

He was right. She had no business burdening that gracious old lady with her problems. But she had to be there to see how the old woman reacted. To see if she recognized the Stone as different, maybe. As less than what it had been before Theo had made off with it. Maybe the old woman would see something the rest of them had missed.

"Well, now, Theo," she said, smiling as she held out the perfectly ordinary oval of quartz, "wouldn't you like to be the gift-bearer, then?"

The boy eyed the Stone as if it would attack. In the end, though, he took it.

"Lovely," Sorcha said, turning him toward the door. "Won't we make a grand parade, now, for your gran?"

Harry just snorted and turned to go.

Again they marched in a line, this time even more purposefully as they descended the stairs from the third floor to the second, where Harry's grandmother lived. Lilly was singing again, something indistinct and atonal, and trying her best to play hide-and-seek over Harry's shoulder. Bea was riding her mother's arms and Theo led the way like a small soldier.

Sorcha spent the time stoking up her courage. Oh, to be able to just disappear right now, she thought. Would they really miss her if she slipped back out to the fairy hall and simply rested? She was so tired. She was so sad.

She was so afraid.

Mary met them at Gran's door. "Please tell me you got good news," she said. "That ole woman been frettin' all night long."

"Theo?" Harry asked, motioning the boy forward.

"Harry!" Gran barked from within her room. "Get in here and tell me what's going on!"

When Theo balked at the sound of his grandmother's voice, Harry gave him a little shove. "Look what Theo found, Gran!" he called, ushering the whole family inside.

Sorcha remained in the doorway. Gran hadn't even made it to her throne chair this morning. She was still abed in the room beyond, propped up by a half dozen pillows and looking even smaller than she had before.

Phyl let Bea down, and the girl raced into her great-grandmother's room, followed more slowly by Theo. Lilly bounced in Harry's arms, singing what must have been her grandmother song, arms wide, face alight.

"My di-mond!" she called.

"You just be patient, young lady," Gran said, laughing as she accepted the Fairy Diamond from her grave great-grandson. "Wait your turn."

"*Your* turn," Lilly answered.

"That's right, you little scamp. It's my turn." The old woman had the crystal cradled in her papery palm, and there were tears streaming down her face. "Excellent job, Theo. You found it?"

"He did, Gran," Harry said, stepping through the door. "The fairies must have tried to steal it back, but he got it before they got away."

He was smiling. Gran was smiling. Phyl was smiling. It was a joke. A celebration wrapped in whimsy. Sorcha was smiling, too. Hers was a lie, though. Gran hadn't noticed a thing. She hadn't jumped up and cried, "But this is a fraud! The real Fairy Diamond was here only last week! This doesn't feel right."

And while Harry's family comforted and cosseted his grandmother, children tumbling around her bed, Lilly tucked up against her shoulder and patting the old woman's cheek, Sorcha stepped away.

She didn't really pay attention to where she was going; she just knew she had to get away. She couldn't bear the sight of that close, happy family, especially not now.

She walked the long hall from Gran's suite and down the endlessly winding stairs that were warmed by the morning sun that poured through the glass dome high above. She thought maybe she would walk back to the kitchen and see if Mrs. Thompson would return her attire to her. She thought she would move on.

The Fairy Diamond had been here. There was no question at all. A hundred years ago, a fairy prince of the *Dubhlainn Sidhe* clan had been caught on the wrong side of the veil and kept by a mortal woman who had loved him, and he had gifted her with the most precious prize in the fairy realm.

Had he meant to bring it? Had he simply not been able to get it back? It didn't matter. He'd kept it here, where his descendants had built a shrine worthy of the Dearann Stone, where they'd spent their lives and fortune trying to find their way back across the veil. And some time during those ensuing years, they had lost the very thing that had given meaning to it all.

Sorcha walked all the way down to the front salon, which Harry's grandfather had painted with the memories of a perfect fairy glen, the sacred trees arched and leafy and sweet, the ceiling a breathtaking sky with just a suggestion of the sun. Here there were painted horses and foxes and salmon to keep a fairy from feeling too homesick. Here there was the hot spring green of Irish fields to salve her soul. Here, even with the formal furniture that kept her from truly believing she was home, Sorcha settled down onto the rug. Bringing her knees up, she crossed her arms atop them and laid her head down. And here she stayed. She had nowhere else to go.

If mortals weren't so ridiculous, Cian could easily hate them. They were insignificant creatures, with no power, no wit, no sense of the gifts they'd been given and certainly no beauty in their pusillanimous little souls. What right had they to hold hostage one of the three Filial Stones? How could they possibly think themselves worthy of it? No mortal being was. Come to think of it, most of the world of faerie wasn't, either.

He was. Born to the clan of the high king himself, cousin to the Avenger and holder of the keys to the treasury, he alone could withstand the pull of so mighty a stone in order to bring it back to the other side, where it could be safely tucked away in a place where it couldn't do any harm. Where it couldn't interfere with the burgeoning power of the *Dubhlainn Sidhe*.

Cian smiled to himself, and it was a terrible thing. He would reclaim the lost Stone. There was no question. No cringing coward of a *Tuatha* would succeed where the *Dubhlainn Sidhe* had not.

As Cian tucked himself into the grove of plane trees out beyond the gardens of the big house, he paid no attention to the cold or the damp or the darkness of the days here. Neither did he waste his time worrying about the Stone's great power or how it could have remained lost in this miserable place for so long. He was much too occupied by just how he would go about reclaiming it. And how much he would enjoy hurting that little blond flyspeck of a child of Mab who thought she could outwit him in time to claim it for herself.

Sorcha wasn't sure how long she sat alone. Time held little meaning for fairies, and here, where she finally gave in to the inevitable, it disappeared completely.

She was caught here, just as surely as Harry's ancestor had been a hundred years earlier. Without the Stone, there was no way home. Without the Stone, there would soon be no home to return to. And yet, what had she here? What worth did she have in a mortal world?

It was much later when she heard the children clattering down the stairs.

"Well, what do we do with her, Harry?" she heard Phyl ask from at least two stories up.

Maybe she should tell them that fairies had exceptional hearing. She didn't want Phyl to be upset at being overheard.

"How the bloody hell do I know?" Harry asked. "Gran won't let her go, and I can't let her stay. So, do we turn her over to the police? I'm sure they'd just love to·hear her fairy story."

"Oh, Harry, you can't do that to her."

"Do *you* want to house her till we find out what's going on? I certainly don't."

And then, silence. Sorcha closed her eyes, completely incapable of reaction. Somehow these last words pierced even beyond the despair she'd felt already. No place in her world, no place in his. And no place, certainly, in his regard. Ah, and wasn't that the worst cut of all?

"Miss Tuatha?" she heard from the doorway.

She didn't bother to lift her head. "Yes, Theo?"

"Are…are you all right?"

"Oh, aye," she said, "Just restin'. I'm after taking a fairy nap."

"Oh. All right. We've been looking for you. You missed dinner."

"Thank you, but I'm grand."

Silence.

"Would you teach me how to ride like you do?"

Finally she lifted her head: "Theo, you're a brilliant rider. Whatever could I teach you?"

"How you talk to the horses," he said, taking a step into the room. Inevitably, just like his uncle, his eyes were drawn to the walls where other horses ran. "They seem to listen to you."

She dredged up a smile. "Ah, sure, that's no secret. You have the ability within you. You just have to take more time to listen. Horses are always telling us what they need to. They just don't talk in words, now, do they?"

"Will you show me?"

She tried very hard to dredge up even an ounce of energy. "Could we postpone it till tomorrow, Theo? I think I've overdone it today altogether."

"Oh…of course."

He looked so very earnest, Sorcha couldn't help but smile. "First thing tomorrow. Before I leave."

His bright young features fell. "You're leaving?"

"Oh, I think I must," she said. "I've seen the Fairy Diamond, now, and I don't think I should be after harassing your uncle anymore."

"Where will you go?"

"Why, back across the veil," she lied, because Theo was a child who would worry.

"Will you take me with you?" he asked.

She gave him the consideration of thinking about her answer. "Maybe one day," she said. "Not now, though. You have too much learning to do right here. And I'm thinking your mam would miss you, now, wouldn't she? And Bea and wee little Lilly? Sure, they're depending on their big brother."

He squirmed a bit, but finally nodded. "As long as I know how to find you again."

Since she had no idea where that would be, she just nodded.

Still, he didn't leave the room. "What about the dreams?" he asked, eyes focused on the carpet at his feet.

Sorcha stiffened. "The nightmares."

He managed to look up. "Did you have them, too?"

"Oh, aye, Theo. I had them. And I'm that sorry you suffered, too. The *Dubhlainn Sidhe* are not respecters of innocence."

"Will they go away?"

Would they? Suddenly Sorcha felt energy flowing back into her. Goddess, she thought. She'd forgotten. The diamond wasn't here. The *Dubhlainn Sidhe,* however, were. And she had to find a way to protect her new family from them.

*Her new family.* She caught herself smiling. Finally she understood how her sister Nuala had found herself adopting a whole family of mortals as her own all those years ago. They were irresistible. Especially the children. The children on this plane were as bright as shooting stars.

Taking one last look around the room, she climbed to her feet and held out a hand. "How 'bout we work on that together?" she asked.

For the first time, Theo really smiled. "Brilliant," he said, and, taking her hand, led her from her exile.

What had happened to his nice, normal, unbearably frustrating life? Harry wondered. Any other weekend of his life, he would be taking the regulation Saturday afternoon away from Gwyneth to sit with Phyl over the estate books as they tried to squeeze money from the estate like blood from a stone, so the two of them could realize their dream of creating the finest breeding program for Irish-bred thoroughbreds in England. They had already made a great start. Phyl had an unerring eye for good horseflesh. The newest mare she'd chosen, a leggy chestnut with beautiful conformation, strong lines and great, intelligent eyes, was proof of that. Now they just had to be able to afford her.

Now was when he and Phyl should have been figuring

out how to do that very thing. Now was when he and
Gwyneth should have been putting the final touches on
the wedding they'd been planning for the last year.

But Phyl was up settling Gran, and Gwyneth was still
in York. On the phone.

"You can't get back down this weekend?" he said to
her, as if she hadn't just told him that very thing.

"I'm sorry, Harry. Something…big has come up."

She sounded stiff and uncertain. And if there was one
thing Gwyneth could never be accused of, it was sounding uncertain. "Gwyn? Are you all right?"

For that he got a long silence and a funny little huffing sound in his ear. "I think I am, Harry. I really think
I am."

And what the bloody hell was *that* supposed to
mean? Harry closed his eyes so he couldn't see the ac-
count books piled up before him in Phyl's meticulously
kept estate office, and rested his head in his hand.

"I think you have to be more specific than that, Gwyn."

"But I can't, Harry. I truly can't. I think it might be
best if we met next week, maybe Thursday after work.
We need to talk."

*Oh, God, not her, too.* "Talk, Gwyn?"

She cleared her throat. "I know I'm not making much
sense right now. I promise I will Thursday. All right?"

Harry rubbed the bridge of his nose. "All right, Gwyn."

He was just about to say goodbye when her voice
came again, and suddenly it sounded small and young
and uncertain. "Harry?"

"Yes?"

"Do you think your grandfather could have been
right all along?"

"*What?*"

"Never mind. Bye, Harry."

Harry hung up and thought seriously about pouring himself a full tumbler of whiskey. What the bloody hell was happening to his world all of a sudden?

Of course, he knew. Nothing had been right since that bedamned fairy had tumbled into it. Nothing looked the same or felt the same. Nothing that had once been enough *was* anymore.

He lurched to his feet and walked to the window, where he could see the paddocks that held his horses. It had been all he'd ever wanted in his life: the ability to stand right here and see the product of his hard work. The chance to interact with these magnificent creatures, to breed the most beautiful horses in England.

To his mind, they had succeeded. Their horses were beginning to be recognized around the country. Harry could name the pedigree and character traits of each one. He had personally picked out Moonrise as their first stud, a magnificent, almost otherworldly gray who had thrown off perfect replicas of himself every time they'd bred him to any mare in the country. Moonrise bred true and Harry had to admit that his get were his favorites. These were the horses that seemed to meet their world with the most intelligence.

It should have been enough. He had his family. He had a fiancée who would match him perfectly. He had a career that could support them all and one day pull them all into not only permanent solvency but true comfort again.

Instead, his fiancée was suddenly unrecognizable, his family was in turmoil, and his own dreams were caught somewhere between impossibility and terror.

And all since she'd stumbled into his life.

She couldn't know.

She couldn't possibly tell the difference. He wouldn't believe it.

He rubbed at his forehead again, when what he really wanted to be rubbing at was the sharp pain in his chest. No one in his entire life had ever thought that bloody stone might do more than just sit like a lump in its cradle. Nobody had once intimated that just being near it could provoke flashes of vision that were no less than impossible. Nobody had ever, *ever* tried to tell him that the bloody thing *sang,* for God's sake.

He was rubbing at his chest now.

How could she *know?*

As if called by just his thoughts, she appeared out by the mares and fillies paddock. She was talking to Theo, motioning to Starchaser, one of his fillies, and Starchaser, the little flirt, was responding as if Theo were her date to a formal, tail up, head nodding, dancing around him in delight. Sorcha and Theo had spent the last couple of hours collecting tree branches and holly leaves. He had no idea why, but now Theo held a short hawthorn branch in his hand, like Harry Potter. Sorcha had holly in her hair. And there, inevitably, were Bea and Lilly, coming to join them at the paddock rails, more branches and leaves decorating them. They all looked like they were rehearsing A *Midsummer Night's Dream.*

A couple more of the fillies joined them at the rails. Moonbright and Starchild. Almost indistinguishable one from the other to anyone but him. The brightest of this generation. The fastest, surest. Breathtaking, both of them, with the dished noses of an Arabian, the strong haunches of an Irish jumper, and the color of a morning mist. Sorcha lifted a hand and Moonbright bent her head as if asking benediction. Bea laughed and Lilly clapped. Sorcha seemed to be instructing.

What was the woman up to now? Harry wondered, and got to his feet. He was not about to have her disrupt his horses with her nonsense.

He made it outside to find Phyl approaching from the other direction.

"She'd better not hurt those horses," Harry growled.

Phyl laughed. "You obviously haven't seen her with them."

He would have answered, but when he looked back, there was his premiere mare, Moondancer, prancing in a circle, with the fairy child already on her bare back.

"Bloody hell," he snapped, ready to take off.

Phyl held him back. "Oh, leave her alone. She's magic, Harry. You know how the Dancer is. She won't allow anybody but me on her back now she's breeding. Well, you would have thought your Sorcha was a big lump of sugar, the way she took to her."

Harry saw perfectly well how the mare took to her. He had seen fine horsemen in his life. He was accounted one of the best himself. Certainly Phyl held her place in the pantheon. But he'd never seen anything like this. Not only did the girl look as if she were one with the animal, but he'd never seen Dancer move with such fluid grace. Dancer was a jumper, a dark bay Irish-bred with powerful movement and the stamina of a warhorse. With that small girl on her back, she looked like a ballerina.

"Me, now!" his niece Bea demanded from the top rail of the fence, already wearing her helmet.

Without seeming to pause, Sorcha rode past and lifted the girl to sit before her. "What do you say to her now, Bea?" Sorcha asked.

"I thank you, Moondancer," Bea recited, patting the great animal's gleaming neck, "for the privilege of your generosity."

"Ah, grand," Sorcha said, briefly laying her cheek against the five-year-old's head. "She'll carry you on forever now."

That was when Harry realized that at least a dozen of his prime stock were standing about as if waiting their turn, the colts leaning their powerful necks over the far fence like children lining up for a ride.

"Unbelievable," he muttered.

Phyl chuckled and patted his arm. "You should hire the girl, Harry."

Harry had no intention of telling Phyl what he really thought. "You want to hire her, go right ahead. That's your job."

Phyl laughed again. "I just might."

"Could I try?" Theo called to Sorcha from the fence.

"Ah, sure, you can do it yourself, Theo," she assured him, still circling with Bea.

For a second Theo just watched. Then he approached Starchild and lifted his hand to her muzzle. The horse dipped her head, and Theo put his own head to hers. Starchild whuffled at him, and he grabbed her mane and vaulted cleanly up atop her.

"Brilliant, Theo!" Sorcha called.

Starchild whinnied and tossed her head. Theo beamed. The little cavalcade went prancing over the grass like a parade.

That was when Harry saw Lilly. There she was, standing at the fence, her little helmet dangling from her pudgy hands, looking as lost and yearning as he'd ever seen.

"Me," she whimpered, almost to herself. "Me."

There were tears on her face. Ah, damn it. He couldn't stand it. He took a step toward her, but Sorcha must have seen her.

"Ah, *mo chroidhe,*" she crooned, swinging off the great bay and setting Bea down before her. "What is it, now?"

Lilly pointed her pudgy little hand toward where Theo trotted happily atop Starchild. "Ride," she said in a hopeless tone. "'Lone."

Sorcha hopped the fence and sat right down at the little girl's feet. "You're wanting to ride, then?"

"She can't, Sorcha," Phyl said. "Not alone. It's too dangerous."

Sorcha looked up, saw Phyl, then saw Harry and bestowed a gleaming smile on him. "Ah, well, that might not be true," she disagreed. "Has she been atop one of the ladies yet?"

"Of course not," Harry said. "Not without one of us holding on to her. She doesn't have the fine motor coordination. She'll *never*—"

Sorcha waved him off and settled the helmet on Lilly's head. "It's just a matter of asking, Harry Wyatt."

And she walked Lilly to where Starchaser stood patiently waiting by the side of the fence.

"Now then, *mo stoir,*" Sorcha said, buckling the helmet on and lifting the little girl into her arms. "What do you say to this fine, gracious lady?"

Harry knew he should interfere, but he couldn't seem

to move. Next to him, Phyl grabbed hold of his sleeve. "Harry…"

"Please," Lilly said in a piping voice, her little hand flat against Chaser's dark gray muzzle. "Carry me."

The horse actually lifted her head, as if considering the little girl.

*"Ogbheann,"* Sorcha crooned with a regal dip of her head, "I ask your favor for this wee sprite here. You see the great heart of her, the pure spirit of her. I give you the greatest honor a fairy can bestow, the chance to guard one of the cherished ones. Will you carry her, then, with all the care you would your queen?"

The horse held still. Everyone in the yard held still, except Lilly, who chortled as she ran her hand down the horse's nose. Then, unbelievabley, Chaser bowed her head, as if in obeisance. Before Harry could protest, Sorcha had Lilly up on the horse's bare back and was wrapping her pudgy little hands in the filly's mane.

"Now then, *mo aoibheann,*" she was saying to the little girl, "you hold on here, and your lovely friend will do the rest. All right?"

Lilly nodded enthusiastically and Sorcha let go.

"No!" Phyl cried, and started running.

Harry followed right behind. But before they could reach the fence, Chaser set off in the most amazing stately trot he'd ever seen. She moved over the ground as if gliding on ice. Lilly, her little legs sticking almost straight out, held on to Chaser's mane as if she'd done it her whole life, and rode her like a rocking horse.

"Get her off, Harry," Phil insisted. "She'll fall."

"Ah, no," Sorcha said, walking over. "I swear an oath, that as long as it's your Starchaser who has her, she'll be perfectly safe. Sure, a fairy horse would rather die than harm a cherished one."

"She is not a bloody fairy horse!" Harry said, trying to step past.

Sorcha took hold of his sleeve. Harry spun on her, ready to fight. Then he heard it, and his heart tumbled right over. Lilly, who just moments ago had been standing alone, left behind by what everybody but she could accomplish, what she ached to do, called to him.

"Ha—rry!" she cried, her little voice shrill with delight. "I ride! I *ride!*"

And then she was laughing. The pure, sweet notes of it skipped through the air like a melody. The horses stopped, each one. Stable boys stepped outside to see and smile. Somehow Harry knew that even his grandmother had heard from her room.

"Yes, my piglet!" Harry called back, his voice rough. "You ride!"

She rode all alone, and she was so happy the sun shone. And seeing that, Harry suddenly wasn't sure what he'd thought could have been dangerous. Chaser literally floated across the ground, carrying that little girl like a precious gift on a cushion, and Lilly, perched motionless atop her, absolutely gleamed.

"Oh…my…God, Harry," Phyl whispered.

"Mama!" Lilly cried out. "See me!"

Phyl was in tears. "Yes, my love. Yes!"

Lilly laughed. Chaser whinnied. Sorcha clapped her hands and laughed, as if she'd created horses just for the pleasure of letting little girls ride. Harry felt the oddest bubble of joy build in his chest. And then he felt the sharp knife of ambivalence. How had she done it? How could he believe it possible? But it was. Lilly, his little miracle of a niece, was doing the thing she most wanted to on earth, something he'd failed to provide for her. But the fairy girl had.

And suddenly he was laughing along with Lilly. Everyone turned. He knew they thought he'd suddenly lost his senses. He couldn't help it. The most unexpected shaft of joy shot clear through his chest, the same chest that had just been hurting so hard. He simply couldn't think of anything more wondrous than to see Lilly atop a horse of her own.

"Ah, Harry," Sorcha said with a beaming smile, "I know Saoirce is one of your most lovely horses, but you see, don't you, that she's Lilly's horse?"

"Saoirce?" Phyl asked.

"Her real name, so. Her fairy name. It means Freedom."

Harry was nodding, wiping tears from his own cheeks. "Lilly!" he called. "How do you like your very own horse?"

At his words, Chaser came to a fluid stop right in front of him and waited as the little girl carefully unwrapped a hand and patted her. "Mine!" she crowed.

"Indeed," Harry assured her. "All yours. Saoirce doesn't mind?"

He knew Phyl was staring at him as if his hair was afire. He didn't care. He couldn't think of anything he'd accomplished in his life as satisfying as this.

"Saoirce says it would be her great honor," Sorcha said.

As if in emphasis, Chaser—Saoirce—carefully bent a knee and lowered her head, as if paying homage.

"Then Lilly's horse she is."

"And just to make sure," Phyl said briskly, as she

scrubbed her cheeks of tears, "the minute she gets off, I'm fitting a saddle with straps."

Harry stayed there for another hour, just watching. Just listening to the laughter that tumbled around the yard like bright water. Just watching that fairy child ensorcell his family. He stood alone outside the paddock fence, wishing he could join them and not knowing how. Sure, though, that if he just had the courage to ask her, Sorcha would make it so easy that he would wonder at his worry.

It shouldn't have surprised him then, that when he finally gave up on sleep hours into the night and headed out to the little fairy house for some peace, it would be to find her there before him.

# Chapter 9

"You couldn't sleep, could you, Harry?" she asked.

There was no electricity here, so she'd lit a candle. Her eyes were luminous in the glow. Her hair tumbled about her like honey, and her beautiful body was draped in that mesmerizing gray dress…blue…violet…that seemed to be whispering in movement even as she held still.

He couldn't take his eyes from her. His heart accelerated. His body caught fire. Desire hit him hard. Impatience. Frustration. This house was the only place where he could find any rest. How dare she invade it?

"I couldn't sleep, either," she admitted, lighting the little lantern that sat on the table. Light flared, sending the shadows skittering into the corners to be caught by the branches that had entwined into walls. The floor, that odd, glittering mirror of a floor, reflected the light and movement as if it were a pool of water. Harry did his level best to keep his eyes on the familiar. He knew damn well that if he looked at her, he'd be lost.

"Go back," he demanded, shoving his hands into his pockets, where they couldn't harm her.

Snatches of dream flashed through his mind. Hot, dark images, terrifying sounds. No more than a whiff of rage and fear and power.

"You wouldn't share the haven you have here?" she asked very quietly.

He could smell her now, and it terrified him.

"Go," he begged. "I don't want to hurt you."

She didn't go. She stepped right up to him. "Oh, Harry," she whispered, lifting an impossibly delicate hand to his cheek. "How could you ever think you could hurt me?"

Fire shot to his toes. His cock went on ready alert, and his chest…his chest just closed off. He closed his eyes against the pain of that contact. "You don't know…."

"But I do. And what you told Theo today was true. No matter what you dream, you could never hurt me. Never, Harry. It is impossible."

He flinched away from her, eyes open and accusing. "You can't possibly be that naive."

Damn her, she smiled. "Not naive. I know you, Harry. More than that, I know that your fairy blood forbids it. A fairy may court, a fairy may seduce or compel. A fairy simply cannot physically force. It would be like a mortal taking wing. It is not possible."

Harry crowded her, needing her to understand. "But I'm not a fairy, Sorcha. I'm a man, and I'm having a damnable time keeping my hands off you. And you have no idea what will happen if I don't."

"Of course I do," she said, smiling even more broadly, so that he could see the shadow of a dimple. "Because you *are* a man, Harry Wyatt. But whatever else you want to believe, you have fairy blood. And that makes all the difference. It is the *Dubhlainn Sidhe* you see in your dreams, Harry. Not you. Never you."

"I'm *not*—"

She stroked his cheek as if he were a fractious child. "You come here to find peace, Harry. Even you, who were born in that great stone behemoth beyond the trees, can't stand to stay there long. You need the living grace of Mother Earth. You need to restore your soul here, in the sacred grove."

"I *need* some bloody sleep!"

Her smile was heartbreaking. "Then sleep. And if you don't mind, I'll curl up here, too. I'm not doing any better than you in that great stone box up the hill."

Harry sucked in a calming breath and shoved his hands through his hair. "You can't sleep out here."

God, just the thought of her curled up against him sent his randy prick dancing. His hands were clenched tight. He was sweating now, struggling to catch his breath. Fighting for control. He could almost feel her soft, round bottom nestled against his groin.

He wanted her. He *wanted* her.

"I know," she whispered, so close that her breasts brushed against the cotton of his shirt. "I want you, too, Harry."

He opened his eyes again to find her too close, too beautiful, too willing. Her eyes were huge and dark. Her skin was flushed and her nostrils were flared, as if she needed his scent as much as he needed hers.

Cinnamon, for God's sake. He was hard over something you put in egg nog.

"You smell like the wind, Harry," she said, not touching him. Not so much as leaning closer in invitation. Only smiling, as if she already saw the end of this discussion in her head. "You smell like freedom and strength and the earth. I can't resist the smell of you, Harry Wyatt."

He lost the fight. Digging his hands into her hair, he pulled her against him. He would show her what kind of game she was playing. He would take her, just like in his dreams. He would force her. He would...

Her mouth was so soft, so open, so welcoming. He wrapped an arm around her and held on, and he kissed her. He kissed her until they both ran out of air, until he could hardly stand anymore, a mating dance of a kiss. A conquest of them both, a surrender never admitted. Tongue and teeth and lips, a hungry, hurried dance of need and want.

She fit against him so perfectly; he couldn't remember any woman fitting so neatly beneath his arm, as if she were meant to be there, where he could guard her, where he could lift her clean off the ground to meet her groin to groin, to measure himself against her and know that she was content.

He didn't remember reaching the bed or laying her down. He didn't remember pulling off her dress. He just knew that she was lying beneath him, her creamy skin glowing in the flickering lantern light, her perfect rose-colored nipples tightening, beckoning. She was small, but God, she was proportioned to cushion a man. Her breasts were so firm, her belly just a bit rounded, her hips lush and soft. He would swear on whatever was holy that he'd never wanted anything as badly as he wanted to be inside her.

He'd no sooner thought it than she smiled, and it was the oldest smile in the world. "You're seriously overdressed, Harry," she said, pulling at his shirt. "I don't think that's fair at all."

God, he wanted to laugh. How could he want to laugh? How could he even be here?

He couldn't. But he couldn't stop. He had gotten a taste of her and needed more. He needed it all. He was ravenous: his hands, his mouth, his aching, straining cock. He wanted to be in her. He wanted to bury himself in her, pound into her, pump himself into her until he'd wrung himself dry.

He knew she was pulling his clothes off. He heard buttons pop. He lifted an arm away from her, then another. But he couldn't stop touching her. He couldn't seem to get enough of her petal-soft skin, her sumptuous curves and valleys, her unbearably beautiful breasts.

He shouldn't be doing this. God, he was taking advantage of a confused young woman who thought she was a fairy. He was *engaged*. What was wrong with him?

She yanked his slacks off, and it didn't matter anymore. He'd found that bright nest of hair at the base of her belly and dipped his fingers into it. He'd discovered the secret, satin-slick folds of her wet and ready and weeping. He heard the breathy little moans she couldn't contain as he inserted a finger into her, as he stroked and fretted over her swelling clitoris, as he suckled on her rose-perfect nipple.

He felt her buck against his hand, and he knew he didn't have to wait. He was dying waiting. But he waited anyway. He tortured her, nipping and suckling at her breast, feathering circles there inside that lovely sunburst nest until finally she shrieked, until she threw her head back, eyes wide, mouth open, her body convulsing around him. Then, just as she climaxed, he lifted her hips to him, and he drove into her, and she climaxed again.

Somewhere in the back of his head he wondered why he wasn't following the script of the dream. Why he wasn't hurting her, terrorizing her. Why she looked up at him with stunned delight instead of dread. Somewhere he knew he would have to look for that answer. But now he feasted on her, and she met him, thrust for thrust, her hands scrabbling over him, her body arching like a bow so he could easily bend again to her breasts. He suckled hard, pulling her nipple into his mouth as he plunged into her, deeper, deeper, faster, until he couldn't remember where he left off and she began, until she pulled his head up to kiss her as thoroughly as he was taking her, until his body clenched and forced his own head back, until he was the one who cried out, his hoarse voice filling the little room, until he pumped himself into her as she laughed and he laughed and his body turned inside out with her, then finally failed him, and he fell senseless into her arms.

For a long while the only sound in the little room was panting. For a long while Harry couldn't think, couldn't move, couldn't regret the most incredible experience of his life. For a long while he lay folded up with her, so that every inch of her skin could meet his, so he could nestle her against him and warm her on what should have been a cold, dreary night.

He knew he should get up. One of them should leave. Hell, both of them should probably leave. He'd never even thought to bring a woman here. But somehow the room was perfectly warm. If Harry had been fanciful, he would have sworn the damned floor glowed. But he wasn't fanciful. He didn't believe in sacred groves or fairies or fate. Even so, for some reason, he knew this was where he was supposed to be.

"And where else would you be?" she asked against his shoulder. "Even you can't deny that this is a sacred place."

"Which we've just sullied."

She lifted her head and stared down at him with a mysterious smile, the kind of mysterious smile that conjured thoughts of goddesses and magic. "Sure, you mortals have a funny view of the most sacred act there is." Shaking her head, she lay down again and sighed. "I'd hoped it would make you happy."

Harry wasn't sure what kept him from answering. He should have assured her that nothing in his frustrating life had ever made him happier. But that would have been admitting too much. It would have been denying everything he believed.

And he simply couldn't do that. So he pulled the blanket up over them, closed his eyes, and realized that for the first time in weeks, he was about to sleep without dreaming.

Darragh, son of Bran, found himself lost in crisp linen and soft flesh. Gwyneth, his Gwyneth, was lying curled in the crook of his shoulder, running her fingers down his chest.

"So smooth," she murmured, sounding amazed. "I've never met anybody like you."

He chuckled. "Sure, I'm not surprised, am I? I've met no one on these streets like me, either."

She lifted her head to reveal sleep-tousled hair and sex-sweetened skin. Darragh didn't know how he could possibly get enough of her. She was laughing, and it seemed to surprise her.

"I thought that poor man at Marks & Spencer would have a coronary when we walked in. I don't think he bought the caught-in-a-Halloween-costume story."

Darragh's gaze wandered over to where his brand-new clothes lay draped over several pieces of furniture, where they'd landed when stripped off in unholy haste. He liked this clothing. He liked the slip and slide of it against him, the way the fabric moved when he did, how the camel-hair coat kept him so warm. Almost as warm as Gwyneth.

"You're sure you can get recompense for the jewels?" he said.

She chuckled. "Darragh, you gave me two rubies and three huge diamonds. Trust me when I tell you that I haven't lost any money."

He stroked the sleek line of her arm. "Good. That's good. I have more to support me in this place till we know what I can do."

She turned serious, of a sudden. "You're sure you want to stay?"

He cupped her face. "You're sure you want me to?"

"Oh, yes," she said, leaning up to kiss him. It seemed they'd been kissing nonstop since she'd first discovered him in the backseat of her car. "I want you to stay."

He smiled at her, amazed at the passion they'd stumbled over in the last forty-eight hours. "Well, that's fine, then. I like your world, altogether. It's loud and busy and full, but there's an energy I'm attracted to."

"Is there?"

He actually thought about it. "Oh, aye. My world flows like a quiet stream, never in a hurry to get from one place to another. After all, what would be the point? Would eternity become shorter with the hurry? Would we get farther than paradise?"

"This isn't paradise," she warned him.

"Paradise can wear after a while if you're not meant for it, I think. Aren't I finding the rush and noise and energy here compelling, then?" He dropped a long, leisurely kiss on her mouth and nuzzled her neck. "Almost as compelling as a certain beautiful woman who's taken me on."

Closing her eyes, she rolled over on her back. "A woman who really isn't free until she sees her fiancé on Thursday."

"Not Thursday," he said instinctively. "Today."

She looked up at him. "What do you mean?"

He shook his head. He'd been plagued by the most inconvenient feeling of anxiety all evening. It had hit right after the moment he'd roused from one of their bouts of lovemaking to realize that he'd woken up.

Odd to think of it so, but he did. It was as if for the first time in decades he suddenly felt clearheaded. As if Gwyneth had swept aside some spell cast on him by his own cupidity and avarice. By the dark magic of Orla, the *leannan sidhe* who had seduced him away from his own good sense.

He'd wanted the Dearann Stone. He'd exiled himself from his own world to obtain it, as if that alone could pay for his crimes. Instead, he'd stumbled over a treasure much more precious to him.

He should have been relieved. Exultant. Excited. All right, then, he was. But at the same time, he had the most gnawing feeling at the pit of his gut that there was something he'd left unfinished back at that great stone house where he'd thought to torment the queen's daughter.

"I'm thinking it might be important for us to get back there in the morning." he said, pulling her close to protect her. "To settle things among us."

And to ease the tightness in his chest.

Something was wrong, and he simply couldn't figure out what.

For a long time Sorcha didn't move from where she was curled in Harry's arms. She didn't even arch her head back so she could watch his sleeping face, no matter how much she wanted to. He needed rest, and she knew he hadn't been getting it. She knew, finally, what had incited part of his self-loathing.

The dreams. The *Dubhlainn Sidhe*-tainted dreams. Even if they'd only been as bad as hers, she could understand how they must have affected him. But she knew that Harry's had been worse than hers. After all, Harry was mostly mortal, and mortals were more susceptible. Especially mortals who didn't believe and so couldn't mount any defense.

Poor Harry. Poor dear, sincere Harry, who only wanted to protect this sacred place and the people who inhabited it, whether he realized it or not. Poor serious Harry, who kept a cauldron of passion tamped down inside him, where he thought it couldn't scorch him. Sorcha actually blushed at the memory of what they'd just shared, and fairies didn't blush. Certainly not over such a natural celebration. But no celebration she'd participated in had been so…so…

She lifted her hand from where it had rested on his taut belly, and she traced the hair that arrowed down that belly, then swept her hand back up to his chest. She couldn't imagine such a thing, such a delicious abrasion against a fairy breast. Just the thought of it caused her nipples to harden. Goddess, how she loved the textures of this mortal. Springy hair on his chest, gravelly beard on his jaw, hard, unrelenting muscle and sinew at elbow and knee and hip. Fairy men were so sleek, like seals. Oddly enough, for beings who did their best to divorce themselves from it, men were more made of the earth from which they came, the warp and weave of them, the contours of them, the scent of them.

Well, the scent of Harry, anyway. She gently ran her fingers over his shoulder—bone and muscle and tendon molding to create an architecture to rival the most beautiful mortal cathedrals. His arms, deceptively smooth in line for the strength that lurked within. Arms that could control the most fractious horse with ease, could lift the heaviest load, could nestle the fragile weight of lovely little Lilly so she felt safe in her world. Sorcha loved his arms.

She loved his legs, his chest, his brow with its constant furrow of worry. She wanted to ease his brow, ease the weight on those magnificent shoulders. She wanted to incite smiles and laughter where they so rarely lived.

She bent over, because she couldn't help it, and she kissed that shoulder. She tasted the man sweat of him, saline and sharp, and felt her belly tighten with wanting. She inhaled him, memorizing his scent just as she did his texture. She knew she dropped tears onto his skin, because of what she'd brought to this man. What she would take away. What he would take away from her.

She would leave. It was inevitable. And he would stay. But Sorcha knew that for all her long fairy life, she would survive knowing that she'd lost her heart, that it would stay here in this cold, wild place in the hands of this honorable man.

"What's this?" he asked, his voice a grainy whisper. Reaching up, he lifted her face to him and began feathering kisses over her eyes. "Was it that awful?"

She couldn't help but chuckle. "Isn't it just like a man, then, to be looking for compliments?"

"I don't understand," he murmured, curling her closer to him so her breasts met his wonderful chest.

"What?" She kissed his chin, testing the grain of his beard with her tongue. "Why it wasn't awful?"

Harry pulled back a bit. "Actually," he said, looking absolutely serious, "yes."

Sorcha rose up on an elbow and stroked a finger across that tense brow. "I told you. This is a sacred place. You're safe here."

He shook his head, and Sorcha knew he was about to bolt. To retreat to denial and rationalization, where he could effectively submerge his faerie soul in mortal responsibilities.

"Of course," she mused, drawing her fingers along

the ridges of his face, "I could be wrong. I mean, we only have this one experience to judge it by."

His pupils grew, and his nostrils flared. "Why would you chance something so terrible?"

"Because I know it won't be, Harry." She smiled and hoped he saw all her desires there. "Shouldn't we find out for sure, though?"

His hands were moving now, unleashing a waterfall of pleasure in her. He drew her closer, and there could be no mistaking his arousal. Sorcha knew she was tormenting him. She knew how likely it was that he would chastise himself in the morning for what they were about to do. She couldn't care. She needed him so badly. She needed to share at least the beauty of creation with the only man she would ever love before she was forced to walk away.

"Please, Harry," she whispered, stretching up to meet his mouth, reaching her hand down to wrap around his arousal, "celebrate with me."

He shuddered at her touch. Sorcha smiled. Another thing fairies lacked, she thought. At least the fairies she'd known. Mortal men were so much more…impressive in size. She couldn't get enough of the silken steel of him, ached deep inside for the return of him to her. Deep, so deep he'd plunged into her, deep enough to touch her very womb. Deep enough to cement her memories of him. Deep enough that she could never question again what it would feel like to accept the weight of the man she loved inside her.

And oh, his touch. Fleeting, furious, so gentle, and yet so thorough she thought he might be memorizing her in return, lighting a swath of fire the length and breadth of her, setting loose a hot, sweet hunger that could only be assuaged by completion.

Oh, Mother Earth, she thought as he bent to take her breast in his mouth, this is creation. This is perfection.

This is love.

She filled her hands with the feel of him, the calluses and the creases, the sensitive, secret places that made him gasp and moan and chuckle against her mouth. She begged for his kisses and melted with the sweep of his tongue against hers, slick and rough at once, just like the rest of him. She let him nudge her legs apart and welcomed the torment of his fingers into the very core of her, where she waited wet and hot for him.

"Now, Harry," she begged, her voice high and thin. "Please. *Now...*"

His chuckle rumbled against her throat, against the unbearably chafed skin of her breasts, against her sore and soaring heart. "My pleasure," he murmured and flipped over on his back, lifting her to straddle him.

He was smiling, the lamplight gleaming off the white of his teeth, the deep wells of his eyes. For the first time since she'd met him, he looked happy, really happy, and it brought tears to the back of her throat. Oh, if she could only give him this. If she could ease his burden just for these few hours in the dark when he would let her. If only she could bring him a bit of peace here in this perfect place. If only...

Bending over, she opened her mouth to him, letting her tongue dance with his, tasting him and testing him and letting him know that she was his, all his, even as she rose up, even as she reached down to cup him and stroke him, even as she took him inside her, deep inside her. All the way inside her, she swore, to the core of her heart, where she could keep him forever, and she sang in the back of her throat, and she rocked, lifting and sinking, tormenting him, tormenting herself, stoking the fire from sweet to unbearable, with his hands on her breasts, with his mouth on hers, with his sweat-slicked body captive to hers, and she rocked, she rocked, she rode him as surely as she rode one of his magnificent horses, until the colors of the earth lit behind her closed eyes, until they spun, until they gathered, collected, sparked and swept through her, until, unable to hold the joy of him to herself, she threw her head back and keened out the bliss and the sweetness and the despair that exploded inside her.

Cian couldn't move any closer to the little hall than that awful circular grove of sacred trees. Dearann's trees, the lifegiver, the motherstone, the goddess-bedamned pain in the arse he was still trying to track down.

He knew where little Sorcha was. Considering the spectacular light display he'd seen burst out of the little windows of the hall and through the roof of twined branches, there could be no mistake. Little Sorcha was creating life in there. A gift to the earth mother, he guessed with a sneer. More likely a gift to the mortal, who didn't deserve fairy bliss.

He would deal with that later. Right now she was vulnerable, no matter how many sacred branches and leaves she'd gathered to surround that house on the hill. Right now, in the depths of night, when the *Dubhlainn Sidhe* crept through the shadows, the world was more open to his kind of persuasion. And he was in the mood for it. He was in need of a bit of chaos.

Turning away from the disgusting swirl of fairy light that was only now dissipating over the roof of the hall, he set himself to a little disruption. Who said you couldn't enjoy yourself while on the hunt for treasure?

## Chapter 10

Sorcha lay very still, listening to the silence of early morning. The sun would edge over the long hills soon. The new day would begin, and she was still wrapped in Harry's arms in the sacred hall. They hadn't gotten much sleep during the night. Every time they'd drifted off, one of them would instinctively reach out to the other, to test the slope of a shoulder with questing fingers, or taste the sweat of exertion on a throat or belly. To begin again the dance of creation. But soon it would be over, for Harry's whimsy wouldn't outlast the sun.

"You live in a blessed place, Harry," she said, her voice so quiet she wasn't sure he even heard her. "And yet you are so angry. I wonder if you could tell me why?"

For a long while he didn't answer. She knew he was

awake, for he was lazily winnowing his fingers through her hair.

"I'm not angry," he said. "I'm terrified. We're living so close to the edge right now that I can see the rocks at the bottom of the cliff. One piece of bad luck would cost us everything."

"It really is that bad?"

"I wouldn't be killing myself in the city if it weren't."

"But you don't seem any more comfortable in that house you fight so hard to keep."

"That's just because of the nightmares, which, according to you, have been brought by your friends."

Sorcha wanted to lift her head and gauge his expression. She had the feeling, though, that only the low light and her closed eyes were allowing truth of any kind right now.

"I'm sorry for that, Harry. It's just that the Dearann Stone is so precious, and didn't we all think it was here with you?"

"And when you found it, what were you going to do?"

"I told you. Protect it."

"No, you weren't," he said, sounding oddly complaisant. "You were going to walk off with it."

She fought for courage. "It would have been the only way to protect it, Harry. If you think your nightmares are bad now, you can't imagine what would happen if the *Dubhlainn Sidhe* managed to capture the great Stone."

"I guess we'll never know," he said.

Sorcha felt the tears well again, the sense of futility swelling in her. "No," she said, wishing she didn't sound so hopeless. "We never will."

She heard the twitter of the first birds, brave souls to sing out against this cold and emptiness. She knew that now she and Harry would measure their time alone in mortal minutes.

"If you could have anything, Harry," she said, focusing on the long, elegant fingers that curled around hers, "anything in your dreams, what would it be?"

"That's not something I ever think of."

She let her fingers drift down his sternum. "If you did think about it. If there had never been any need for you to go to the city. If…"

"*If* is a futile word, Sorcha."

She shook her head. "Then how about *pretend,* Harry? Could you pretend with me, here, where nobody can touch us? Where we're safe from the outside and all its problems? What would you do?"

For a long moment he continued to draw his fingers through her hair, and she could feel the tension in his shoulder. But as the peace of the early darkness settled on them like fine dust, he seemed to ease a bit.

"I'd spend all my time with the horses," he said. "Horses never lie to you. They never make promises they can't keep or lose themselves in the impossible or…or…"

"Throw good money after bad?"

"Yes." The word was abrupt, his tone stone cold.

"Were they so very terrible, these parents of yours?"

"I don't really know," he said. "They were dead by the time I was nine. I don't remember much of them or my grandfather."

She lifted her head to meet him with her compassion. "Ah, I'm sorry, then, Harry. How did you lose them?"

He laughed, a small, wry sound. "I wasn't the one

who lost them, Sorcha. They did that all by themselves. They wandered off and never came home."

"How?"

"The three of them went down in a hurricane when they were looking for Atlantis."

"Which ocean?"

He glared at her.

She tried her best to smile. "Well, it might help if you knew it was the correct ocean, don't you think?"

"I do not. And there is no correct ocean. Just con men more than happy to sell supposed artifacts to gullible believers, right along with pieces of the true cross."

She considered him for a minute, her fairy heart heavy. "Don't you believe at all, Harry? In anything?"

"Of course I do. I believe in me. In Phyl and Gran and Ned. In the beauty of a well-made business deal. In the grace of a horse on the move, and the responsibility of being steward of land you pass on to the next generation."

She laid her head back down, sighing. "I wonder if you'd be thinking differently if your parents had lived longer. If they'd given you a bit of magic with the madness."

"I doubt it. It's a child's obligation to rebel against a parent."

"Oh, aye," she said softly. "I imagine it's so." Focusing on his hair-roughened chest, she considered Harry's life. "No matter how disagreeable the parents, it's still a loss not to have known them."

She actually surprised a small smile out of him. She could hear it in his voice. "Are your parents so disagreeable, then, Sorcha?"

She smiled back, and it was just as wry. "She is Mab, Harry. Queen of the *Tuatha de Dannan*. Sure, queens have little time for their offspring, unless they're happening to blacken the family name or interfere with the ruling of the clan." She shrugged, laying her hand across the steady beat of his heart. "She was as good a parent as a queen can be, I imagine. I always knew she was there. I'll say that for her."

"And your father?"

"Is not my business to know."

She could tell he was staring at the top of her head. "You're joking."

She shrugged. "Sure, it's the way of our queens. Their consorts are theirs to choose and theirs to discard. And my mother the queen has been inordinately fond of the discarding."

For a long moment there was nothing but the sound of the waking birds; then Harry made a small huffing sound, and his fingers returned to her hair. "Huh. And here I thought having an imperious grandmother was tough."

"Ah, sure your gran is a lovely woman altogether, Harry. And my respect for her has just risen quite a lot, knowing she had you to raise. Don't I have the sneakin' suspicion that you weren't all that easy to teach."

"I was a righteous prick," he admitted ruefully. "Still am, sometimes. But a person can only stand so much of the world of fairy tales before he's forced to object."

"And so you dedicate yourself to reason."

"Exactly."

The birds had multiplied, more than any she'd heard around the house. Even these mortal birds knew a holy place, it seemed.

"What is your perfect world, then, Harry? When you close your eyes and imagine yourself with your horses, where is it?"

This time she was met with a long silence, with a stiffening of every muscle in Harry's body. She was afraid that he would bolt. That he would run from the answer she knew he refused to allow.

"I don't," he said starkly.

"Oh, aye," she whispered. "I think you do. Is it so terrible because you don't believe in the world on your walls, or because you know you can never go there?"

"Don't," he said, even the planes of his body unrelenting.

"Because it hurts?"

"Because it's a fantasy."

"If it were," she said, "I don't think it would plague you so. It's not just an image in your mind, Harry. It's a memory."

He jerked away, but she held on to him. She made him stay right where he was.

"Don't be absurd," he snapped. "*It* is the fanciful paintings of a delusional man. It's all bollocks."

"And yet you can't stay away from those walls, can you?"

"How did you…?" He went silent, and she knew he was appalled at his inadvertent admission.

She began to stroke his skin, calming and nurturing so the truth wouldn't be so difficult. "Because I find myself in those rooms without knowing how, as if there is a lodestone there. Those aren't my fairy hills he painted there, you know. Not my home. I think, maybe, your ancestor described the southern mountains where the *Dubhlainn Sidhe* hold court. And yet, they *are* fairy hills, fairy horses, fairy flowers. And every time I see them, I ache so fiercely for home it almost brings the tears, and fairies have no place for tears. And I've seen the land of faerie. I've been there. I know, sure, there's always a chance I can go home. But to see those hills and not know why I was hurting so…I can't imagine it."

She felt the pain rise in him then, a tide of red that filled the little room. She rose up and kissed Harry, a long, gentle, healing kiss that led to more kisses, that led to quiet murmurs and surprised gasps, and finally the sweet agony of completion.

"I don't…I don't believe in any of it," he insisted finally, his voice already sounding harsher.

"Of course you do," she said gently, easing back into his embrace, her heart still thundering with the exquisite flight of climax. "If you didn't, you never would have allowed Lilly up on that horse. Sure, you wouldn't have let her anywhere near me."

Silence, throbbing with the staccato beat of his heart, with the stiff restraint he'd donned again. With the waking of the morning around them, still too early for the sun, but unfurling along a thousand coverts and meadows.

"Let's pretend again," she said. "For only now, and only here, to never be taken past that door. Here, where it's safe. Your wildest dream, Harry. The one you haven't even told your cousin, who knows you better than any. What would it be, Harry?"

She'd thought her voice held pain. She couldn't imagine the wasteland that echoed in Harry's. "To walk out of this world into the one on the walls."

The words seemed to propel him up. He lurched to his feet, away from her, and began searching around for his clothes.

Sorcha kept her eyes closed. "Ah, I was afraid of that."

"Because it's *insane*."

"Because I believe you. Haven't I felt it in you from the first, the fact that no matter how hard you try, you simply don't fit here in this place? Even in these wide open hills."

"Don't be absurd," he said, struggling into those wonderful things they called boxers. "I was born here. It's my legacy to pass down to my children. To pass down *intact,* not with bits and pieces bitten off to satisfy the whims and delusions of the people who came before. *That's* where I belong. The reason I'm so unhappy is because I have to spend most of my time in the city to make sure it happens."

"If that were true," Sorcha said, rising herself to sit on the edge of the well-tumbled bed, "then you would have found ease here with your horses, with your family. Especially with Lilly for, Goddess, isn't she life's own gift to you of pure light and joy? But you're not, Harry. You're not happy, and that is a sadness too great to bear."

He swung around on her and froze. It didn't occur to Sorcha that she was naked, that that might be a distraction. Sure, she'd spent much of her life like this. Evidently mortals didn't. It was obvious in an instant that Harry was affected.

"Put something on," he rasped, turning away again.

She looked down, bemused. "Am I unsightly, then?"

He bowed his head and laughed, a harsh bark of a sound. "Just...do it."

Sorcha reached over to pick up her dress and was struck anew by the difference in mortal textures. She couldn't say she wasn't intrigued by the rough edge of their fabrics. She didn't think she could survive in them, though. They erected too stiff a barrier between her and the goddess. She wondered, head tilted in consideration, what Harry would look like in faerie attire.

Elegant, she thought, instinctively seeing the weave of his colors in her mind, a shimmering array of greens.

"Should I tell you about my home, Harry?" she asked, properly clad and watching out of the corner of her eye for the first edge of the sun to breach the horizon.

He stepped into his trousers and pulled them up. "No," he said, a curious yearning in his voice. "It wouldn't do any good."

"Because you could never go?"

He glared at her. "Don't be absurd. Of course I can't go. There is no *there* to go to."

"But there is," she said with a soft smile. "And you know it, so. You've known it all along, no matter what you tried to believe. And you could go, if you wanted. I promise you that on the name of the goddess."

"Ah," he said with a sharp, disdainful nod, "of course. I'd run away into the mists, just as every one of my ancestors wished they could do, and I'd leave this place to…who, exactly? Creditors? The tax man? Lovely. Then my grandmother would end up in an old folks' home, eating pap, and the children you're so fond of would be living in a housing estate somewhere and never see a horse again. The closest Lilly would come to her very own horse would be the kind you slot coins into at the arcade. Brilliant. I think I'll just go along with you now, shall I?"

"If we could figure a way," Sorcha said, "if everything were possible, a savior for your estate, a place for everyone where they'd be happy, what then?"

He closed his eyes, standing there in the shadows, and Sorcha thought how unbearably handsome he was, the sharp edge of a knife, a mortal hewn from fairy stone.

"Everything hasn't been possible since the day I was born," he said. "This discussion is moot."

"If you left, who would own the house?"

He sighed, not moving. "Phyl."

"She'd be an earl?"

A small smile curled the edge of his mouth. "A baroness in her own right, heir to Gran. Theo would be the Earl."

"Would that be a bad thing?"

His eyes snapped open, and he turned on her again, as if ready to strike. This lovely little hall was simply too small to hold all his pain.

"Would it?" she asked, very, very quietly.

And she saw her answer there in his eyes, the longing, the disbelief, the rage at the responsibilities all those feckless forebears had dropped on his shoulders.

"It's not possible. The responsibility is mine."

"So Phyl would lose the house? She'd ruin the horses? She'd shame the barony?"

"You know perfectly well she would do none of those things. She would do an admirable job of stepping into Gran's shoes. But she shouldn't have to. Not with the burden of this place to add to it."

Sorcha nodded distractedly. She could see it, too, she thought. Phyl was a strong woman, with a sharp mind and generous soul. She could make this place bloom in her time. If she had the time. Which, as Harry understood better than a wandering fairy, wasn't there.

"There must be a way, Harry," Sorcha said. "I simply can't believe that we met by chance and will have to part again the same way. We are meant to be together, here in this place. We're meant to change the future of faerie and mortal alike."

"We're meant to do no such thing," he assured her, his shirt clenched in his hand like a battle flag. "I'm going back to work tomorrow, and you…"

Sorcha knew how sad her smile was. "I can't leave until I find the Dearann Stone, Harry. It was the task that brought me here, and if I don't accomplish it, all will be lost."

Why it should be, she didn't know, but that seemed to be the thing to give Harry pause. "Tell me why."

She pulled in a breath. "Aye, you do deserve the whole truth, don't you?"

Focusing on her hands, entwined in her lap, Sorcha told him the truth. Of the three great Filial Stones, of the loss of one and the theft of another, and the imbalance that would begin to betray itself as the days went on in the world of faerie and mortal alike. Of the desperate need for the recovery of the Stone that would bring life back to the world in its prescribed time.

"And the *Dubhlainn Sidhe* don't want this to happen?"

She shrugged. "Sure, I'm not at all positive they're able to think at all right now," she admitted. "The Dearann Stone has always given balance to their masculine rages and quests for power. Without it, what kind of sense would they have? Do they realize, do you think, that in their quest to gain the greatest power, they have doomed themselves even before they've doomed the rest? There will be no life in the land of the *Dubhlainn Sidhe*. No birth, no regrowth, no warmth. They've lived on dreams of revenge for so long that I'm not sure they can see what their revenge will reap."

He seemed so still all of a sudden. So wary, a wild thing caught in the sights of a hunter. "And this Dearann Stone would change that?"

She lifted her hands to show how empty her palms were. "Ah, now *there* is a moot point, Harry. You don't have the Stone, and you don't know who does. Which means I'll have to leave very soon and seek it, and hope to pull the *Dubhlainn Sidhe* along with me. If I don't, then I'm afraid they'll stay in your dreams, you and young Theo and, to be frank, Harry, without the Dearann Stone, I don't know at all how to stop them."

Fury gathered in his eyes. "Can they be killed?"

Sorcha felt the weight of his words catch in her chest. "It isn't something to consider, Harry. If you harm one of the fair folk, you gain a curse I am not entitled to lift. And as you said, too many people depend on you to chance such a thing."

He lifted an eyebrow. "A curse?"

She drew a breath. "Your nightmares would only grow worse, Harry, until they drove you mad."

"I thought fairies couldn't force."

"I'm afraid that this falls under the category of suggestion. And haven't I had the dreams myself, Harry? So I know how bad they are. You truly can't imagine how fierce they could grow."

He shoved a hand through his hair. "Brilliant. So I

imagine that everything else we've *pretended* is a moot point, too."

"Unless I recover the Dearann Stone and get it safely back to the court of the *Tuatha,* yes. For without its power, we won't ever see spring again."

He was shaking his head, his focus on the floor, and Sorcha couldn't help but hurt. For herself, for him, for his wonderful family. For sweet little Lilly, who truly wouldn't understand.

"All right, then," he said, shoving his arms into his shirt and buttoning it up. "I guess it's time to go."

Even his posture said it. Their interlude was over, forgotten as if it had never begun.

Except for one thing. In the way of her ancestors, Sorcha knew that before the loss of all life, there would be one more, created in the beauty of this place, and what they'd done and the light of Harry's eyes. Sometime in the height of the months of summer—sure, she had to believe it would come again—she would have his child.

Did it help or hurt? Was it something she should tell him, when he was still trying to deal with what she was? Soon, she thought, letting him slip a coat over her shoulders in preparation for stepping outside. Soon she would decide whether it would be better for them both for him to know. Better for the babe who even now hovered near enough to join herself to Sorcha's soul.

"Do you believe, then, Harry?" she asked, because she had to know.

"Of course not," he said, but his smile was wry. Against his better judgment, he believed. She could tell. "I'd be a laughing—"

Suddenly he stopped, his head lifting. He went perfectly still. She followed the direction of his suddenly hard gaze and wondered what had gone wrong now.

Then she heard it. A distant sound of voices, of pounding, of a horse trumpeting like a charger at the forefront of an army.

She and Harry looked at each other. "What the…"

Again she heard the horse, and suddenly Sorcha recognized it. "It's Saoirce," she said, stepping toward the door.

This time Saoirce screamed a pure war cry of fury, and the two of them spun on each other.

"Lilly," they said at the same time.

They left the door open as they fled down the hill.

# Chapter 11

Lights were on all over the stableyard. Harry could see some of the grooms running for the block that held the mares. He saw lights pop on in the estate manager's house on the other side of the far pasture. And then he heard the most terrible sound he thought he would ever hear in his life. Small, thin, a keening in the wind unlike anything he'd ever experienced, a terrible, despairing cry that could threaten a person's soul.

Lilly.

Saoirce screamed again, and battered at her stall.

"She needs to get out," Sorcha panted behind him. "Please, Harry."

"Let her go!" he yelled as he neared the stable yard.

His stable manager, still shrugging into his coat, turned on him. "Are you sure, sir?"

"Do it!"

"Open her box!" the gnarled old man yelled to the men inside.

There was another burst of thudding, hooves against wood, and suddenly a second of silence. Then Saoirce came bolting out of the building, her nostrils flared, white showing around her eyes, her lips curled in a snarl of fury. The men scattered before her, but she had no time for them. She thundered out of the yard, her coat gleaming wet in the harsh halogens as she pounded straight at Harry and Sorcha.

Harry pulled Sorcha aside just as the horse clattered past, not even seeming to notice them.

"She's getting loose!" one of the lads yelled.

"She's after the one who's hurting Lilly," Sorcha told Harry.

"Let her go!" Harry told his staff. "Follow her if you can, but don't stop her."

They stared as if Harry had just gone mad. Maybe he had. He didn't have time to discuss it, though. Lilly was still keening up in her room, a room Phyl had painted with bright clouds and whimsical storybook characters. The sound Lilly was making was a violation of such a special place.

Harry didn't wait for anybody to answer Phyl's front door. He reached into the flower pot by the porch, grabbed the key and shoved it into the lock, his hands shaking so hard he could hardly work it. Then, unlocking it, he pushed the door open and led the way inside.

He could hear Phyl's panic-stricken voice all the way down in her front foyer, a pragmatic horse house space crowded with cast-off boots, anoraks and helmets. Not a place for what he was hearing. He could hear Theo, and he heard Lilly, who couldn't seem to stop. Who was ripping his heart out with her wild, endless cries.

He was hearing the screams he'd been hearing in his head for the last four weeks.

Oh, God. Not Lilly. Please, *please,* not Lilly. It was too obscene to even consider. Harry took the stairs two at a time, up two stories, not even hearing Sorcha's feet strike wood behind him as she followed. He didn't think he was breathing. He couldn't imagine what was in Lilly's head. Worse—dear God, worse—he couldn't imagine how to stop it.

Phyl must have heard them coming. When Harry slammed through the nursery door, she was already looking for him, her eyes wild, her body, incongruously clad in a frothy lace nightgown above bare feet, taut, her arms filled with Lilly, who was arched and stiff, her eyes open and staring, her mouth gaping, letting loose those terrible sounds. Tears coursed down Phyl's face, and Theo, standing to the side in his pajamas and sleep-tumbled hair, had his hand up on Lilly's back, his own eyes far too knowing.

"Oh, God, Harry," Phyl choked, "do something!"

That brought Harry to a crashing halt. There was nothing he could do. He had no idea how to stop this. He couldn't even stop the screams in his own head. As if he'd heard Harry, Theo looked over at him, and Harry knew he was thinking the same thing.

"Piglet," Harry crooned, lifting his arms to take her from her mother, "hush, piglet, hush…"

But Lilly didn't see him. She didn't react at all when he took her to his chest. She vibrated with the terror that infected her and kept shrilling as if it were the only thing left in her.

"Goddess," Sorcha breathed, sounding shattered. "How could he? This breaks ever fairy oath, every one!"

She reached out to Lilly, but Harry stepped away. It was illogical, but he couldn't help it. She'd brought this to his niece. The baby they'd long since dubbed their own fairy child. Well, he wouldn't have it. He wouldn't allow some malevolent creature to rip at her soul this way.

"*You* do something," he snarled, knowing he looked much like his horse had as she'd stormed past him. "This is a plague *you* visited on this house."

She flinched at his words, but he couldn't seem to stop. He couldn't bear the terrible weight of Lilly in his arms, so stiff and staring. So tormented that he was sure people were crying in their sleep miles away.

"Well?" he snapped. "Have any brilliant ideas? Any tree branches or holly leaves you think will suffice?"

Her eyes gleamed with unshed tears. "I thought I'd kept them protected," she said. "I thought…" She shook her head and looked away, and Harry could feel her own despair.

"Theo," she said, very quietly. "You must go to that room where I've been sleeping and bring my bag to me."

"What bag?" Harry demanded, as if his niece weren't shrieking her sanity away in his arms. "You have no bag."

"I have one. You can't see it unless I will it so." She turned to the boy. "Get on your coat and shoes. The bag is tucked under my pillow. There's a smaller bag inside, green and soft, yes? Bring it to me as fast as you can."

Theo never questioned her. He just spun on his heel

and ran. Then Sorcha faced Harry and held out her hands for Lilly. He backed away.

"Oh, no," he said. "I think you've done quite enough already, don't you?"

Her breathing hitched, but she didn't back down. "Maybe so, Harry, maybe so. But I can also do you the only good that can be done this night. Theo will bring my herbs, the ones that saved me from the mortal illness—"

He snorted. "It was a *cold*," he growled.

She briefly closed her eyes. "To you, it was. Not to a fairy body."

"And what good would those herbs do you now?"

"Nothing. But there's another mixture in the bag that would. Our *bean tighe* gave it me to help any mortal struck with a fairy ill. I think it will help Lilly."

"You *think?* That's not a hell of a lot of help, Sorcha."

"Harry," Phyl said, "enough. If she can help Lilly, let her. Unless you have another idea?"

Harry curled himself around the tiny body in his arms and battled the wash of fury. Of course he had no other idea. He'd never been faced with anything like this in his life. He could never have imagined in his wildest fears something like this. He closed his eyes and rested his cheek against Lilly's head.

She never reacted, never softened, her tiny body rigid with distress. It ripped into him like a saw, and he couldn't bear it.

"If you hurt her worse…" was all he could say.

They waited, second by second, the sharp, terrifying thread of Lilly's voice slicing them into bits as the sun finally topped the far moors and sent a shaft of pure gold into the bright room.

Pooh Bear smiled down from the wall, along with his friends. The Three Little Pigs, whom Lilly had named Spot, Bill and Harry, danced a jig to the Pied Piper's playing. Little Red Riding Hood stood defiant over the vanquished wolf. All bright, whimsical, playful. Harry swore they all looked frightened.

He couldn't stand this. God, he couldn't.

He saw Theo slide around the front corner of the house and disappear beneath him. He heard frantic footsteps and turned to the door. He saw that Bea was already there, the hem of her fairy princess nightgown pooled around her feet and her thumb in her mouth. He wanted to go to her. He couldn't bear to put Lilly down.

"Phyl," he whispered.

She jerked as if pulled by strings, but then she caught sight of her other daughter and rushed over to gather her into her arms. "It's all right, baby," she said, clutching Bea to her.

"Lilly," the little girl whispered, every question and fear resonating in her voice.

"Yes," her mother said. "Lilly."

Phyl came and stood beside him so that the girls were together. So that *they* were together to bolster each other. It wasn't until he heard Theo approach and turned to the door that he realized Sorcha was standing apart from them, completely alone, rigid and silent in the shadows at the edge of the sunlight.

His chest caught at the sight of her. He suddenly wanted to pull her to him, to collect her to his family. And yet he couldn't help but blame her. As if he'd said the words aloud, she raised her eyes to him, and he saw her raw pain.

"Here, Sorcha," Theo gasped as he skidded into the room.

Sorcha accepted what looked like a small green drawstring felt bag, the kind jewelers loved to fill with silver chains. She thanked him and balanced the bag in her hand.

Harry could almost hear it in her head. There wasn't much in the bag. Would it be enough? Would it be what Lilly needed? He wanted to shout at her that of course it wasn't what Lilly needed. She needed Sorcha and all her freakish friends to just leave them all the hell alone.

"We need to get her to swallow this," Sorcha said, pulling open the drawstring. "I'll begin with a small amount and increase it every few minutes until we see a result."

She sounded so hesitant.

"What's in it?" Phyl asked.

Sorcha gave her a sad little smile. "Ah, sure, I don't know. Our healer mixed it. But she'd never hurt a cherished one, I swear that oath on the goddess. The herbs are to help a mortal overcome any fairy ill. I think they can help Lilly."

Phyl gave Bea a strong, quick hug and then set her down by Theo. "Then do it," she said, the warrior queen, looking oddly like Boadicea, even in her nightgown.

Sorcha nodded and bent to spill a tiny amount of dusty green herb into her palm. "If you have a bit of water, that might help her manage this. But carefully. The herb has to go down, but, sure, we don't want her chokin' on it."

It was a struggle. Harry changed his hold on Lilly so she lay back in his arms, still stiff and unyielding. Phyl wet a little T-shirt in the pitcher on Lilly's dresser. Sorcha reached over and dropped a few grains of herb in Lilly's mouth, and then Phyl squeezed the cloth so that a few drops of water followed. At first Lilly sputtered. She coughed. She screamed, her face unchanged.

Sorcha waited. She watched. Harry couldn't bear the wait. He wanted to scream himself. He wanted to batter something to splinters with his hands. He wanted to emulate his own horse, and charge after the enemy with a battle cry echoing in his head.

Sorcha stroked little Lilly's throat, as if encouraging the herb to slide down it. She brushed the little girl's hair back off her forehead and caught the tears that slid from her eyes with her fingers. She chanted in Gaelic and shook her head.

"Again," she whispered.

They repeated the process with much the same results.

"This is bollocks," Harry grated, his heart beating like a bass drum. "We need to call the doctor and get her sedated."

Sorcha stiffened. "No! Mortal medicine will kill her sure. Let the *bean tighe*'s remedy work. Give it a bit of time."

"She doesn't *have* a bit of time!" he all but howled. "Look at her!"

Sorcha looked at him, and he saw that pain ravaged her, as well. "I can see her perfectly well, Harry. Please. Trust me."

He opened his mouth to tell her exactly what he thought of that bit of absurdity but somehow couldn't say it. He couldn't look away from her, from the soft well of determination in her eyes, from the sudden, sharp memories of what they'd shared not an hour earlier. She stepped forward, and the rising sun caught her, bathing her in warmth, and suddenly Harry couldn't think why he shouldn't trust her.

"Do it again," he snapped, and turned back to Lilly.

Sorcha tipped the bag over her hand. Phyl wet the shirt. Harry held Lilly where they could reach her to feed her whatever the hell it was Sorcha carried in her magic bag.

And by damn if almost immediately Lilly's cries didn't wane a bit. She softened by millimeters in his arms. The room, where the Three Little Pigs were friends with the Cowardly Lion, began, oddly, to warm.

"Ah, there," Sorcha breathed, stroking Lilly's face. "There, *mo chroidhe,* see? You're feelin' better already."

"Lilly?" Phyl said in a strange hiccup. "My piglet?"

Harry felt it before he saw it. He saw it before he heard it. He heard it before he believed it. Lilly's terror was easing. The dream, or whatever it was, was loosening its hold on her. Her body softened in his arms. Her cries eased away into sporadic sobs. Her eyes, those horrible, staring eyes, slid closed.

Suddenly, shockingly, the room was silent. The four of them stood there wide-eyed and stared at the now-sleeping child in Harry's arms.

"Oh…my God," Phyl breathed, taking Lilly from Harry's arms. "Oh, my God." Then, burying her face in Lilly's hair, she burst into sobs.

"Mama?" Bea said, staring.

It was Sorcha who knelt to her. "Let your mama comfort Lilly a bit, sweetheart. Would it be all right, then, if you comforted me?"

Bea said not a word, but lifted her arms. Sorcha picked her up and just held her. Just stroked her bright hair and rubbed her back. And Harry, because he knew just how Theo felt, held the little boy to him until both their trembling eased.

"Crikey," the little boy said. "I never want to see *that* again."

Harry met Sorcha's gaze and saw the uncertainty there.

"Why didn't the hawthorn work?" Theo asked. "And the holly and hazel? I thought they were supposed to protect us?"

Sorcha gave him a chagrined smile. "We only surrounded the big house with them." She shook her head. "We just didn't think about this one."

His eyes grew great. "I forgot...."

Harry knelt before him. "You didn't forget anything. Who could figure something like this?"

Theo's eyes were grave. "Sorcha did. She said that we had to protect ourselves when she left to find the Dearann Stone. She said she'd make sure to—"

"Ah, now, Theo," she said from where she was still holding Bea, "it doesn't matter now. What matters is that we spend this morning laying the circle around your home, too."

"And the stables," Theo said. "I thought I heard one of the horses scream."

Sorcha looked out the window, as if she could see the path Saoirce had taken. "Ah, no," she said. "That was Saoirce fulfilling her responsibility as Lilly's guardian. She's after the beast that visited this on you tonight."

Theo looked in the same direction. "Will she find him?"

Sorcha shook her head. "I don't know, Theo. I do know that if she does, he can't possibly outrun the punishment due him."

"Mama?"

Everybody turned to see Lilly's eyes open.

"Yes, my piglet?" Phyl asked, tears once again streaming down her face.

Lilly rubbed a hand over her own cheeks, where Phyl's tears still gleamed. She scowled. "Wet."

Phyl's laugh was a bark of surprise. "Well, that's because I was watering you, Lilly."

Lilly's frown grew. "Why?"

"To help you grow, of course," Harry said, taking Lilly from Phyl's arms. He couldn't help it. He had to hold that little body to him. "Don't you want to grow?"

"I grow," she assured him, then gave a great yawn. "Tired."

"Yes, piglet," he said. "I imagine you are. If we let you get back to bed, do you think you could take care of that?"

She nodded and nestled her head against his shoulder. Harry couldn't think of any sweeter feeling on this earth. He looked down to see that her eyes had closed again, her little hand splayed against his chest.

"'Lo, fairy," she said to Sorcha.

Sorcha's smile held a myriad of conflicting emotions. "'Lo, Lilly."

Harry was just about to turn and settle Lilly in her bed when he heard footsteps clambering up the stair. Two sets. Every person in the room turned for the door, ready to do battle to protect the little girl in Harry's arms.

When the two reached the door, they were winded and wide-eyed.

"Gwyneth?" Harry said, stunned at the windblown woman leaning against Lilly's door.

Beside him, Sorcha stiffened. *"Darragh?"*

The beautiful young man standing next to Gwyneth proffered a sheepish smile.

"Who's he?" Theo asked.

Sorcha opened her mouth but couldn't seem to get any words out.

"Sure, I'm a bit of extra help, if you'll have me," the man Sorcha called Darragh said in a soft, melodic voice.

Then, by damn, he wrapped his arm around Gwyneth.

Harry let an eyebrow rise. "I assume this is what we were going to talk about Thursday, Gwyn?"

She at least had the grace to blush. "I'm sorry, Harry. I can't explain it."

He sighed. *He* could. There was just something about these fairy folk that set reality on end.

"Are you the one who flew over the car?" Theo asked.

Darragh nodded. "Aren't those beasts a marvel, then? Sure, they're the fastest things in two worlds altogether."

"And as interesting as that is," Harry spoke up, "I think it would be a better discussion for downstairs. Right now, we need to settle Lilly."

Darragh turned to Sorcha. "I heard her all the way across the moors. The *Dubhlainn Sidhe?*"

She nodded her head, and Harry thought he'd never seen her look so dispirited. The young man's shoulders slumped. "I brought him," he said. "When I kept the gate path open. Ah, Goddess, Sorcha, I'm that sorry."

Sorcha gave him a brisk nod. "Well, if you are, you can help us track him down and force him back. See what he did, Darragh? See who he did it to?"

Which was when, Harry assumed, Darragh realized that it was Lilly who had been tormented. Darragh sucked in a sibilant breath and shook his head.

"It's so much worse than we thought. What, then, are you to do, Sorcha?"

"Me?" she echoed, looking small. "What can I do? At least you could visit storms on them."

"Ahem," Phyl interrupted, reaching over to reclaim a sleeping Lilly from Harry's arms. "Downstairs, all of you. I'll join you when I know Lilly's really asleep."

Harry handed off his burden, and thought again how precious the feel of that trusting little body was in his arms. How empty they suddenly were. And would stay, if the look Gwyneth was giving Darragh was any indication.

He stopped long enough to help Theo and Bea settle back into bed. Then he made a brief sojourn out to the stables to find that his filly hadn't returned to her stall. Half a dozen men had set off in Land Rovers and on horseback to follow her across the moors.

There was nothing he could do to help there, so he returned inside to join the other three in the back salon, where comfortable overstuffed furniture shared space with paintings of the Wyatt horses of the past. Gwyneth was all but sitting in Darragh's lap on the sofa, her hand wrapped in his, and Sorcha was perched on a footstool, a fairy on a lily pad. Harry shook his head at the whimsical thought. There was no place for that now. Not considering what had just happened in this house.

"You're really staying?" Sorcha was asking Darragh.

He nodded, looking a bit sheepish. "It's better, so," he said, taking hold of Gwyneth's hand. "Didn't I forfeit my place in court when I conspired with Orla to bring herself the queen low? I've nothing to return to."

"And what would you be doin' here?"

His grin was bright. "Sure, my Gwynnie says that there's a calling for a man who can predict the weather. Especially to someone who trades futures, as she does."

"Futures?" Sorcha asked.

Darragh shrugged. "It's a mortal thing, I'm told."

"All well and good," Harry interrupted, leaning against the door. "Right now, though, we have a more immediate problem."

Sorcha leapt to her feet. "Is Saoirce back?"

He shook his head. "Will she find him, do you think?"

Gwyneth was closely watching. "Saoirce? Who—"

"Starchaser," Harry clarified.

"What's she got to do with this?" Gwyneth asked.

"She's after, bein' Lilly's guardian," Sorcha said, as if Gwyneth would simply understand. "She's trying to track down the fairy who did this thing."

Gwyneth didn't even hesitate. "And if she does?"

"She'll do what we couldn't. She'll stop him."

"And if she doesn't?"

Slowly Sorcha sat back down. "Ah, then, I don't know."

"You're going to stop him," Darragh said. "Aren't you?"

"I don't know," Sorcha said. "The Stone is lost, and without it…"

This time Darragh went on alert, looking over at Gwyneth. "Lost? But Gwyn said it was here."

"So everyone thought. The Stone here isn't the Dearann Stone, though. It isn't a fairy stone at all, I'm afraid."

Harry saw Darragh slump in sick surprise and felt at least a bit better. So Darragh hadn't been the one to bring this poison then. Darragh, it seemed, had been off charming his fiancée. And out of all this, the only thing that surprised him was how little that thought bothered him.

"You must do something, Sorcha," Darragh demanded. "Without the Stone, we are lost."

Sorcha seemed to shrink from those words. "Me? What can I do? I'm but a teacher of children, Darragh. I have no great power, no mighty gift for the settling of nations."

"Sure, you're the daughter of Mab," Darragh protested. "She chose you as her heir. She sent you on this task. She must believe you have the gifts."

Sorcha shook her head. "She believes nothing, except that it's her time to go. I have failed my own people, and now I have failed the world of mortals, as well. There is nothing I can do that will matter, Darragh. Nothing."

Harry saw the true despair in those otherworldly eyes and pushed himself away from the door. "Then I guess I'll have to," he said.

Everybody looked at him. Sorcha sat very still, her hands clasped tightly together, her posture rigid with distress. "Ah, no, Harry," she said. "I'm afraid it's not possible."

"What can you do, Harry?" Gwyneth asked.

Harry rubbed at the bridge of his nose, where a headache had taken up residence. He'd known all along he couldn't keep this secret. That one day he would at least have to tell Theo, to pass along the truth he'd so assiduously hidden to protect his own sanity. He just hadn't anticipated having to take care of it himself.

"I can recover the true Dearann Stone," he said.

"Harry," Sorcha gently admonished, climbing to her feet. "Even a fairy might not be able to find it."

"They could if they knew where it was."

Now even Gwyneth was on her feet. "You know?"

There was no more chance to back down. "Yes. I'm quite afraid I do."

# Chapter 12

Sorcha felt as if the air had been taken from the room. She thought she might actually be swaying on her feet. "This might be something worth explaining, don't you think, Harry?"

Harry motioned for everyone to sit back down. He remained on his feet by the back window, where the sun glinted blue on the raven's wing of his hair. Sorcha kept trying to push her brain into motion. She couldn't seem to make it past Harry, though, standing in the sunlight and looking so torn.

"Harry?" Gwyneth said from where she'd returned on the sofa.

He nodded. "Yes. The Stone." Then, closing his eyes, he sucked in a breath. "I can't believe I'm saying this.

I can't believe I'm telling you, Gwyneth. You were always the last person I thought would understand."

"I was," she admitted with a sheepish grin and a squeeze of Darragh's hand. "Until yesterday."

Harry opened his eyes and Sorcha saw the amazement in them. "Yesterday," he murmured. "Yes."

"You know where the true Dearann Stone is?" Sorcha asked, struggling to keep her voice low.

He didn't look at her, only watched the sun warm the sere grasses of the moors. "I seemed to be the only one affected by it. My father never seemed to notice. Neither did my grandfather, and they were the ones obsessed by it. But it never…*spoke* to them. It never…" He shook his head, trembling.

Sorcha wanted desperately to go to him, to hold him as he made his confession, but she couldn't seem to move.

"Sang?" was all she could manage.

He turned to her. "Yes. I saw things, even as a child. Places, people, the…the beings who lived on the walls, where grandfather painted them."

"You were the one who provided the details."

Harry looked stricken. "I thought I was going mad. I couldn't stay here. I begged to be sent to Eton, then Cambridge. Anywhere but here, where that bloody damned hunk of rock infected my dreams. But I couldn't stay away, either."

"And then you and Phyl took over the estate," Sorcha said.

He nodded, still trying so hard to say it.

"Oh, my God," Phyl said. "It's in the bank. Isn't it?"

They all tuned to see her standing in the doorway, now clad in regular riding attire.

Harry's expression was even more bleak. "Since nobody but me noticed, I switched the stones the day I came into my majority. I hid it where it couldn't hurt me."

"And replaced it with an exact replica," Sorcha said.

He nodded.

Phyl shook her head. "I was wondering what was so terribly important about getting to York that day. Especially since Gran had set up such a huge birthday crush for you. We were late getting back. You barely had time to dress for dinner."

"And felt like a traitor the whole time. No, a lunatic. I couldn't believe not one person at the party noticed that the Fairy Diamond was different than it had been the day before. Not *one* of you."

"But we weren't you, Harry."

"What do we do now?" Gwyneth asked.

Harry stepped away from the window. "If I leave now, I can be in York by the time the bank opens."

That brought Sorcha to her feet. "No. First we have to make sure everyone is protected here. Because once we get the Stone, I'll have to get it back through the gates, and I'm not sure I'll be able to pull the *Dubhlainn Sidhe* with me."

Darragh leaned forward. "If we—"

Sorcha lifted her hand to stop him speaking. She heard it, and then Darragh heard it, and finally Harry. The thunder of approaching hooves.

Phyl turned for the door. "Star…"

"And once we get the Stone," Sorcha said, staring Phyl into stopping, "we'll bring it right to the gate. We won't come back here at all. So I'd like to say my goodbyes now."

Everyone looked at each other as the hoofbeats grew closer.

"Then let's be after it," Darragh said. "I'll get the salt, girl. You get the branches."

"But Saoirce is back," Phyl protested.

Sorcha made it a point to pause. "Ah, so she is. I wonder if she's caught the *Dubhlainn Sidhe*."

She hadn't. If she had, she wouldn't be approaching at a dead gallop. But anybody listening might not have figured that, and—Sorcha hoped with all her heart that somebody was listening.

"Let's see what Saoirce has to tell us, then," she said and ushered everyone out the door.


A curse on that horse, Cian thought, as he ran into the woods. How could she have followed him so far and back, and made it here just in time to interrupt his surveillance? Especially since they had just been about to tell him absolutely everything he needed to know to intercept them?

In a bank. Wasn't that a vault of some kind, made of the terrible iron metal? He would never be able to sneak into a vault. But he could wait for the mortal to walk into it. All Cian had to do was wait by the gate to confiscate the Stone before they could carry it through. Then, because he could, he would destroy the mortal, and maybe destroy the *Tuatha* princess, as well. After all, hadn't she just given her precious protective herbs to the little girl? She would be vulnerable now, and Cian felt his groin tighten just with that thought.

He shook his head even as he literally flew over the ground. It had been a tactical error, infecting the child.

He'd thought he'd struck the other little girl, sneaking silently into her dreams to lay the seeds of madness. Who knew a cherished one occupied that bed?

Now there was no question. If he didn't confiscate the Dearann Stone and present it to the king, he would be banished for all his fairy life. And that he simply would not tolerate.

If he could just rid himself of the horse, he would set himself to wait. After all, there wasn't any other place to return to the land of faerie than that bare hilltop. Why expend his energy, when he could simply sit in the sun, plotting the queen's demise?

Yes, that was a grand idea. Besides, if he stayed close, he would have a much better chance to make one of those children part of the equation.

Now, to throw his scent off. That horse was getting too close again.

Sorcha made it out into the back garden just as Saoirce approached. Sorcha lifted her hands, calling the horse to her. Saoirce, lathered and trembling, stumbled to a halt right in front of her, whinnying as if in frustration.

"*Fuist,*" Sorcha crooned, gentling the high-strung animal. "*Fuist,* all is well. The cherished one sleeps in peace, and we go now to protect her. Rest, Saoirce."

The horse bobbed her head, her sides still heaving, and turned her head to look back beyond the buildings into the woods.

"Oh, aye," Sorcha agreed. "He's still on the run, my fine lady. But I know we can leave you here to watch the children. Can't we?" The horse nodded again, her ghostly coat shimmering in the early-morning sun. Sorcha smiled and stroked her velvety muzzle. "Grand, that's grand. I thank you. The queen herself thanks you."

The horse raised her head, just like Gran peering down her nose. Sorcha couldn't help but smile even more broadly. Her friend was just a bit outraged by the idea that it would take the queen's approbation for her to guard one of the cherished ones. Her very own, given to her by Sorcha not a day before.

Sorcha gave her a formal, court bow. "My apologies, *a bhantiarna.* I should have known better. Now then, go down and rest. You will be needed."

The horse gave her another bow and turned to amble down to the stable block.

"Leave her box open," Sorcha instructed the head groom.

"But…"

"It's all right, Jacks," Harry said, stepping up beside her. "Starchaser won't go anywhere unless one of the children is threatened."

Jacks, a short, squat mass of wrinkles, scratched his thinning hair and turned to look after the horse. "I heard of guard dogs," he muttered. "But a guard horse…"

"What do we do now?" Harry asked.

Sorcha looked out toward the woods. "If we're lucky and all, the *Dubhlainn Sidhe* heard my plans, and he'll think it a waste of time to do more than wait by the gate to intercept us. But I'll not be taking that chance, so we need to get the protection laid in for the children. Then you can take me to this place where the Stone lies."

"And then?"

She faced him, wishing with all her heart she had another answer. "And then I take it back through the gates to my home."

Sorcha didn't have to share Harry's mind to know every emotion he battled just then. She saw his feelings on his face: loss, longing, grief. And yet he said not a word. Just turned away from her. Sorcha realized that she'd reached her hand to him, but he was already walking away.

For the first time, she knew for certain how this was all going to end. She would rescue the Stone. She would return it to its proper home. And she would return to her own world, where she belonged, where she had worth and purpose. Where she would live her long, long fairy life with no heart left in her, because she would be leaving that sore thing here with this stern man who would never think to leave his needful family just to be with her.

Fairies did not weep. It was as alien to them as this cold and wet weather. But standing there in the cold sunshine, Sorcha felt what she knew had to be tears crowd the back of her throat.

It would be over soon. She would succeed where she'd thought she would fail. And for the first time, it wasn't enough.

"I assume you have a plan," Phyl said as she stepped up to wrap a coat around Sorcha's shoulders.

Sorcha looked up at Harry's cousin and thought what a magnificent person she was. "A plan?"

"To keep everyone safe and get that bloody thing back where it came from."

Sorcha sighed. "I'm after working on it."

Phyl looked after Harry as he walked back into the house. "I don't suppose fairies grant wishes, do they?"

"And if they did?" Sorcha asked, following her gaze and felling the weight on Harry's shoulders.

Phyl took a second to look down at Sorcha, and in her eyes Sorcha saw the complexity of these mortals. "I'd want his happiness."

Then Phyl turned away herself, because she knew as well as Sorcha did that it wasn't something Sorcha could guarantee. Especially now that she knew what would have brought him happiness. And what its cost would be. A cost he would never ask of his family. Sorcha had thought she couldn't love him more. She should have known better.

She slipped her arms into the sleeves of Phyl's coat. "We need to gather up hawthorn branches, and hazel and oak, holly leaves and sea salt. And we need to surround the house and the stables with them for protection against what has just visited here."

"Are you sure it'll be enough?" Phyl asked.

Sorcha couldn't lie. "No. But I'm hoping that our friend will find himself more interested in following us than tormenting you. You don't have what he wants, after all."

Except hostages. Sorcha fought the instinctive panic that idea incited.

"But if he follows you, won't you be in danger?"

"Ah, no. I can deal with him."

"And Harry?"

"To Harry I'll give the rest of the *bean tighe*'s herbs, just as a precaution."

"But that would leave nothing for you."

Sorcha smiled and shook her head. "I have a knife as sharp as my mother's tongue. And to tell you the truth, I find I'm just aching to use it on anyone who would have thought himself immune to punishment for visiting his poison on our Lilly."

"She really will be all right?"

"It's a blessing of a cherished one. Her memory only holds joy."

Phyl's shoulders eased. "Thank you for that."

Sorcha's laugh was sore. "For what?" she asked. "Bringing such obscenity to this hallowed place? Torturing one of the true innocents in creation? Don't be after thanking me for that, if you don't mind."

"After you leave," Phyl said, walking along with Sorcha toward the sacred grove, where they would find all the branches they would need, "what guarantee do we have that the other fairy, the *dove*..."

*"Dubhlainn Sidhe."*

"Yes. What guarantee do we have that he won't stay behind and continue his reign of terror?"

"Well," Sorcha said, "with both Darragh and I workin' on it, I think we'll manage to get him caught in an impossible place. Then, with the Stone back, his power will wane, and his crimes will have to be paid for."

"I certainly like the sound of that."

All that morning, the four adults and Phyl's two oldest children collected sacred branches and purloined the cook's sea salt, and with Sorcha intoning prayers and Darragh setting the pattern, laid a protection around all the areas mortals inhabited on this hill. Sorcha knew that Gran was watching from her suite window, but she never demanded an explanation. She never asked about the terrible sounds that even she must have heard during the early-morning hours. Nor did she smile as she watched the industry in her gardens.

Sorcha did her best to make it a game for the children, but even they were quiet.

"I think this is better," Theo said after they'd finished. "It feels safer here."

Sorcha nodded. "Good. Then you'll know where you can go and where you can't. Don't leave here, Theo. Don't let Bea or Lilly or your Gran try and step beyond the array until you see your uncle Harry come back. Will you do that for me?"

They were standing in the front salon of the great house, and Sorcha was dressed for the trip to York. She was just waiting her turn to say goodbye to Gran. Harry was up there now.

"Are you coming back with Uncle Harry?" Theo asked, looking very young all of a sudden.

Sorcha knelt down to meet him eye-to-eye. "Ah, no, *a chara*. I must carry the great Stone back to the world of faerie, where it will be safe. And aren't you meant to stay here and watch over your sisters?"

"But I want to come with you."

Sorcha didn't even answer, because both she and Theo knew there was no answer to give.

"Will I see you again?" he asked at last.

"Ah, sure, I hope so," she said, brushing his guinea-bright hair out of his eyes. "Lilly will see us. Trust her."

He just nodded and wrapped his arms around her neck. Sorcha held him tight, those tears welling in her again. "Sure it's a hard thing to have to straddle two worlds, Theo. Hopefully one day we'll find a way for you to visit back and forth, for you are as much a man of our world as your uncle Harry is."

Finally Theo pulled back and smiled. "No, I'm not," he said. "He sees things nobody else can. Not even me."

Sorcha just nodded. *"Slan, a chroi."*

"Be careful."

Her farewells to Gran and Mary were brief and dry, with Gran simply nodding her away. Sorcha desperately wished she could have thrown her arms around the old woman, but she knew it would overset her completely. So she made some lighthearted jest about how they took in perfect strangers off the moors, and accepted a quick, firm hug from Mary.

"Tell me," that soft, small woman said in Sorcha's ear. "In your world, would that old woman walk?"

Sorcha couldn't even form the words to answer. But Mary saw the truth in her eyes, and nodded. "Ah, well. She wouldn't leave that boy to his fate without her, anyway."

There was no way Sorcha would get past Lilly without hugs. She didn't. She sat on her floor up in that wonderful, whimsical room and nestled the little girl in her lap.

"Take me," Lilly begged, tugging on the coat Harry had made Sorcha don over her own attire. "Take me, fairy."

"Ah, no, *mo chroi.* Your place is here, with Theo and Bea. And your uncle Harry. Why, wouldn't he cry, then, if you left him all alone?"

Lilly considered that, her little face puckered in thought. Then she shook her head. "Harry go," she said, and sounded mournful. "Not me."

"But he'll be comin' back," Sorcha assured her, and

thought her own heart would shatter just at saying the words.

It seemed that Lilly knew that perfectly well, because she lifted one of her little hands and just laid it against Sorcha's cheek. And when a tear fell onto her fingers, she gently patted. "Bye, fairy."

Her voice sounded so soft, so sad. Sorcha gathered her close, fortifying herself one final time on that sweet innocence. And then she set Lilly on her feet and gave her a little push in Theo's direction. How was a fairy meant to survive such loss? she wondered. Even when she knew she carried a child of her own.

She climbed to her feet and walked down the stairs to where Harry waited in the front hall with the other adults.

"You're all ready, then, girl?" Darragh asked.

She nodded. "Are you?"

"Sure. All you have to do is call, and we'll be ready and waiting at the top of the hill. And the goddess willing, himself our *Dubhlainn Sidhe* will be so tied to your tail he'll never see the door shut on him until it's done."

"Now, the timing of the thing is delicate, Darragh. He must be caught solid between this world and ours, or we'll have no control of him."

"Leave it to me." He, too, gave her a brisk hug. "Offer my apologies to your mother for deserting her."

"She'll understand." Sorcha turned to the woman standing so close beside him. "Gwyneth, sure I wish I'd had a chance to make a better acquaintance of you."

Gwyneth gave the brightest, most unfettered smile Sorcha had seen on her. "Maybe you can step through next Halloween, when the veil is thin."

Harry shook his head. "You're the last person I'd ever expect to hear that from, Gwynnie."

She chuckled. "Yes, aren't I? Good luck, you two. And be careful."

It was Gwyneth's car they slid into, since Harry said it was faster and less liable to break down than his. Sorcha settled herself against the seatback, let Harry close her in all that metal, and fought to breathe. She couldn't imagine how Darragh could have enjoyed this thing. It was an elevator that moved sideways.

And very fast. Sorcha didn't really understand that until Harry had strapped her in, obviously afraid she would try to run. Well, and wasn't he in the right of it? If she'd had the courage, she would have unclamped herself and pushed open this cage, and escaped back out onto the moors.

"Would there be a way I could get some air, then, Harry?" she begged, her voice embarrassingly small and weak.

He pressed a button, and the side window of the car slid down to let in a breeze for her starving lungs. She lifted her face to it and closed her eyes, her hands clamped around the handles. Goddess, Harry didn't so much as hiccup in the thing. In fact, he seemed to *like* it.

"Think of it as a mechanical horse." he said.

She managed to crack one eye open to see the landscape hurtling past at an unconscionable speed. "I don't suppose we could go back and get an actual horse, Harry, could we?"

His laugh was lighter than she'd ever heard it, even for the fell thing they were about to do. "Ah, no, Sorcha," he mimicked her. "We'd be hours longer at the job. And the shambles of York is no place for a horse. Besides, we have no place to leave it."

She sighed, leaning her head against the window. "And wasn't the queen right about me?" she asked forlornly. "A failure even to have the courage for such a simple thing that even little Lilly isn't afraid of."

He reached over and took her hand, and Sorcha immediately felt warmer. "Little Lilly was raised in these things, Sorcha. She might be a bit more reticent to be seated atop one of your flying fairies."

Sorcha managed a laugh. "Ah, sure, Lilly wouldn't be afraid of the end of the world."

Harry chuckled in return. "We're lucky to have her."

"Oh, aye. You are. I can't wait to tell the queen that I was privileged enough to give a cherished one her guardian. There will be celebrating in the high hall."

For a while the only sounds Sorcha heard were the whisper of wind rushing just beyond her ear, the throaty purr of the car's voice, and the wash of it over the road. She began to ease her hold on Harry by increments.

"Does your home really look so very much like the murals in the hall?" he asked, and she knew just what it had taken him to do so.

She straightened and opened her eyes. Eager to soak in the rare spring of his eye, she smiled for him, because she felt his raw pain at finally knowing the truth and never being able to partake of it.

"Aye, Harry," she said, holding him tight. "It does. Even in the land of *Dubhlainn Sidhe,* the light is rare and soft, the flowers bursting with color, and the animals and fish alive with poetry and grace. Would you come over with me, Harry?" she asked. "Just to bring the

Stone home? The queen would allow your visit and usher you back through again. You would be able to see this place you've only dreamed of. You could know for sure that it's real and finally have no more need for fury."

For a second he looked away from the road, then lifted her hand and kissed it. "No, my fairy princess. I cannot. It would be too much for me to bear to know it's as much as I'd ever thought it to be. Especially since I wouldn't be able to stay."

Ah, Goddess, he broke her heart for sure, Sorcha thought, feeling the pressure of his lips on her hand like a brand.

"I know this won't help, Harry," she said, "but I must say it, and I must say it now, before we become occupied with the task we are sent to do. It's you I love. It's you I'll love until the day my ship sails for the West and I inhabit the land of eternal youth. Yours will be the last name on my lips."

There was a wetness on her cheeks, and she knew that the tears had finally come in full. And when she turned to Harry, there were tears on his cheeks, as well.

"And you," he said, dragging in an unsteady breath, "are the only one I'll love. I'll wake up with the memory of you, and fall asleep to dream your face."

It was what she'd wanted, wasn't it? The certainty that of all the beings in this vast and complex place, she and Harry had found each other, even for a few moments? Hadn't she always wanted a love of her own, one name she could call when she hurt, or was happy or frightened? Well, then, she had one. And it fair destroyed her. And she couldn't even tell him about the child she would bear him, who would never have the right to return home to his father. Ah, it was too much for her. It was a burden even the queen couldn't have anticipated.

The miles passed, and the minutes with them, those human inventions that compartmentalized existence. Fairies had no need for them, and now Sorcha knew why. They were a measurement of endings. Of loss. Only sixty of them left now. Only forty. She felt them collect in her chest until she couldn't breathe for the weight of them, until she couldn't think or smile for the panic of their ending.

So consumed was she by these things that she barely registered the houses that appeared, then multiplied, then seemed to crowd against each other like children trying to see over a wall, until the sun had to struggle to find its way through. Sorcha shivered. She knew this was the city where the Dearann Stone was, and it should have given her joy. Instead, it pierced her with loss. Minutes fled, tumbled behind them like leaves from these mortal trees, until Sorcha felt the heart of her slowly die with the ending of her time with Harry.

The car stopped, and Sorcha looked around. "Is this a bank, then?" she asked, wondering why a man stood in uniform in front of the doors.

"When was the last time you ate?" Harry asked, ignoring her question.

Sorcha turned to him. "Ate?" She shook her head. "Last night?"

He nodded. "Well, a girl needs her strength to tackle the big problems in life."

He shut the car down, and the man stepped up to open the door.

"It isn't the bank then, is it?" Sorcha asked.

"No, ma'am," the gentleman said with a stiff little bow. "I'd like to welcome you to the Royal York Hotel."

"Harry," she said, "we can't afford to do this."

Harry stepped around the car and took the man's place. "We can't afford not to. Trust me, Sorcha."

She did. Of course she did. But she couldn't figure why she should go to a hotel to look for the Stone in a bank.

# Chapter 13

It was another stone building. And it had elevators. But by the time Harry opened the door to the room he'd rented, Sorcha wasn't sure she cared.

"I don't understand," she said, turning to him.

He was handing something to the young man who had led them here and accepting a key in return. Tossing it on a table, Harry shut the door and turned to her. "I'm being unpardonably selfish."

How could those simple words lodge so tightly in her throat?

"You'll not get the Stone?"

He stepped nearer. "Of course I'll get the Stone. But right now you look pale and shaky, and that's just not the optimum condition for conducting an assault."

"It's all those metal cages you mortals love so, Harry. I'll be grand once I get my feet under me."

"Then there's the fact that I very much want to make love to you."

Sorcha stopped breathing. "I…"

He stepped right up to her and took her shoulders in his fine, elegant hands. "We're out of time, Sorcha, and we didn't even know we were on a countdown till this morning. I'm sorry. I can't send you back just yet. I have to… I need to…"

"I could stay here in your world," she offered, feeling her fairy soul shrivel at the thought.

Tears welled in his eyes, where she knew he'd never allowed them before this day. "I couldn't allow it," he said. "It would kill you faster than despair. You don't fit here, Sorcha. You wouldn't survive what this world is."

"You shouldn't have to, either," she couldn't help but say, matching him tear for tear.

He was right, of course. She knew it. She knew, too, that he would sacrifice their happiness for their own good.

He combed his fingers through her hair. "But I have to be here, my love. I'm needed too much to go. And you have generations of children to train. We have only these moments, and I don't want to squander them."

*But we'll not be safe till the Stone is home,* she almost said. She knew, though, that they would be, at least for now. She couldn't imagine the *Dubhlainn Sidhe* wasting his time scouring the house or grounds when he could more easily lie out on that vast, lonely moor and wait for the sound of a car engine.

If he'd overheard her as she'd hoped. If he didn't think it would be better to find himself some leverage.

"We have a little time," Harry said, as if he'd heard her, leaning his forehead against hers. "There's no way that fairy's going to find us till we get back to Waverly Close. And you've managed to strip almost every single tree on the property to protect those children. All I ask is an hour or two, Sorcha. Just enough time to pretend we don't have to do this."

She couldn't bear the pain in those sweet eyes; she couldn't bear to walk away, either. Even for the sake of her world and the goddess and Mother Earth herself. He was right. There would be no other time for them.

"We'll still have time to get the Stone?" she asked, knowing how small and uncertain her voice sounded. Knowing that her body sparked with sudden, intense life in his hands. She laid her own hands on his chest to measure the pounding of his heart and knew she was home. "I know that mortals run on clocks we fairies have no need of."

"We have time to get the Stone and even a meal to see us through the next hours." He kissed the tip of her nose, and he smiled. "I promise."

She managed a nod. "All right, then. But only if you'll do one thing for me first."

"Anything," he said, and she knew he meant it. He meant all of his heart and his wealth and his life. He meant everything that he was and would be.

She smiled and struggled to draw a complete breath. Already she saw it in her head, his eyes darkening, his skin sheening with the sweat of arousal, his body taut-ening in her arms. She heard the rasping of his breath and felt the thunder of his heart against her questing hands, all in her head where it did her no good. She had to hurry now, or she would never have the time to realize those wonderful imaginings.

Pulling a hand away, she reached into the coat Harry had lent her and pulled out the smallest of her packets. "For me, Harry," she begged. "Take the herbs with which the *bean sidhe* gifted me. Protect yourself against the evil of the fairy we fight."

He looked down at the small green bag and then back up to her. "But I'm not having the dreams anymore."

"He'll fight you, Harry. When we reach him, sure he'll use every weapon in his arsenal, and in doing, would stop me cold, for I'd have to help you. Please, Harry. For me."

Still he just looked. "And what about you? Shouldn't you be protected?"

"The herbs are for mortals. Sure, they don't work on a fairy life. It's his assault on you that would kill this fairy heart, Harry. Please."

Finally, just when she was sure he would ask the question she couldn't answer, just what would happen if the *Dubhlainn Sidhe* attacked her, he reached over and took the little bag from her.

"I don't suppose these taste at all good," he said.

Sorcha's laugh was sore. "Sure, the *bean tighe* herself said that nothing is worth the cure that doesn't hurt. The thing is, though, I'm thinking it would be after hurting much less if you're using it for prevention instead of cure."

He squinted at her, as if trying to decipher a riddle. "Uh-huh. Well, then, let's get on with it." He took another look at the little bag in his hand, weighing it. "Not much here. Is it enough?"

"Oh, aye, I think so. It might help with a bit of water, though."

He managed that. He opened the bag and just tossed back the herbs, following them with a large swallow of water. And before the reaction set in, Sorcha pushed them both onto the sofa in the corner and wrapped her arms around him.

It didn't take long. He bucked like a young colt to rein, and his mouth opened. "Ah…"

"Aye," she said, holding on tight. "I'm that sorry, Harry."

"It's like…fire…."

She just nodded. He was sweating, and his hands were clenched around her arms as if trying to hold on for dear life.

"I have you, Harry," she assured him, her lips against his cheek, her arms tight around him. "I'll not let you go."

"Good thing," he gasped, "I have…the strangest feeling…I'd explode."

"Sure, you're safe. It's just the fairy version of a cold."

His laugh was sore and short. But his frantic grasp on her eased a bit, and he drew a full breath.

"Ah, now it's passin'," she said, stroking his damp cheek. "Grand, grand…it'll be over soon, and you'll be impervious."

"For how…long?"

"Long enough for us to get our enemy back through the gate and into my mother's loving arms, anyway."

"Loving?" he echoed.

Sorcha grinned. "Sure, haven't they acquainted you with sarcasm in your world, Harry?"

He just closed his eyes and rested against her.

"Not exactly my idea of foreplay…" he muttered.

She chuckled and rested her head on his shoulder. "Well, then, how would this be?"

Closing her eyes, she spent a long moment just listening to the steady beat of his heart, then settled herself against the hard wall of his chest. She did what she'd never consciously done in her life, what her mother and sister had tried to teach her. She crept into Harry's head and prepared to seduce him.

It wasn't as easy as it would have been in her world, but Sorcha was determined. In her mind, where all was possible, she created a picture. She sparked the image to life with her will and whirled it into colors, into intent and imagination. Like clay, she molded it to her will: crafting, refining, until the general feelings were honed into sharp, clear edges, and she could recognize them for what they were.

Hunger. Lust. Delight. Love.

Harry in her arms. Harry at her mercy.

She knew the minute the images appeared in Harry's mind. He stiffened, just about to object, she thought. She thought he moved to look down at her, but her eyes were still closed as she focused on the scene she would play out in his head.

His eyes drifted shut, and his hands loosened a bit around her arms. But his heart, that great, giving heart, sped up. His skin warmed, and fresh beads of perspiration appeared on his forehead and upper lip.

*Yes, Harry, yes,* she thought, molding those images to perfection. And there, in her mind, she stood before him and slowly, very slowly, lowered herself to kneel between his thighs. She lifted her hands and laid them on his chest, against his shirt, which was suddenly damp and hot, where his heart beat hard and the breath of him rasped beneath her fingers. And slowly, so slowly, she drew her hands down, over his chest, his belly, his groin, down to his thighs to feel them tauten, hard and sleek as a stallion's, and she edged them apart.

She smiled for him, the most potent smile Orla had ever taught her. She thought briefly of the oils Orla had given her, seductive scents that would drive a man to insanity if shared. But Sorcha didn't want Harry by sorcery. She wanted him truly, with honesty and delight between them, instead of seduction.

"Good God," he rasped in her mind, breathing hard. "What are you doing to me?"

"*Fuist,*" she whispered out loud, holding on to him, letting the scene play out in her head. "Isn't it just a bit of an appetizer before we have our luncheon?"

She felt the growl of laughter against her fingers. "I don't think this is legal," he managed, his body arching against the suggestion of what she was painting in his mind.

It was there she was reaching out to him, to that interesting fastener they called a zipper. Not just something to close and hold, something to seduce just with the opening. Even imagining it, it made the most interesting rasping sound as Sorcha pictured catching it in between her fingers and pulling.

Even before she touched him, Harry was hard; she felt him against the sides of her hand, and it exhilarated her. She unbuttoned the waist of his slacks and stroked her hand down the silken line of his boxers. She needed to bring boxers back with her. Sure, weren't they a sensual treat, to intimate the pleasures beneath without forfeiting the delicious texture altogether? Sleek and hot, and hiding him away from her.

"Oh, God, Sorcha…" he rasped. "Enough!"

"Aye," she whispered, taking her arms from around him. "It is."

And so she let the images in her mind fade, slowly, like the last stroke of a hand or the final invasion of a tongue. She gently disentangled herself from his embrace and got to her feet. Then, before he could recover, she stepped out of his mind and in between his thighs. She lowered herself to her knees and with her fingers trembling with the hunger in her, she took hold of that zipper at last and made it growl. She thumbed the cool, round button above it, letting it slide free, and reached in to savor the hard, thick lines of him that he'd wrapped away in silk.

"Ah, Goddess, Harry, I'm not sure fairies are made for mortal men."

"Don't tell me that," he groaned, his head thrown back.

She did away with the silk, as well, and took him in her hands, the steel length of him, the velvety tip that already pearled his essence for her. Ah, how she loved mortal textures, the wiry coil of hair, the sleek satin of skin. She loved his scent, musk and salt and man. Harry. She bent to taste him and loved that, too, so she ran her tongue along the length of him. She nibbled the tip of him with her teeth and took him in her mouth to pleasure them both.

She felt his hands in her hair, his fingers strong and elegant. She heard the harsh rasp of his breathing, the odd growl of frustration in the back of his throat, and she smiled. She did this to him. She brought him to this place where he lay helpless before her.

Not totally helpless, evidently. Before she even realized what had happened, he slipped his hands beneath her arms and pulled her up to him. She didn't even remember him kicking his pants away, but suddenly he was walking her over to the great, pillow-filled bed, where he dropped her. And somehow she found that her dress had been left behind with his clothes.

They were both naked as the day the goddess had made them, so that it was his hair-roughened body that met hers, that tormented her with its delicious abrasion. Her breasts swelled. Her nipples tightened. She was the one moaning now, because he kept his hands to himself. He lay above her, just looking, as if memorizing every inch of her. Touching her only where his chest met her breasts, her tender, aching breasts.

Her skin was shot through with lightning at the sense of his gaze on her. She shivered, hot and cold at once, and he hadn't yet touched her with hand or mouth or tongue.

"Is it begging you want?" she asked, reaching up to delight herself with the feel of his chest. "I'll beg, then."

"Don't beg," he murmured, and bent to her. "I couldn't bear it if you begged."

"Then I'll command," she said on a breathy sigh, as he nipped at her breast. "Touch me, Harry. Give me enough memories to last me my long fairy life."

He didn't answer, not in words. He smiled, and Sorcha thought she'd never seen a more bittersweet sight. It was the smile she would take with her, the smile she would try to remember when she felt lost and forgotten back in her world. It was the smile she would cherish until her memories winked out.

She lifted her hands to him, cupping his face, claiming him for hers, calling him to her. She brought him to her, mouth to mouth, tongue to tongue, heart to heart, and she loved him. With her hands and her body and her soft sighs of delight. With her lips and head and heart.

She, too, memorized, but with her hands: his throat, his shoulders, his arms, oh, his arms, his chest with its crinkly hair and copper nipples. His belly, his flat, hard belly and its whimsical navel that, sure, had been created for nothing more than dipping into with her tongue. His thighs, those thighs that could control a stallion and protect a woman; ah, sweet Goddess, there wasn't poetry enough to speak of his thighs.

And his hands, those hands that set fire loose in her, sweeping over her, settling in her most sensitive nooks and crannies, cupping her breasts and holding them up, one after the other, for the worship of his mouth. Those hands that measured every inch of her and seemed to offer him delight, for he murmured, too.

He sighed into her mouth, as if all breath should be shared between them. He chuckled when he slipped his fingers into her, and she gasped, she writhed, she arched to him, begging without words, because words weren't needed between them anymore.

She knew, because before she could even think to ask, to coerce, to, Goddess, yes, *beg,* he rose over her, nudged her thighs wide and drove himself home.

"Ah…my love…" he moaned against her throat.

She wrapped her arms around him, wrapped her legs

around him, pulling him hard into her, so hot and deep
that she'd never lose him, so full that she'd carry the
imprint of him to her very core, tears sliding down her
cheeks at the sweet beauty of it, her mouth open to gasp
for air, her hands desperate to hold him to her, to keep
him in her, to bring him ecstasy inside her.

"Yes, Harry," she heard herself saying. "Yes, yes,
love me, please, love me…."

"I couldn't love you more," he answered, and drove
into her, harder and harder, deeper, until she thought she
would die of the delight of it, so much more visceral
than anything she'd ever known, so immediate and alive
and true, a swirl of color and sound and impatience that
gathered, that tightened inside her, that urged her on to
meet him, thrust for thrust, seeking, climbing, soaring,
the air around her thinning, the temperature climbing,
until suddenly she heard herself keening, because her
body was keening at the wild, impossible knifepoint of
pleasure that suddenly cut through her and simply destroyed her.

She threw her head back, scrabbling to keep hold of
his slick back, opening herself impossibly to him, completely, utterly, as he thrust home once, twice and again,
one final time, until he shattered right along with her,
his guttural cry echoing around the pale, dim walls.

He wasn't asleep. As much as he ached for it, there
was no way he was missing a second with Sorcha in his
arms. He was panting like one of his racehorses after a
long uphill course. His skin was sweat-sheened and
cooling fast in the autumnal room. He probably should
think about pulling up covers or rearranging pillows, but

he simply didn't have the energy. He didn't want to take his concentration away from his beautiful fairy princess.

"Ah, Harry," she said, her breath washing over his chest where she lay nestled beneath his shoulder. "Sure, it's a good thing we have other appointments. I think if I got used to this, I'd never get another thing done."

He couldn't help chuckling. "I'm not sure I'd let you. You feel too good right here."

*Against his heart,* he thought. Two days ago, he would have groaned aloud at such a maudlin thought. Today, all he could think of was how little time they had like this, in perfect accord, sated and settled and exhausted by the most spectacular lovemaking he could ever imagine.

Who would ever believe it? He, Harry Wyatt, wrapped up in the arms of a woman he'd met only two days before, right in the middle of the day in a hotel in York. Harry Wyatt didn't indulge in flights of fancy like that. Harry Wyatt didn't believe in them.

Harry Wyatt *hadn't* believed in them.

It was just too bad he'd finally begun to believe only when it was too late.

He closed his eyes against the shard of pain that lodged in his chest. He was losing her. Hell, he'd hardly found her, and he was having to sacrifice her. It wasn't fair.

He almost laughed. He was an adult. He knew how often life was fair. And he knew damn well his was more fair than most. He had a close family, a beautiful home and a successful career. How could he have known that he would come to realize how little most of that meant when faced with the loss of love?

"I love you," he said, because he couldn't help it.

She ran her fingers down his chest. "Ah, just so I love you. And I thank you, Harry, for sharing such beauty with me this day."

He slipped his own hand along her waist, over the slope of her hips, obsessed with the feel of her. They had so little time.

"Tell me," he said, just to put off the inevitable, "What's your world like?"

She brushed her satin-soft fingers along his cheek. "Ah, well, it's pretty much like you see on your wall."

"You said you had a sister."

She was looking at him as if he'd lost his mind. "Harry, I don't think…"

"I know nothing about you, Sorcha. Give me this. Please."

Tears trickled down her cheeks, and he couldn't bear it. But she nodded briskly, as if this weren't killing her, too.

"Two. I have two sisters: Nuala, the oldest, and Orla, the baby." She smiled a bit wryly. "Although I doubt it would be wise or accurate to describe her as a baby of any kind. Until very recently, she was one of the *leannan sidhe.*"

*"Leannan sidhe?"*

She nodded, her attention more on the patterns she was now drawing on his chest. "Aye, one of the legendary fairy sirens. A seducer of mortal men, who counts her successes in the slaves she's created."

Harry caught her hand, too distracted by the touch of her to attend to her words. "Slaves?"

She kissed the tip of his nose instead. "Aye. Once she's had them, they pine for her until they waste away. It's a fearsome thing to be, but such she was."

He scowled and kissed the tips of her fingers. "I can certainly sympathize with the poor bastards."

"Sure, I'm no *leannan sidhe*," she protested.

"You've enslaved *me*."

There seemed to be no amusement to be found in that answer. They both knew it was true. They both knew the enslavement was total and mutual. Harry felt the despair of it in his chest. Silence stretched to discomfort. He couldn't tell whether either of them was breathing. The injustice of their situation was suddenly overwhelming, and the minutes were ticking away.

"But I used no fairy power," she finally said, her voice a bit rough. "Orla was a master at it."

Harry was awed by her. "Was?" he asked, just to keep her talking.

She nodded. "She was the one talked Darragh into trying to usurp our mother's throne. Sure, there could be no punishment greater for her. She now must face the world without her powers, or the knowledge of how to go on without them."

"And you like her?"

Sorcha smiled at him. "She's my sister. She can't help it she was given that soul-gift from the creator. And I'm thinking she'll be better for it now that she's lost it."

"And your other sister?"

Her eyes grew wistful at the question. "Ah, Nuala. I'm going to miss her, altogether. She has gone to her mortal, and happily. She was to be queen until she met him."

"I'm sorry."

She smiled. "I'm not. She won her love, and I'm thinking that's a rare thing."

Another punch to the gut. Harry smiled for her,

though, and used his thumb to wipe away the tears that escaped down her cheeks.

"And your mother?"

"Ah, my mother. She is a queen, as queens are, I suppose, controlling and inspiring her clan since the days when the poet walked our land in Ireland."

"Which poet?" he asked. "The place is jammed full of them."

"The one who wrote the poem to her. 'The Faerie Queen,' he called it. Sure, you must know him."

His eyes widened. "Spenser?"

She smiled and nodded. "Oh, aye. That's the lad's name. And didn't he spend time at the very castle where our seer was born?"

"Your seer. What's a seer?"

"Ah, well, he who is a prophet, the interpreter of the great design. The one who sees the threads of existence." She looked down at him for a moment, then shook her head. "Ah, Harry, would that I could show them to you—the queen, my mother; Kieran, who is our seer; my Uncle Mick, who is master of the horse. Sure, you'd be a perfect heir to him, as he's longing for the West himself. I can see you now, with your magic with the horses, gentling the great horses of faerie to your hand."

"They really look like my stock?"

"They are the same as your stock, Harry. Maybe brought over when your ancestor came, maybe just happily yours by serendipity. Fairy horses are always gray, so pale they fade into the mist and disappear in the early morning. So fleet their step can't even be felt. And you, with your fairy eyes, recognized them."

He snorted. "I saw a beautiful horse."

She just smiled. "Aye, you did that."

"What about you?" he asked. "What was your childhood like?"

She looked wistful again. "It was a fairy's life, Harry. I had the glen and the hills and the rivers to wander, the animals and birds as friends, the trees as teachers. I had the rarest of music and the finest of bards to entertain me every night as we feasted in the great hall." She paused, and Harry thought this the most important part. "I had the children. It's they who are my responsibility, not the throne. I have no business being queen, and so my mother the queen should know."

He pulled back a bit, as if that would help him see her better. "She wants you to be queen?"

She huffed a bit and shook her head. "Sure, I'm not made for it, and so I told her." Suddenly, she chuckled. "And wasn't that the best thing I've done in my life? Because I refused her, she sent me on my quest in a place she said was so hostile my fairy soul would shrivel." For the first time, there was whimsy in her eyes. "I'd say there's been precious little shriveling between us, Harry."

He couldn't help a chuckle. "I think the opposite has been more the case. So, what happens when you get back?"

She looked off into the distance, as if visualizing the event. "Why, I refuse her again. Sure, how can she argue if I'm holding the Dearann Stone at the time?"

Somewhere in the town, a clock struck the hour, bonging dolefully. Harry felt each strike in his chest, counting down the time they had left. He saw the realization dawn in Sorcha's eyes, as well. God, he wanted to keep talking, nestled together like an old married couple on a Saturday morning, unhurried and easy. He wanted to just keep holding her, here, where no one could find them. He wanted more time.

"We don't have it, Harry," she said, as if hearing him. "We had this, though. It will keep me, I promise. I couldn't ask for a more perfect memory. A more gentle or considerate lover."

"I didn't have any violent thoughts," he mused, surprised that he hadn't even worried about it before now.

Sorcha didn't move. "I'll tell the *bean tighe* thank you for you."

"That's all it took? Some herbs?"

"A temporary measure, Harry. We have to think about getting the rest of this day done."

For a second all he could do was hold her as tightly as he could. Damn, where had those tears come from again? Harry Wyatt never wept. Not when his parents died, not when he'd realized what kind of condition they'd left his world in. Not when his gran had lost her legs, or he'd lost his chance to spend his days wandering the moors and glens he loved so much.

"We'll get the day done," he said. "I have some food coming up first. You need some nourishment."

She actually chuckled. "Sure, after the exercise I've just had, I should think so."

"Will I ever see you again after this?"

She went very still. He kept his hold on her, wrapping himself around her so that he could stay skin to skin with her, as if that would imprint her on his memory any better.

"Do you think it wise?" she asked. "Since I can't stay and *you* can't go?"

He closed his eyes and pulled her head to his chest. And for a long while he just inhaled her, cinnamon and honey and wildflowers. He satisfied himself with the silk of her body in his arms. He pretended they had all the time in the world.

"Well, then, we'd better make the most of the time we do have," he managed, his voice raspy and sore.

And when she lifted her face to him, he met her with a kiss. They turned to each other, wordless, eyes open and mouths meeting. They kissed, a slow, sensual mating of tongues and teeth and lips, a branding and a leaving. He took her mouth as he would take her body, gently, insistently, completely. He kissed her cheeks, her eyes, her nose. He licked the salt from her throat and wrapped her hair around his hands. He tasted and touched and tortured himself with her body, until his own was taut as a bowstring and hurting hard with the waiting. He weighed her breasts in his hands and pulled her nipples deep into his mouth, until she mewled in the back of her throat, her hands tangled in his hair as she held him to her. He slid down the silk of her belly and fingered the damp curls below.

"Open for me, love," he begged, his hands on her thighs, and she opened.

He bent lower to spread her open with his fingers, and he bent to taste her. He inhaled the scent of her so he would never forget. She shuddered at the touch of his tongue, and he smiled, hungry for the slip of that satiny flesh, for the swelling sex that smelled of her, tasted of her, that wept with the waiting.

Ah, he could feast here forever, and yet his body was shrieking in protest. She was rubbing her legs against him, tormenting him into agony. She was humming in her chest, and trying her best to pull him up to her. But he persisted, licking, dipping, nipping at her until he could feel her climax gather, until her muscles clenched and her mouth opened, and she arched impossibly so he could reach her more easily, and he laughed, because she was singing for him, a high, sweet keening sound of wonder, wonder he'd brought her.

Before the spasms eased, he lifted himself up and plunged into her. She met his gaze with one of demand, of delight, and Harry thought he would do anything for that look. He caught her hands and pulled them above her head, so he could be eye to eye with her, and he began to slowly drive into her, a slick deep glide, then just the tip of him to tease her into moving, into clawing at him. He smiled at her, and then he kissed her, sharing her own taste with her, and he plunged in, harder, until he pushed her up, until they were slamming the bed against the wall, until she had to hold hard on to his hands, her legs thrown around him, her hair tangled and wet, her gaze only on him.

And it was at the moment she smiled, a cat's smile, a siren's smile, the smile of a seductress, that he felt the spasms begin again, clenching around him, milking him, and oh, God, he couldn't hold out any longer, couldn't control himself. He bent to her, forehead to forehead, hands clenched above her head, bodies meeting in a fierce mating, and he exploded into her with a growl that sounded primeval and felt as if it had consumed him whole.

"Sweet…Goddess, Harry," she gasped, as he collapsed into her arms.

Harry nestled against her breasts and closed his eyes. "Indeed, Sorcha."

Her heart was racing. She was the one panting this time. Her hands trembled when she wrapped her arms around his chest. He wasn't surprised. He was chilled with sweat, and shaking as if he had the ague. He didn't think he'd ever held on to anything as tightly as he held on to her for those few minutes.

And then, inevitably, there came a knock on the door.

"Who's that, then?" Sorcha asked him, not so much as twitching.

If he didn't answer, maybe they would go away. Maybe the rest of the day wouldn't matter so much, and he could stay here in her arms.

"It's undoubtedly the room service I ordered."

"Room service?"

"Our food."

He felt the reaction in her body. "Ah. I see. We'll be after moving on, then?"

"We'll be after moving on."

The beginning of the end had come.

## Chapter 14

For some reason, Sorcha had thought she would be better able to handle the bank than she had the other mortal buildings she'd been in. But she hadn't figured on having to deal with Harry's city.

"It's not *my* city," he protested calmly as they walked hand-in-hand down the impossibly narrow street that seemed to wind in around itself like a snake. "I just use it on occasion."

"It's *all* stone," she protested, looking down at the strange lumpy variety that made up the streets. "How can anyone breathe?"

"They're not fairies."

"Obviously."

Finally, though, they stood before another huge box constructed of stone and fronted with pillars nobody really needed. It would be such an easy thing to go in. Grab the Stone and run away back to where the grass stretched away to the horizon without a building in sight.

For a very long moment they couldn't move. Sorcha found that her breath had left her again, and she thought even Harry should have been able to hear her heart.

"It really is in there?" she asked, wondering why all the people who walked past them like river water over boulders didn't realize the import of what was about to happen. All those rocks, she thought miserably. How could a person feel a thing?

"It's really in there," Harry said. "And if we don't go in and get it soon, they'll be closing on us, and we'll have to wait until tomorrow."

And yes, didn't Sorcha have the brief cowardly impulse to nod and turn away, and hide back in that pillow-strewn room? *Sure, we'll be after getting it tomorrow, when the omens will be better. The sun will shine, the air will warm....*

Somewhere over her shoulder, a building let out another of those slow bonging noises. Harry turned, then checked the timepiece he wore around his wrist.

"Time's up," he said and pulled her to him for one last kiss before they walked inside.

She was a muddle of emotions: terror, anger, grief, anxiety. She was about to hold one of the great Stones of Creation in her hand, the one lost to them for so long, the harbinger of spring and renewal. She it would be who would welcome it home.

She was about to change the course of not only faerie history but mortal history. She, Sorcha, who sought only to sit with the little ones and teach them the cycles of the earth. Her heart was stumbling about, and she swore someone had stolen the air. She was almost finished here.

She was almost finished. The thought all but killed her.

The inside of the place echoed. People moved about impatiently, and there was a constant clicking of machines. Sorcha didn't want to be here. Electricity was bad enough for fairies, but there were other energies altogether shuddering through this high, cold place. She couldn't imagine what the Dearann Stone had suffered, being caught in this place for so long. Suddenly she couldn't wait to get it out.

"I'm sorry," Harry said, as if he'd heard her. "I really had no idea what I was dealing with."

"Ah, sure, she knows that, Harry. How could the goddess punish you for what you couldn't understand? Even so, it might be a good idea to think about apologizing when you hold the Dearann Stone again."

"That'll be fine," he said, leading them through a grilled door. "I'd just appreciate it if we could wait for the apologies until we're alone again."

Sorcha looked around to see how blank the faces around her were. "Oh, aye, I see. They wouldn't be after understanding, would they?"

"Not if you're thinking of singing to it or falling to your knees."

She actually managed a smile. "Sure, fairies aren't that dramatic, Harry. You must be thinking of some mortal ritual."

He led her to a group of chairs and motioned her toward one. "You'll need to wait here," he said. "Only I can go in."

Sorcha sat. She took a deep breath. She wrapped her hands around each other and set them on her lap to keep still. Moments. They had only moments left to be together. And only moments remained until she could see the Stone. The air clogged in her chest and refused to soothe her.

She watched as Harry approached one of the people who seemed to work here and spoke to her. The woman barely noticed him. He signed a book of some kind and waited for her to finish some business. Sorcha held perfectly still, terrified and excited at once. Please, Goddess, let this be the Stone. Let there not be another of those awful surprises, the likes of which she'd suffered when Theo had handed her a silent stone of quartz.

The woman unlocked another door and walked through, and Harry followed her. Sorcha held her breath. She tried desperately to look as if the fate of two worlds wasn't at stake. Truly, she did her best to notice the world around her. But it seemed as if she were sitting under water, the light filtered badly from the high windows and the air thickened by the odd energy that seemed to reside in those clacking machines. She waited. She tried to breathe. She prayed.

And then she knew.

It was as if a shaft of sunlight had spilled into the room. She didn't see Harry or the other woman. She heard nothing. But she knew the instant the Stone had been released.

Harry had been right to warn her. She did want to drop to her knees. She wanted to laugh and sing and dance. She wanted to grab the nearest person to her and swing them around with the unspeakable, unbearable joy of it.

The Dearann Stone was free. It was here. It was whole and beautiful and strong, and soon she, Sorcha, daughter of Mab, would have the privilege of holding it in her hand.

Pictures tumbled through her mind: fairy woods, so deep and green and dark that the sun failed to find them; endless, arching skies of blue and white and gray; mountains, great, harsh mountains, with white shoulders and wooded skirts.

Sounds rushed past: the soughing of the wind through the trees; brooks chattering along their courses; lambs searching for their mothers; birdsong and moonsong and the sweet music of unfurling leaves. And scents, ah, sweet eternity, the scents that assailed her: fresh mown hay and wild iris; oceans and bonfires; birth and growth and spring, sweet, sweet spring.

Tears welled in her eyes: tears of joy, of anguish, of awe. And when she saw Harry walk back out of that metal room with the velvet-wrapped stone in his hands like an offering, she saw that there were tears in his eyes, too. She heard in his mind the awe of discovery as he finally allowed himself to appreciate the miracle he alone had seen for so long a time.

Reverently, she got to her feet, her head bowed in obeisance to the great power in Harry's hands.

"I guess I really am glad you found me," he said with a rather silly smile as he approached. "If you hadn't, I never would have had the chance to enjoy what this thing makes me see."

She reached out a tentative hand to greet the great Stone, and she laughed. "Isn't it brilliant, Harry? Didn't I tell you?"

"Yes, Sorcha," he said, carrying the Stone in one hand and guiding her with the other. "It's brilliant."

It was one of the most difficult things Sorcha had ever done, but she kept her promise. It wasn't until they'd locked themselves into the car and driven it out of the narrow streets that she slipped the Dearann Stone from its home. Harry pulled over to the side of the road in a place where the clouds skated over endlessly undulating earth, and they took a moment to greet the Dearann Stone as she deserved.

"You do have my apologies for imprisoning you," Harry said to it, and it sounded as if he meant it. "I wouldn't have, if I'd had even one person around me who could have explained things."

"To your satisfaction," Sorcha said, smiling at him. "A much more difficult accomplishment altogether."

He smiled back. "I guess so."

Sorcha sat in humble joy and, whether it was a good idea or not, sang a song of spring to the harbinger of it. She bathed in the glittering white warmth the Stone exuded and reached over to hold Harry's hand, so they could experience it as one.

"Ah, to think I'd actually see this day," she sighed. "For so long the Dearann Stone has been lost to the mists of legend. Who would think such as I would be granted the privilege of carrying it home?"

"Why would it be such a surprise?" Harry asked. "Didn't you think you'd succeed?"

She knew her eyebrows had risen. "Me? Of course not, Harry. After all, I'm only—"

"If you say you're only a teacher one more time, I'll toss the car keys into the river and let you walk back.

Don't you understand? Your mother didn't send you here because she thought you'd fail. She sent you because she knew you'd succeed."

His words lodged in her chest like stars. "Ah, sure I'd like to think so, Harry."

"Then do." He started the car. "Now, what's the plan?"

She shrugged. "Darragh should have been keeping an eye on the gatesite. Among us, we have to make sure the Stone gets through and the *Dubhlainn Sidhe* does not."

Harry looked over at her. "But I thought the whole point was to take him with you."

"Sure, we're hoping he gets caught in the antechamber, if you'd like. The space between the worlds of mortal and fairy. If we can keep him locked up for a bit, the queen will have time to decide how to deal with him. And you'll be safe here."

"So you're not just the courier, you're the bait?"

"Pardon?"

"I won't let him hurt you."

"You'll not cross him, Harry. You don't know what he can do."

"I know what I can do. He hurt Lilly. He's not going home without a memento of his visit."

She clutched his hand tightly, suddenly fearful of letting him go at all. "No. You mustn't. Please, Harry. Promise me."

This time, when he turned to her, his eyes were hard. "I'm afraid I can't."

She closed her eyes, fresh fear washing over her. What was she to do? How could she keep him safe, when her goal must be safe passage home for the Dearann Stone? Yet how could she bear to desert him if he were in danger?

"How about if I call Gwyneth?" Harry asked. "Let them know we're coming."

She nodded. "Sure, it'll give Darragh time to work a bit of weather to our aid. It would also help him to know we've succeeded. Won't he be surprised altogether?"

Harry pulled that little box out of his pocket again. "You're sure now that you can trust him not to steal it for himself?"

She actually smiled. "Ah, no, I believe he's much too interested in stealing Gwyneth for himself."

He gave a little "humph" and punched buttons on his box. "I can't wait to see him at his first restaurant.... Gwyn? Success."

Sorcha waited patiently as Harry informed his one-time fiancée of the completion of their mission. She basked in the warmth of the Stone she held and noticed that even in November, the skies had grown soft and the shadows less harsh. Where there had been emptiness, a few birds now flew. How could she regret her success? How could she resent her part in bringing harmony to her people? Yet how could she walk away from the only man she would ever love?

"Are you ready, lass?" Harry asked.

She drew a breath. "Aye. Have they had any trouble?"

Harry looked into the mirror and then back before pulling out onto the long, lonely road into the moors. "Evidently Darragh knows just where our friend is and is keeping a close eye on him. The good news is that you were right. He's biding his time on the moor. The bad news is that Darragh says he's powerful."

Sorcha nodded. "Sure, and how can that be a surprise, when you think of what he did to Lilly?"

"Yes," he said, his eyes on the road. "What he did to Lilly."

Sorcha swung around to him. "It's not your job to punish him, Harry. Let it be up to the queen, please. I'm not sure there's another who can contain him."

Harry didn't argue. But he didn't agree, either.

"We'll call Darragh again when we're close," Sorcha said, as if closing the argument. "The *Dubh-lainn Sidhe* will feel the approach of the Stone, but if Darragh works fast, he'll have a mist formed to confuse him. We'll hide inside, so, and not let him see us till I walk through."

"We hope."

She tried to smile. "Sure, don't you mortals thrive on a positive attitude, Harry?"

"Only when we know what we're facing."

Sorcha couldn't think of a thing to say to that. She slipped the Stone back into its bag and watched the miles slide by out the window of the car. Time passed, and the hills gathered and multiplied as they traveled west toward Waverly Close. She once again heard the air rush by and thought she saw a hawk testing the air currents far above the hills. She didn't know how to break Harry's silence or change his mind. She didn't know how to salvage these last few minutes they had together.

Then, without a word, he reached over and wrapped his fingers around hers and held on. And Sorcha closed her eyes and bathed in his light for as long as she would be given.

The warning came almost imperceptibly. At first Sorcha thought it might just be a change of weather, a darkness creeping across the afternoon sky. The Dearann

Stone sat in her lap singing of rebirth and the cycle of life, but Sorcha began to grow afraid. Not just that she would have to leave Harry, but that she would somehow lose her way before she got the Stone across. She felt anger latch on to that fear, its tentacles sly and tenacious.

"What's going on?" Harry demanded all of a sudden. "I'm seeing things in my head again."

Sorcha looked down at the Stone that glittered in her hands. "Different things."

He nodded. "Oh, yes. But at a distance, if you understand. It's as if I'm watching it on a screen. Violence. Disaster. It's as if I'm being visited by portents of doom, and it's making me afraid."

Sorcha snapped to attention. "Faith. I should have anticipated this. He's there."

"The *Dubhlainn Sidhe?*"

"This is his advance attack, Harry. Doubt and frustration and fear. Ambiguous, amorphous, too uncertain to name."

For a long moment Harry seemed to think about that. Then, abruptly, he nodded. "All right, then. As long as I know what it is, I can deal with it."

"I just hope Darragh can."

He looked over at her, and she saw the weight of what they were about to do in his eyes. "He'll have to, won't he?"

The clouds gathered, real and imagined, the closer they drew. Could Darragh be gathering a storm to protect them? Was it he who sent the wind skirling along the moors like an advancing army? The car rocked about a bit with it, and the clouds shredded and tumbled over the higher elevations. Sorcha shivered in her seat and curled her hand more tightly around the Dearann Stone, as if that would keep it safe.

She wondered if the *Dubhlainn Sidhe* could feel its approach. If it gave him joy or satisfaction or annoyance. After all, the *Dubhlainn Sidhe* had suffered the most from its loss. Would they be glad at its return or resentful? Anymore, Sorcha simply didn't know the mind of the *Dubhlainn Sidhe,* especially now that they carried the Coilin Stone with them.

It would all be over soon, though. She would bring the Dearann Stone back to the land of faerie, and Orla would return it to its true home.

Another thought that brought grief: she would lose Harry. She had done her best to come to grips with that.

And she'd just met the Stone. And like her love for Harry, the joy of the Stone had swept through her like a sweet wind. Now she would lose that, as well. The Dearann Stone would return to her place among the *Dubhlainn Sidhe,* and Sorcha would be left behind.

Thank the goddess she would have her child or she might think her chance for renewal had been forfeited in this cold land where mortals spent their lives oblivious to the miracle of life.

She saw Darragh's plan from all the way up the valley. Thin fingers of fog shrouded the hill that held the gate. Farther down, a shaft of sunlight swept over the valley like a spotlight searching for prey. She didn't see anything, which meant the *Dubhlainn Sidhe* wouldn't be seen until he struck. Hopefully his vision would be no better than hers.

Harry brought the car to a halt well before the place where they had to begin their climb and pulled out his communication box. After punching some buttons and greeting Gwyneth, he handed the thing to her.

"I'm not sure I can hold him," were Darragh's first words.

"Where is he?" Sorcha asked, her hand instinctively clutching the Stone more tightly.

"I'm not sure. He's a master at subterfuge, my girl. I may have mist and fog, but he has nightmares."

"Ah, sure, and don't I know it," she agreed, her focus on the fog that was slowly eating up the hill she sought. "We don't have time, Darragh. If he thinks we've skirted him, he'll go back for the children. Hold them hostage."

"I know. Can you see the trees on the south flank?"

"Trees. Oh, aye, I can."

"Use those as camouflage as far as you can. As you draw him, I'll try to track him."

"Is Gwyneth safe?"

"I've sent her on. She thinks she's bringing help."

Sorcha dragged in a thready breath. "Help Harry, then."

There was a pause. "I will."

She closed the little box and set it on her lap.

"Are we ready?" Harry asked.

Sorcha clutched the Stone in one hand and took Harry's hand in the other. "No," she admitted, the moment clotting up in her chest. "Faith, I'll never be ready."

"Yes, you will and you are, Sorcha. You're a princess of the blood. No one else could get the Stone through but you."

She locked her gaze with his then, reinforcing her will with his belief in her. Taking this last moment to be most important to him.

There was no time, but they made time anyway,

spending their last moments memorizing each other for all the years they wouldn't have. Harry curled his hand around her neck and pulled her gently toward him. He kissed her, his eyes open, his heart there for her to see. Sorcha let her tears fall, her gift to him, and she saw his tears gleam in his eyes before he willed them away. And when she broke the kiss, he let her.

"I have to go now," she said.

He nodded. Ah, how could her heart hold against the grief in his eyes? "I'll help hold him till you're safely through."

"Trust Darragh to know when to let him go."

"I will."

She bent her head to focus once again on the Stone as Harry restarted the car and finished their journey to the bottom of the hill. Sorcha washed herself in the white light of the Dearann Stone. She asked the goddess to keep Harry and his family safe, no matter what happened. And she said goodbye to this mortal world she would never see again.

As Sorcha finished, Harry pulled to a stop at the edge of the trees. Already Darragh's mist curled in among the tree trunks and muted the lines of the bare branches. The rest of the long hill was hidden in soft gray. Sorcha looked up, hoping for inspiration. Instead, the first tendrils of terror seeped past Darragh's magic to embed themselves in her heart. The *Dubhlainn Sidhe* was waiting, and he was fully armed.

Sorcha turned away from Harry before she couldn't and opened the door. The wind Darragh had gathered slapped at her. Icy fingers of fog slithered across her face. She stepped from the car and almost collapsed.

"Sorcha?" Harry asked, sounding anxious.

"Fine," she managed, even as the *Dubhlainn Sidhe* struck her again, his poison like a spear to her heart.

Hot, sick terror poured over her like hot oil from a battlement. It was only a psychic attack, but the pain shuddered through her.

She heard Harry scramble from the car and wanted to tell him to run. Goddess, how could a person walk with such fear on her shoulders? How could she manage this task? Images sprouted full-blown, not sweet images brought by the Stone she carried, but violent, vile scenes that played in her head until she cringed before them. Her own fairy family, tortured and bleeding, scattered across a sere, dry earth. The fairy children, oh, the children, twisted and keening like Lilly, vacant-eyed, their souls defiled with the *Dubhlainn Sidhe*'s rage, their bodies shattered from his venom.

She couldn't hide from such an attack. The *Dubhlainn Sidhe* didn't have to see her to batter at her will. But he *did* have to see her to keep her from the gates. Her only hope was that the trees would hide her movements until the last moment. She stumbled again, her stomach heaving with the poison he unleashed.

"Steady on, girl," Harry whispered to her, and took her by the elbow to help her up the hill.

She knew she was shaking. She could barely set one foot before the other. It was worse than the violence offered on the plains of faerie by armed hordes of *Dubhlainn Sidhe* warriors. There was no death here, only madness. It crept in on her, foul fingers of despair that ate away the light.

The trees rose abruptly through the fog, an army that

stood in uneven ranks. She slipped through them, wishing she were as insubstantial as the fog. Wishing she could hide here forever, though she knew she would have to step out to face her enemy.

"Darragh," she whispered, wondering where he was. How he was faring against this attack.

She heard nothing in return, only the sly laughter of a madman on the breeze. She sucked in great lungfuls of air and struggled to walk faster. She clutched the Dearann Stone and prayed it would protect her. But even the Dearann Stone, so far away from its rightful place, seemed to dim before this defilement.

She had to send Harry away. She had to protect him, or his family would be lost. *He* would be lost, and it would destroy her more surely than any injury the *Dubhlainn Sidhe* could inflict.

The mortal children. She could hear them now, terrible, soul-emptying cries of loss, of pain, of anguish. She had to get that beast through the gate before he could get back to them. Before he had the chance to make his threat a reality.

"Harry," she begged, giving him an ineffectual push. "Go. Please."

The ground was so cold beneath her feet. The shoes they'd forced on her hurt. From one step to the next, she kicked them off, needing the mother earth to fortify her.

"He knows we're here," Harry said.

She wanted to warn him again. She couldn't manage it. The attack was so fierce that her senses were beginning to fail.

Grass beneath her feet. The wind snarling through

her hair. The fog slipping down to cover her, to protect her from fairy eyes. Harry walking alongside, his strength unbowed, his hand so gentle it hurt her as he guided her to the end of the trees.

"If I don't get through…" she rasped.

She felt him startle. "What do you mean?"

Somewhere in that fog, the *Dubhlainn Sidhe* was focused on her. He was pulling at her soul, as surely as a leech drew blood. He was battering at every defense she had. She was afraid; she was furious; she was weakening.

"Carry it through, Harry," she begged, never taking her eyes from where the top of the hill should be. "Promise me."

"Of course," he said, wrapping an arm around her shoulders.

She wanted to smile. She wanted to thank him. To tell him how she loved him. It was becoming difficult to hold herself together enough to remember how to speak.

Lilly, little Lilly, there in her head, writhing in agony, keening away what was left of her special light, lost to the darkness, sacrificed to the greed of one fairy. Sorcha shuddered with the image. It surrounded her, consumed her, took away the sight of the hill. There was only Lilly, crying out to her with the last, gasping cries of sanity.

"Tell me he's not really doing that," Harry begged.

So he'd seen. He'd felt it, even protected as he was.

"Not yet." One foot in front of the other. Another breath. A prayer to the earth and the goddess and the great Creator Stone to give her the strength to go on. To step out onto the bare rise of the hill, where she could be seen. "We have to find the gate."

Another searing breath. "Cease, *Dubhlainn Sidhe!*"

she cried in her mind, where he couldn't locate her. "You befoul the grace of faerie with your attack on the innocent. Run, for fear of your very soul!"

He heard her. He laughed. He crept closer.

"Run, Sorcha!" She heard Darragh's voice, and knew that he was already on his knees. "I can't...I can't hold him...."

It was time, then. She'd run out of protection, run out of time. Separating herself from Harry, she stumbled into a run. He followed her. She closed her eyes and saw the gate before her. All she had to do was lift the Stone before her to have it open. She could barely get her legs to move, couldn't lift her arm even to save her life. She felt Harry stumble next to her and knew that the herbs had reached their limit. If she didn't succeed in the next few moments, he would be lost, his mind and heart shattered beneath the power of the fairy evil. And by the goddess, she would not allow that.

From one step to the next, she realized that they'd been wrong. It wouldn't be enough to capture the *Dubhlainn Sidhe*. He had to be stopped. He couldn't have the chance to do what he threatened. They couldn't allow him to visit his revenge on those children. Because he would. She knew he would, no matter what, as punishment for her challenge.

Taking the life of one of the fair folk was the ultimate crime. Sorcha no longer cared. Her mother the queen would have to understand. And if she did not, Sorcha would gladly pay the price to protect those she loved.

She stumbled, forcing her legs up that hill, pulling air into her tortured lungs, dragging the last bits of light into her mind before madness took her completely. She held on to the Stone, and she held on to Harry, and she ran through the fog, already knowing that her enemy would materialize inside long before she reached the haven of her home.

She felt him nearby, her enemy. She knew it was time. She set the Stone into Harry's hand and reached down to draw her knife. That sharp, elf-crafted knife that had to protect her.

"Get it through, Harry," she panted.

"Sorcha, no...."

And then she saw him, the *Dubhlainn Sidhe,* a shadow in the mist, not more than ten steps away, barring them from the gate, taunting them with the gate. A beautiful fairy with black, black hair that gleamed like a seal's pelt, and eyes the color of midnight. Milk-pale skin and a lithe, elegant body. One of her own who had given himself over to corruption. He smiled, and that smile sent a shudder through her.

"I will destroy you, *Tuatha!*" he called out into the twilight of the swirling mist. "Let it go, or I destroy all that you love."

"You will not stop me!" Sorcha cried out. "And you will, by the goddess, not destroy another living being. So I swear, *Dubhlainn Sidhe.*"

She saw him lift his hand and felt the strike of it like a bolt of lightning against her head. She staggered and almost fell. She was sweating now, cold and hot, and so weak that her muscles couldn't remember how to function. Her head shrieked in anguish, in a cacophony of terror and pain. Harry put his hand against her back, and it was the only thing that kept her upright.

Harry. His love. His belief in her, a teacher of small children.

Harry believed she could do it. And so she *would* do it.

She had no strength left, but somehow she pulled herself upright. She donned the mantle of her rank and faced her enemy.

"Stand aside, *Dubhlainn Sidhe*," she commanded, not even recognizing her own voice, hearing the voice of her mother, of her sister Nuala, when she'd led the cavalry in a charge. The voice of power, of command. "The Dearann Stone will return of her own accord, and you will not stop her."

"Oh, but I will," he said, his voice slithering through the dimness like a viper.

He began to lift his arm again, attempting to throw his poison directly at Harry. Harry stumbled, but he didn't fall. He didn't speak. He just supported her.

"Ah, so you wasted your protection on a mortal," the fairy drawled. "Precipitate of you, *Tuatha*. You have none left for yourself, then, do you?"

He actually blew on his fingers, as if cooling them. Sorcha refused to notice. She collected the strength Harry gave her. She gathered her fury, the might born of her ancestors. She curled her fingers tight around the jeweled hilt of her dagger.

"Sorcha, watch out!" Darragh cried, and she saw him at the edge of the mist, stumbling toward her.

The *Dubhlainn Sidhe* lifted his hand. Sorcha charged him.

He began to laugh. He laughed as he flung another lightning bolt that all but brought her down. He laughed until she ran right into him. Until she lifted her own arm and plunged that sharp knife right into his throat. Until she met him face-to-face, eye to eye, so she could see the surprise, the disbelief, the dawning rage, as his fairy blood pumped out over her wrist and her throat and her chest.

"You will…not…stop…me," Sorcha gasped with the last of her strength.

She almost made it. She heard Darragh running toward her from the other side of the hill, his gait erratic and slow. She felt Harry approach from behind her, obviously ready to hand the Stone back to her. But she would never see the Stone through the gate.

As he died, the *Dubhlainn Sidhe* clamped his hand around hers. He clawed at her face. Sorcha struggled, but he'd already taken her energy. She bucked back, kicked, fought, but he had an unbreakable hold on her.

"Do it, Harry," she begged. "Get it through."

And then, caught in the embrace of the dying *Dubhlainn Sidhe,* she suffered his final assault. He died, and in his dying, took Sorcha with him.

The last thing she heard as she began the long fall into darkness was Harry's voice, so far off.

He would see the world of fairy after all. He would have to bring the Stone home.

# Chapter 15

Harry dropped the Dearann Stone at his feet.

"Noooooo!"

He was only a step away when Sorcha fell, still caught in the clutches of the other fairy. Her eyes were open. She was completely limp, a rag doll tossed aside by an impatient child. Harry's heart stopped as he reached for her. He unwound her from the clutches of those bloody, rigid fingers and clutched her to his chest.

"Ah, Goddess," he heard behind him as he pulled her into his arms. "No. Not Sorcha."

Harry looked up to see Darragh collapse to the ground not three feet away.

"Do something!" he demanded.

Darragh closed his eyes and shook his head. "Get her

across," he said, sounding lost. "Her and the Stone. It's her only chance."

Harry looked down at her, but he couldn't tell if she still breathed. He couldn't feel her heart beating. "God, Sorcha, please don't do this. Not now. Not *now!*"

He wanted to crush her to him, to beat on her, to force air into her mouth.

"Now, man! She doesn't have any time!"

Harry looked up, and suddenly there, right in front of them, not five feet from where the other fairy lay, twisted and blackening even as he watched, the mists cleared to reveal a gate. Ornate, stone, empty. Harry couldn't think, could do only what he'd been told. Grabbing the Dearann Stone, he lifted Sorcha into his arms. Then he carried them both through the gate.

He didn't know what he'd expected. What he first saw wasn't that different from what he'd left: long, cold hills and an indifferent sky. In fact, he turned back to make sure, because he was certain only fairy magic would save Sorcha, and if this wasn't the land of fairies, they were lost.

"Please," he prayed, tightening his hold on her.

She was warm. Wasn't she warm? Could she be alive, in some place mortals didn't know how to get to? He looked around the long valley, where trees were shedding their leaves, and he panicked.

"Help me!" he yelled as loudly as he could. "Help Sorcha! I have—"

He never got out the rest. Suddenly there were throngs of people there. No, not people. Beings. Some rode on horseback. Some flew. He would think about that later. Right now, he ran toward them.

"Save her. Please, save her. She brought the Dearann Stone home to you. You have to help her!"

In the front of the throng a woman stepped forward. Tall, lithe, elegant, so blond that the sun seemed to shine from her hair. Harry didn't even have to see the crown on her head to know who she was.

"You're her *mother,*" he begged. "Do something!"

She slowed to a regal halt and smiled, her green cat's eyes amused. "And what have you brought me, then, mortal?"

He shook suddenly with rage. "Your daughter, damn it. And if you don't help her, you'll lose her faster than you lost your precious bloody Stone."

Her eyebrow lifted in regal disdain. "You certainly have a way with an insult, little man. Do you know who it is you accuse?"

"A woman who worries more for her prestige than the life of her daughter." He turned away from her. "Is there *anybody* here who can help us?"

The queen waved a languid arm. "*Fuist,* little man. Even a queen would never forfeit her own daughter. Let the *bean tighe* see her."

Cold bitch. He wasn't sure he should leave Sorcha here after all. She would be better off with *his* family, even if the mortal world fretted at her. At least she would know his gran loved her, that Lilly would always delight her.

"Peace, mortal," the queen soothed, her voice suddenly soft. "Leave her with us. I promise she will be well."

Harry didn't move. He didn't let go of his precious burden. He looked down at Sorcha's face, so unspeakably pale, the circles beneath her eyes darkened, the life that was so much a part of her absent. He saw a tear splash against her cheek and thought how he never cried.

"Here," he said, not bothering to look up. "It may not mean as much to you as it did to her, but she brought this to you."

He lifted his arm and opened his hand. The green velvet pouch that had protected the Dearann Stone fell away, and the sun struck what was left behind. A thousand colors of light shattered over the hills and seemed to make the trees shudder. A long, heartfelt sigh rose from the throng. The queen went perfectly still.

"Ah, well, and didn't I say that our Sorcha was the very one to recover our precious Dearann Stone?"

Harry thought he heard singing in his head. He saw the sea of fairies bow as reverently as priests at high mass. Then the crowd parted, and a tiny, unspeakably ugly being came trotting up.

Harry took an instinctive step back, pulling Sorcha closer. The gnarled, wrinkled old woman seemed to be grinning.

"Hasn't the girl spoken of her own *bean tighe,* then?" she asked. "If I'm not much mistaken, it's the smell of my own herbs that's about you."

Harry bent over and squinted, as if it would help pull her into some kind of focus. "You gave her those?"

She squinted right back. "And weren't they after helping?"

"Will you cure her?"

The little creature settled a nut-brown hand on Sorcha's forehead and closed her eyes. Harry swore her pointed little ears quivered. The vast plain fell into absolute silence as every creature waited for the *bean tighe*'s words. He held his breath, frantic with impatience. *Please. God, please...*

Finally, drawing a great breath, the old woman lifted her head. "Aye, mortal," she said, her voice impossibly soft, a mother's voice that conjured memories Harry didn't even think he had. "She'll do. Leave her with me, so she can heal."

"Will she be whole again?"

She nodded. "In time. In time. But first we'll put her to her own bed, so she recognizes herself as being home. She's suffered greatly in your mortal world, hasn't she?"

He could barely get the words out. "She has."

Suddenly the *bean tighe* beamed and patted his arm, just like Lilly. "And she has gained much, as well. The queen there might be a bit stiff on it, but we who revere our princess thank you for bringing her home to us."

This time he could get no words out at all. His throat simply closed up. Two tall men stepped forward and held out their arms for her. Harry couldn't let go. He couldn't give her up after all. He couldn't go home.

"Take care with her," he warned, not caring that there were tears in his voice. He handed her over to them, where she would be safe. Where she would be home.

"Tell her..." He shook his head. "Tell her..."

The tiny woman reached up to pat his hand. "Aye, lad. I'll tell her, and be happy to."

He nodded. He watched as they carried her away. He didn't notice that the queen had stepped forward.

"Will you stay and tell us what adventures our little Sorcha has had?" she asked.

From the reaction of the crowd, he knew not many

people got such an invitation. He looked around at them and finally saw what had existed beyond his focus. And he recognized it all. The soft glen, the creatures, the horses that looked so much like his own, the trees that seemed as if they could talk to you.

For the second time in moments, his heart broke. He had brought Sorcha home, only to realize that he was home, too. Except that he wasn't. He had no place here while his family needed him.

"Mortal?"

He turned back to see the queen assessing him with her odd cat's eyes. "Harry," he corrected her, straightening to his elegant best. "Harold George Cormac Augustus Beverly Wyatt, ninth Earl of Hartley."

For some reason that caught the queen's attention. She offered a frosty smile and seemed to suddenly look more closely at him. She stepped closer and stilled. Harry thought for sure that her eyes widened in surprise.

"Yes," a little boy alongside her said. "He bears the look."

"Goddess," the queen said. "He's the very butter stamp of him."

"You knew my ancestor, did you?" Harry asked.

For some reason the queen and the boy exchanged significant looks.

"And it's you who's had the Dearann Stone all this while?" she asked him, her posture minimally different. Less haughty.

"My family. It's said that Cathal was the one who left it with us."

She nodded. "And you allowed Sorcha to bring it back?"

"Sorcha fought like a warrior for it. You might want to know that there's a dead *Dubhlainn Sidhe* just on the other side of your gates."

She frowned. "And who might have been responsible?"

"Your daughter."

He thought he actually saw a smile on her face. She nodded again. "Will you stay and give us the tale?"

Harry took another look around and thought how magnificently eccentric it was that he felt more at home with these creatures than the population of London. Too much at home. The longer he stayed, the harder it would be to leave. He handed the stone to the queen.

"No," he said. "It's Sorcha's story to tell. I was just there to help."

The queen lifted a regal eyebrow. "And you've no curiosity about what lies on the underside of the hill?"

He lied, and he knew she knew he lied. "No, thank you. I need to be getting home. My family will be worried."

She looked as if she were about to object again. Harry never gave her the chance. He simply turned around and walked back through the gate. Back to the only world he'd always known. Back where he didn't belong anymore.

Sorcha healed slowly. She wasn't sure how long she spent lost in the nightmare of a *Dubhlainn Sidhe*'s revenge. Time, after all, wasn't a faerie concept. She just knew that again and again she woke screaming, sure he'd come back for Lilly or Theo, or that he'd stripped Harry of his soul out on that barren hilltop.

Every time she woke, it was to find the *bean tighe* by her bedside, when it was Harry she looked for. Every time she begged to know if her bairn would be harmed by what had happened.

"Ah, no, child. How could you be thinkin' I'd let any harm come to such a precious gift as you're bringing us? The babe is protected and will retain nothing of this on his journey to us."

Each time Sorcha eased back to sleep, to the realm of healing and renewal. Each time she checked out the window to see that the spring had reawakened in the land of faerie with the return of the Dearann Stone. She felt her in her heart, the soft singing of her, the sweet spring greenness of her.

She had no idea what her mother the queen had done with her. No one would say. She knew, though, that the queen had set a plan in motion, and that her sister Orla was involved. And didn't she wish she had the energy to enjoy the idea of that? But the only energy she wasted was in thinking about Harry. Wondering whether he'd settled in back home. Wondering if he missed her with the same bone-deep pain with which she missed him. Wondering how she would ever raise his babe without him.

She wasn't sure how long it took, because time was elastic, but one day she woke to hear birdsong and smell the sharp spice of wild iris, and she knew it was time to rise. And when she did, it was to find her mother at her bedside.

"Well, little Sorcha," the queen said where she sat looking unconcerned. "You've decided to return to us, then."

Sorcha lay very still. "I have."

Her mother nodded slowly, and Sorcha thought there

was something different about her. Something that bespoke new flexibility, maybe. With some care, she rose to sit before her mother.

"And have you great stories to tell us that will be sung by the bards when we meet at the great hall?" Mab asked.

"I have no great stories, lady. Just a small one, as befits a teacher of children."

Her mother smiled, and Sorcha saw something she had never seen in Mab's eyes before. A measure of pride. "Oh, I wouldn't be saying that, daughter. You are a princess of the blood. No matter your gift, it could never be small. And now you have the tale of the Dearann Stone to add to your song."

"She is safe, then? She is back where she belongs?"

"Well, she's still here, now, isn't she? She was needed to heal one who is precious to her queen." Her mother raised an imperious eyebrow. "Lookin' at you, though, I'd say her work is fair finished altogether. It's time you were returning to court, little girl."

"I will not be queen," Sorcha said, just to be getting that out of the way.

There was a long silence, and Sorcha thought even the birds had gone quiet. Sorcha knew her voice carried the change in her. She wondered how her mother would accept it.

"You have the right," the queen said with a vague wave of her hand, as if it had never mattered. "Haven't you carried out the task I set you? You brought honor to your clan, and, whether you like it or not, with your small claims and your humble aspirations, your name *will* be recorded in the list of great deeds."

"And I have your blessing to continue as I am?"

"You would want that?"

Sorcha wasn't surprised anymore by the shaft of pain that seared her at the thought of what she really wanted.

"Aye, my lady. It is what I would want."

"And what of the mortal who looked on you with besotted eyes, little Sorcha? You mean to tell me you'll not keep him?"

"He doesn't belong here." Her voice was small and sad.

"Faith," her mother snapped. "If that isn't a statement I'm tired of hearing. First from your sister and now from you. Just how doesn't he belong here when he bears the perfect stamp of his faerie blood? When he looked at these hills as a man in exile looks on his homeland?"

Sorcha felt tears welling in her eyes and thought her mother would be appalled. "Ah, no. Did he?"

"As well you know, or you wouldn't be after threatening to water your linen. What is it keeps this one away, then?"

Sorcha would never have thought she could share such a thing with her mother. She never would have thought the great queen could care for such mundane problems. But then, would she ever have thought to hear the queen call her precious? Suddenly, she found herself opening up to her mother.

"Just as the queen can't leave her people for her own comfort when they are in need, so an honorable mortal man cannot leave his family to ruin so he might find his own peace."

"And doesn't it serve them right for holding the great Dearann Stone hostage all these years?"

"It does not," Sorcha said, sitting straighter. "How could they know, then, what a treasure it was they had?

The one who brought it is long gone, and Harry was the first to even feel the pull of her. For all the faerie blood in them, only a few are fully aware."

"Did he tell you of the one who brought it across?"

"Just his name. Cathal. A royal name for certain."

"Oh, aye, and all that." The queen enjoyed a private smile. "And another surprise for the mortal if he would wish to discover it."

"Why?" Sorcha asked.

Her mother shook her head. "Ah, no, little one. He'd have to come for it himself. Now then, what ruin does he face, this mortal you love so deeply you'd bear his child?"

"Conceived in a sacred grove, lady," Sorcha said, her hand protective over her belly. "A gift to us all, I'm thinking."

"A gift he'll never share, for want of a walk through the gates."

"Ah, but he can't. The place where they've guarded the Stone these years, a good place with the sacred grove and black bog oak for comfort, would be lost to them without Harry's help. His family would be lost, for his ancestors, once acquainted with the land of faerie, spent all their gains trying to get back. There is nothing left to sustain them. And not simply those he loves, but one we of faerie love, as well. A cherished one, who is in great risk if he fails. How in honor could he desert them simply to be with me?"

Her mother's face actually softened. "A cherished one? You had the privilege?"

"Oh, aye. And no matter the pain to me, I would never cost Harry the safety and comfort of that child."

"No," the queen mused, looking out the window. "No, you couldn't. What of the copy stone I sent with you, Sorcha? Did you give it to them?"

She shook her head. "They already had a copy. One that didn't torment my poor Harry with visions of places he could never go."

Her mother looked up at her. "Where is it?" she asked. "The stone you carried away?"

Sorcha shrugged. "It was carried home with me."

The queen laughed suddenly, a short, harsh bark that sounded odd coming from one so elegant. "And you never thought to tell them, Sorcha. Did you?"

"Tell them what?"

It was the weekend, and Harry was on horseback. It was the only place he felt alive anymore, throwing himself over jumps and measuring the moors on one of his ghost-gray horses. It had been five months since he'd left Sorcha on the other side of the gate. Five months of sleepless nights and long silences. Five months of trying to convince Lilly that her fairy was gone. Five months of Phyl's sympathy and Gwyneth's delight. She'd married her own fairy, and they were madly happy. Harry wanted to hurt them both.

He couldn't help it. He felt more out of place than ever before. He found himself again and again standing before the murals in the front salon, aching to walk back through that gate. He found himself hearing Sorcha's voice in the dawn, smelling the cinnamon and honey scent of her on the wind.

He was on Moonsilver today, one of his fey gray colts who looked to be an excellent eventer. Harry was taking him over the low jumps, getting him used to the rhythm and pace of them.

He should quit. It was getting on toward dusk, and he knew Phyl would be yelling at him to for heaven's sake eat something, but he wasn't hungry. He was in need of a way to exhaust himself to sleep. The nightmares were gone. The sense that he should wake to find Sorcha next to him wasn't.

He heard Lilly over by the stables, but he couldn't turn his horse toward her. Every time he'd seen her lately, she'd patted him and sighed.

"You go, Harry. You go."

He didn't even want to ask her what she meant. He knew what he wanted, and that was hard enough. At least she was thriving. They could hardly keep her off Soairce these days, and it was helping her coordination and stamina. Whatever else Harry did, he would make sure that little girl never lost her home.

"Hi, fairy," he heard her say, and jumped so hard in the saddle that he startled his horse.

He shook his head. She shouldn't do that. A man could die of disappointment when he turned around to find she was playing a game. He turned around anyway. And almost fell off his horse.

Moonsilver came to a shuddering stop, almost upending him. The horse whinnied. The horse bowed. The other horses perked up ears and heads and headed for Lilly's voice.

Harry couldn't breathe. He couldn't think. He couldn't move.

It was the dying light, he swore. It was his own wishful thinking taking form in the shadows.

"Is it so disappointed you are, then, to see me, Harry Wyatt?" she asked.

Here. She was here. The enormity of it lodged in his chest and blocked his breath.

"Sorcha?"

She laughed and walked toward him. She was in her fairy dress, and it swirled around her lovely legs. Her hair shone like gold, and her eyes were the color of spring leaves. And she was here. He swung down off Moonsilver and stalked toward her.

"What are you doing here?" he demanded.

"You go, Harry!" Lilly yelled from over by the paddock fence.

Sorcha walked right into his arms. He couldn't believe it. He pulled her so tightly against him that he was sure she couldn't breathe. "What have you done, Sorcha?"

"I'm in good health, thank you, Harry," she said with a chuckle. "You're a bit thin, altogether. Are you well?"

"I'm dying for want of you."

She cupped his face in her hands and kissed him. He met her openmouthed and all but devoured her. "Please tell me you haven't sacrificed anything."

She pulled back a bit, so she could see him better. "You wouldn't want me to?"

"God, no." He couldn't help it. He kissed her again. He hugged her hard, as if he could better convince himself of her presence that way. He closed his eyes and buried his face in the silk of her hair and never wanted to leave.

"Ah, I've missed you so, Harry," she whispered, her arms just as tight around him.

"You have no idea, Sorcha." He straightened and ran

a finger down her cheek. "The Dearann Stone. Were we successful?"

"Oh, aye. Haven't you noticed the spring, then, Harry? The lambs are birthing."

"And it's over?"

"Well, now, that's a different story entirely. The tale isn't full told yet, as Orla is still completing her part of the mission."

"What's that?"

"Ah, well, herself the queen won't say. We're all supposed to wait like good subjects."

"Hi, queen," Lilly was saying.

It took Harry a minute to pull himself away from the beauty of Sorcha's eyes to comprehend that.

"Queen?" he finally asked.

By then his entire family was out there. He picked every one of them out of the gloom, even Gran in her chair. The staff was clustered in the nearest doorway, staring at their surprise guest. And not at Sorcha.

"Good God," he muttered.

"Ah, well, it was the cherished one," Sorcha admitted. "Herself couldn't pass up the opportunity to meet our Lilly. She also thought to deliver the invitation in person, which I thought to be unusually generous of her. Don't you?"

He couldn't quite take his eyes off the queen where she knelt in the grass before Lilly, her white dress only a shade lighter than her moon-pale hair. Phyl and Ted stood a few feet away, mouths agape. Mary stood behind Gran's chair, with Sims and Tommie beyond her. Theo had placed himself next to Lilly, as if to protect her from the queen.

Harry was already smiling. Lilly needed no protection.

"Harry go," Lilly demanded of the queen, patting that impossibly sleek cheek. "Gran go."

"Ah, and aren't you the wise one?" the queen said with a startlingly sweet smile. "They're just who I've come for. Is it all right, then?"

Lilly considered the queen as if Mab herself were the supplicant. "I not go."

"Ah, no, sweet. Wouldn't your parents weep for it if you did? But we'll always be nearby, sure, to watch you."

Lilly nodded emphatically. "Good."

Harry's heart stumbled at the words. "Sorcha, I told you—"

"*Fuist,* Harry," she said, and lifted something in her hand. "I've brought you a gift."

He looked down to see the last light of day gleam on the egg-shaped stone in her hand. "You don't have to bring us another stone," he said. "We have one."

"Not like this," she said, and smiled. Reaching over, she took his hand and dropped the stone into it. Then she curled his fingers around the stone. "How big would you say this is, Harry?"

He wasn't sure what to say. "Size of a cricket ball, I'd say. Why?"

"Is that considered a big diamond, Harry?"

"Of course. But this is quartz. You know that."

"No, Harry. The other stone is a quartz. This, I'm afraid, is a diamond. It was what I brought to replace the stone I stole."

"A *diamond?*"

She looked chagrined. "And how was I to know how important the thing was? Sure, we've got them by the wagonload. Else how could we give fairies their soulstones?"

"Diamonds."

She grinned. "Herself the queen rather thought you might accept it as thanks for your help."

Harry couldn't think. Suddenly the rock was heavy in his hands. Impossibly large, if it was, in fact, a diamond.

"And she has a few more, as well," Sorcha said. "She doesn't want the cherished one to ever find herself in need, Harry. I'm thinking she found the way to do it."

"Lilly isn't the only cherished one, Sorcha."

"Oh, aye, that we know. But she's crossed the world of fairy, and when that happens, she becomes a thread in our weave. We are obliged to protect her."

As if to punctuate Sorcha's words, the queen was even then standing to raise a hand to Lilly's horse, who was literally kneeling before her.

"I honor you, my lovely Soairce," the queen proclaimed, "and make official my daughter's choice of you as guardian for this cherished one. Your name will be linked to hers in the rolls of honor."

Harry was sure the horse shivered. She bent her head to receive the queen's benediction, and Lilly laughed in pure delight. Harry looked back at the glittering egg in his hand. "Good sweet God," he breathed. The thing had to be worth millions.

Millions.

He was having trouble breathing again. Dragging air into his lungs, he raised his head and looked at his surroundings. The universe of his early life. The only home he'd known, the one he'd fought for and protected and sacrificed for.

The one in which he'd never really belonged.

Did he have the courage? Did he have a choice?

"Phyl," he said, focusing on Sorcha's hesitant smile rather than the anxiety in his voice. "Do you think you and Ted would like to take over this enterprise for your son?"

His heart was beginning to beat hard. It couldn't be possible.

Phyl never hesitated. "Hand over the diamond and I'll work for your investment bank if you want, Harry."

He looked over to his cousin to see the wistful smile on her face. "Truly?"

"I want you to be happy, Harry."

Harry reached out to take Sorcha's hand and turned to face the gathered audience. Especially the queen, who was now holding on to Lilly's hand.

"I hear you have need of a master of horse," he said to her.

The queen's smile was ghostly in the fading light. "That I do. Are you interested in the position, then, little man?"

Harry grinned like a ten-year-old. "That depends on what's being offered."

"I see. You have demands, I presume."

"A request, rather." He turned to Sorcha, unable to believe this moment. "Your daughter."

"Ah, you wish to be consort."

"I wish her to be my wife."

Sorcha folded her arms around him. "A good thing," she said. "I know you mortals are fierce protective of your children."

Which was when she laid his hand against the new roundness of her belly. Harry stopped breathing all over again. Then she was in his arms again, and he didn't think he would ever let her go.

"Gran?" he asked, his eyes closed as he inhaled cinnamon and honey. "What would you say to a bit of a trip?"

"Me?" He'd never heard her voice so small and uncertain.

"Go, old woman," Mary said. "I want to go back to the sun. You want to ride your horses and meet fairies."

And so it was. It took longer than that evening, because good wishes demanded legal documents in the mortal world and goodbyes were never swift. But by the time spring was in full bloom, with new foals to fill the paddocks and Sorcha swollen with their child, Harry and Sorcha said farewell to his family, whom they would see on the odd Halloween and through Lilly's eyes, and they accompanied his grandmother through the great gate into the world of fairies.

The story of the Dearann Stone was still not finished, but with the Stone back in the world of fairy, there was hope. There was new life, and there was a new master of the horse, who was often seen mounted alongside his new wife and his laughing grandmother as they raced over the fairy hills into the sunset.

Left behind, the family happily embellished the tale of the Fairy Prince and his great-great grandson. They closed the house back up and built a small shrine at the far edge of the property to house the rock the world thought was the Fairy Diamond and let the hordes ogle it there. They cashed in the real fairy diamond and built one of the finest horsebreeding estates in the world. Nobody had to know that not all their stock came from Ireland. Some came through a gate on a high hill on the moors. And as they arrived, each paid obeisance to the laughing girl named Lilly, who was so beloved to two worlds, and gave greeting to her brother, who protected her.

And in the land of faerie, Harry kept track of it all. Well, when he wasn't too busy cherishing his new role and the love who had tumbled into his arms on a cold moor. He wore clothing that made him look like Robin Hood and rode horses that spoke in his mind, and he made love with the woman he'd married beneath a bower in a fairy glen. And there in that glen was where he found his peace. Because it was there, with a fairy princess named Sorcha, that well into his thirtieth year, Harold George Cormac Augustus Beverly Wyatt finally came home.

* * * * *

*Look for BLOODRUNNERS—a brand-new
miniseries
from Rhyannon Byrd
beginning next month
from Silhouette Nocturne!*

*Dark, sensual and fierce.
Welcome to the world of the Bloodrunners,
a band of hunters and protectors,
half human, half Lycan,
caught between two worlds—yet belonging to neither.*

*Turn the page for a sneak preview of book one,
LAST WOLF STANDING.*

If not for the bustling noise of the crowd, anyone standing within five feet of Mason Dillinger would have easily heard the two halting, roughly drawled words that slipped slowly past the tightening lines of his mouth.

*"Damn you."*

Perhaps not the most erudite of phrases, but what it lacked in eloquence it more than made up for in conviction. In fact, in Mason's opinion it summed the situation up to perfection.

After all, it wasn't every day that one of his kind found his life mate in a throng of jacked-up caffeine addicts. Five seconds ago he'd have sworn that it could never happen—that a woman who had been created as his perfect match, the other half of his self, even existed—but there was no denying what that scent was doing to his head, not to mention his quickly thickening body parts.

The second he'd stepped through the doorway into the bustling interior of The Coffee and Croissant, the smell of her had hit him like a fist upside the head, rolling across his tongue like the sweetest sin, the most wicked of temptations.

He wanted to eat her alive…and he didn't even know who she was.

But he knew *where* she was. She was somewhere in this crowded, prepped-out joint that Jeremy had insisted they duck into before the entire day had passed without their eating. With their accelerated metabolisms, it was unhealthy to go too long without sustenance, not to mention dangerous as hell to the population at large.

Yeah, he knew where she was. And he knew *what* she was, too.

She was *his*.

Mason's narrowed eyes quickly scanned his surroundings, taking everything in. And then his head tilted back and he allowed inhuman senses so much sharper than mere sight to take over and read the room. The myriad of sounds and scents assailed him, chaotic and full, and yet, she burned through sharp and crisp like a radiant beam of light. Vibrant, breathtaking sunshine on a bone-chilling, cloud-smothered day. Something warm and comforting like home.

Hunger clawed its way up his spine, ripping through his system with such force that he expected to look down and see blood seeping through the thin cotton of his navy T-shirt and dark gray flannel, spreading like death down to the ragged denim of his jeans. Ripping him open quicker than teeth or claws ever could.

His nostrils flared as another wave of scent crashed through him. Yes, it was right *there*…lingering on the air.

The smell alone had him tied in knots, his body feeling tight and hot and swollen. It was something succulent and rich that sat on the tip of his tongue like a warm drop of honey. He wanted to roll it around for a deeper taste. Draw it into the cavern of his mouth and bite down on it. Hold it. Keep it and fight for it.

A hard shudder racked the long length of his body, his skin going hot and damp as a low, unfamiliar burn began in his belly. An animal lust…but different. There was the unmistakable hunger for hard, grinding, gritty sex, but this was utterly foreign to the driving need he'd known in the past. Hell, he'd had his share of women in his lifetime, leaving them quickly, but always with their well-used bodies heavy with pleasure, steeped in satisfaction. This sensation was more, though. Harder. Deeper. A sharp-edged, driving need unlike anything he'd ever experienced, raging and explosive.

He didn't just *want* to bury himself inside her—he *had* to.

But first he had to find her.

\* \* \* \* \*

*Follow Mason in his battle for the passion he can't
live without...
Look for LAST WOLF STANDING
by Rhyannon Byrd.
In stores March 2008*

# REQUEST YOUR FREE BOOKS!

## 2 FREE NOVELS PLUS 2 FREE GIFTS!

Silhouette®

# nocturne™

## Dramatic and Sensual Tales of Paranormal Romance.

**YES!** Please send me 2 FREE Silhouette® Nocturne™ novels and my 2 FREE gifts. After receiving them, if I don't wish to receive any more books, I can return the shipping statement marked "cancel." If I don't cancel, I will receive 4 brand-new novels every other month and be billed just $4.47 per book in the U.S. or $4.99 per book in Canada, plus 25¢ shipping and handling per book plus applicable taxes, if any*. That's a savings of about 15% off the cover price! I understand that accepting the 2 free books and gifts places me under no obligation to buy anything. I can always return a shipment and cancel at any time. Even if I never buy another book from Silhouette, the two free books and gifts are mine to keep forever.

238 SDN ELS4   338 SDN ELXG

Name _____ (PLEASE PRINT)

Address _____ Apt. #

City _____ State/Prov. _____ Zip/Postal Code

Signature (if under 18, a parent or guardian must sign)

### Mail to the Silhouette Reader Service™:
**IN U.S.A.:** P.O. Box 1867, Buffalo, NY 14240-1867
**IN CANADA:** P.O. Box 609, Fort Erie, Ontario L2A 5X3

Not valid to current Silhouette Nocturne subscribers.

**Want to try two free books from another line?**
**Call 1-800-873-8635 or visit www.morefreebooks.com.**

* Terms and prices subject to change without notice. NY residents add applicable sales tax. Canadian residents will be charged applicable provincial taxes and GST. This offer is limited to one order per household. All orders subject to approval. Credit or debit balances in a customer's account(s) may be offset by any other outstanding balance owed by or to the customer. Please allow 4 to 6 weeks for delivery.

SN07

# Silhouette
# Desire

Buy 2 Silhouette Desire books and receive

# $1.⁰⁰ off

your purchase of the Silhouette Desire novel
*Iron Cowboy* by *New York Times* bestselling author

# DIANA PALMER

on sale March 2008.

---

## Receive $1.⁰⁰ off

**the Silhouette Desire novel IRON COWBOY,
on sale March 2008, when you purchase
2 Silhouette Desire books.**

*Available wherever books are sold including most bookstores,
supermarkets, drugstores and discount stores.*

Coupon expires August 31, 2008. Redeemable at participating retail
outlets in the U.S. only. Limit one coupon per customer.

11470

5 65373 00076 2 (8100) 0 11470

SDCPNUS0208

## Buy 2 Silhouette Desire books and receive

# $1.<sup>00</sup> off

your purchase of the Silhouette Desire novel
*Iron Cowboy* by *New York Times* bestselling author

# DIANA PALMER

## on sale March 2008.

---

# Receive $1.<sup>00</sup> off

### the Silhouette Desire novel IRON COWBOY,
### on sale March 2008, when you purchase
### 2 Silhouette Desire books.

*Available wherever books are sold including most bookstores,*
*supermarkets, drugstores and discount stores.*

Coupon expires August 31, 2008. Redeemable at participating retail
outlets in Canada only. Limit one coupon per customer.

52608214

SDCPNCAN0208